BIKER BA

MW00655034

BIKER
Beauties
Volume I

#1 *NEW YORK TIMES* BESTSELLING AUTHOR

AUDREY
CARLAN

Copyright 2019 Audrey Carlan, Inc.

All rights reserved.

No part of this publication may be reproduced, distributed, or transmitted in any form or by any means, including photocopying, recording, or other electronic or mechanical methods, without the prior written permission of the publisher, except in the case of brief quotations embodied in critical reviews and certain other noncommercial uses permitted by copyright law.

This book is a work of fiction. All names, characters, locations, and incidents are products of the author's imagination. Any resemblance to actual persons, living or dead, locales, or events is entirely coincidental.

Cover Design: Jena Brignola

Copy Editing: Red Quill Editing

ISBN: 978-1-943340-12-5

BIKER

Babe

Ceej Chargualaf
(December 21, 1981 – May 5, 2019)

Because I miss you every day.

Chapter 1

Shay

"I T'S EVERYTHING I DREAMED OF AND MORE," I GASPED AS tears pricked the back of my eyes. I closed them tight, trying to stave off the deluge of emotion as it plowed against my chest.

I held my hands over my mouth and stared lovingly at my store's sign. The old-fashioned round bulbs surrounding it blinked prettily, like the ones found in the old Hollywood movies or outlining hotels along the Vegas strip. Definitely not something you see regularly in Grants Pass, Oregon, my hometown.

The lights twinkled and flickered, then lit up in a line around the words that meant the world to me.

"Biker Babe," I whispered, a gigantic smile on my face.

A roar of applause, cheers, and the growling of motorcycle engines being revved blasted the air around me. A pair of thick arms encircled me from behind and held me close against a big barrel chest smashed against my back. A scratchy beard and the scent of motor oil and leather hit my senses at the same time the most familiar voice in the world spoke.

AUDREY CARLAN

"Proud of you, Princess. You done good. My girl. My baby girl is now the owner of a business." My father's voice was thick with pride. I knew in that moment I'd never forget those words or that feeling of absolute joy as it settled over me.

I smiled proudly and held onto my father's arms. His brothers, their old ladies, even the club girls made an appearance, though the girls stood way in the back, nowhere near the wives and girlfriends. All were here for the reveal of my new store, Biker Babe.

My mom pushed at my dad's arms. "Riot, give me some time with my girl!"

"My girl, my princess, my baby." Dad growled and kissed my temple.

Mags to the club, Magdalene on her birth certificate, and also my mother, cocked a leather-clad hip and put her hand on it. Her black matching leather property vest was fitted to her tiny waist perfectly, showing off her hourglass figure, something I also got from her stellar genetics, alongside her temper.

She narrowed her gaze, shooting daggers at my father, who simply smirked and grinned in response. Dad loved when my mother got fired up. Usually that type of response ended with my father physically lifting my mother over his shoulder and taking her to his room where he could give her a "talking to"— code word for a *hard fuck* to cool that fire he loved so much.

"Your girl, your princess, your baby..." she repeated in a sarcastic tone.

Dad squeezed me again and kissed my cheek that time. "That's right, woman."

"You forget that she's *my* daughter too, and I had a hand in making her all that she is." She waved her hand up and down. "Look at her. She's my spitting image."

And she was right. Thank God. My mom was hot as hell,

2

even at fifty. My hair hung down my back in long dark waves, my eyes as blue as the sky on a good day, icy gray-blue normally, just like hers.

"Not her height or her grit, Mag Pie. That's all me. Right, Princess?" He snuggled my neck and gave me a bunch of scruffy kisses until I giggled and pushed away.

I held my arms out to my mother.

She pulled me into her embrace. Mom was only five feet four inches. Me, I'm five ten, so I tucked my head into the crook of her neck. My mom held me tight and sniffed. "You did it, Shay-la-la. I knew you could, and you did."

I swallowed down the lump in my throat and held on to Mom even tighter, soaking in her own brand of roses and leather scent. "Thank you, Mom."

Dad hooked his arms around both of us.

"I couldn't have done it without both your help, especially financially," I murmured into our huddle.

I stepped out of their arms and looked at all the brothers lined up, arms crossed over their large chests. Every single one of them big, badass, scary as all get out, and the most beautiful family anyone could ever hope to have. All of these men, their old ladies, heck, even the club girls, supported my decision to open my own business.

"I want to thank you all for everything you did. From gutting the old building, to creating and painting new walls, to the plumping, and windows and décor..." I shook my head as the tears started up again. Biker babes are taught to be tough, so I did what I could to hold the tears at bay. "This is my dream, and I know you all gave up a lot to help me."

"It's what families are for!" Tank, the Sergeant-at-Arms, hollered out. He handled the security for the club and assigned the duties for the Enforcer.

"Fuck yeah," Champ agreed. Champ is my father's Enforcer. He kicks ass first, takes names later. For his day job, he runs the club gym and boxing league, one of the many businesses the Hero's Pride Motorcycle Club owns in Grants Pass and the surrounding cities.

A warm hand landed on my shoulder from behind and squeezed. I jumped back, clutching my chest and turned to find Shadow grinning.

"Jesus! What did I tell you about sneaking up on me! Make some noise once in a while, you freak!" I pushed at his chest playfully.

Shadow chuckled and pulled me into a hug. "Happy for you, Princess." Shadow is one of the younger members of the club but seemed to be wise well beyond his years. Then again, he was a covert operative in the CIA. Got his road name because he's sneaky as a ninja. Not to mention, he can be in a crowded room and not be noticed. Also tends to disappear from the club, sometimes for months, but he always comes back.

"As I was saying..." I raised my voice. "You are the best and most supportive family a girl could ever ask for. I love you. You're welcome in my store any time. In fact, I demand it!"

Everyone cheered again and took their turns to hug me and shake hands with my father, who was standing by my side, chest puffed up, beaming with pride and love.

God, I have the best family in the world.

Speaking of family, I saw a little blonde head and a giggling face attached to a small body being held on the shoulders of none other than my twin brother, Shane. Though no one but me and Mom call him Shane. He's known as Whip to the club.

"Now, who is this beauty? I think you grew. What are you, seven feet tall now?" I smiled up at my gorgeous niece.

"No, silly. Daddy is here!" She patted his dark head.

"All right, Sunflower, down you go." My brother dipped his head and pulled his daughter off his shoulders. She bum rushed me, hugging my legs quickly but then went right over to my father who scooped her up into a teddy bear hug. She's a total Daddy and Grandpa's girl. Which I got, because I am too.

"Sis, sorry I'm late." My brother hooked an arm around my neck and plastered me against his chest. I held onto his cut and squeezed until the nearness of my twin settled my heart. We'd always been thick as thieves. I guess sharing a womb fosters such a connection. It's never been easy for us to be apart for any real length of time. Even now, he rents the apartment next to mine. We literally share a wall, and that's the way we like it. Sometimes, however, the number of women that come through his pad and the sounds through those walls are hard to swallow. Those are ear plug nights.

For us, though, the hardest separation came when he was serving in the military. I tried to forget about that time because I was completely off kilter and listless without my bro in the area.

The deal with The Pride is everyone has or is currently serving the community or the country in some way. Whether it be military, a civil service branch, firemen, doctors, or all the way up the chain of government. That's the one rule of entry into the club. Service. Hence the name, Hero's Pride.

"Shayna was being a pill about getting dressed. You know how it is with her sometimes." My brother sighed and rubbed at the back of his neck.

I could see the dark circles under his eyes. Being a single dad, taking care of a four-year-old, being a member of the club, and working at the club's bar was a lot for a twenty-five-year-old man trying to make a life for himself and his daughter.

I clapped a hand on his bicep. "It's cool. I'm just glad

you're here. Just look at it!" I gestured to my new store. He looped his arm around my shoulders and gazed at the shop with its black painted concrete walls and big display windows. In one window was a full-sized Harley Davidson. It was our grandfather's, and Dad thought it would be a great display in his memory. Everyone agreed. Next to the bike is a mannequin wearing a pair of skintight jeans, badass suede heels, a studded leather belt, and a Harley tank complete with sequins around the collar. I've got a sharp black bobbed wig on her, like the one Uma Thurman wore in *Pulp Fiction*, with hooped earrings and a horde of dangling necklaces, as well as silver bangles around her wrists. There's a leather vest displayed, jeans, jewelry and all kinds of biker babe necessities. The other window has a male and a female mannequin dressed to the nines. Leather. Studs. Accessories. Everything biker babes and bikers drool over.

I made sure when I designed my store to have seventy percent of the product be geared toward women; however, women love to shop for their men. I know for a fact the old ladies do. Which means I've got the staple tees, Harley merchandise, Zippo lighters, men's rings, brass knuckles, and silver jewelry galore, which is handmade by a local kickass artist. Basically all the things a man would like and his woman would want to buy for him. I even have a saucy little section of some sexy lingerie, whips, floggers, and toys behind a beaded curtain. I also transformed a walk-in closet into a small adults only section where I could display pipes and other paraphernalia the brothers liked to enjoy.

The best part, and the reason why I'll have brothers all over the West Coast coming in, is my leather tooler or tailor depending on the needs. He's my ace in the hole. Cricket is the grandfather of the club and a master of all things leather.

A veteran in every sense of the word from his time in 'Nam to his time in the club. He helped found it with my dad, the President, but he didn't want to take on a leadership role. Just wanted to be part of a team again.

For me, he tailors the leather for the babes, makes the cuts and sews the patches on cuts for the brothers, and creates custom pieces for a hefty price, of which I get fifty percent. He comes and goes as he pleases, but that's the life of a biker. I could never tell a brother what hours he's supposed to work. It's just not something one does. Besides, I like my beauty sleep and never had a problem with late hours, so my store is open from eleven to seven for now. Cricket usually rolls in after lunch sometime and leaves for dinner at the clubhouse. When I get bigger and really start raking in the cash, I'll hire more help to work whatever hours are needed. For now, I'm just happy it's finished. And it's absolutely beautiful.

"Princess, you gonna open the doors or what? My old lady is drooling over a tank she can see in the window that she swears is going to show off her sweet titties. And you know I'm a man who likes my woman's tits," Hammer, one of the brothers, hollered.

I sighed. "You're a pig."

"Oink, oink," he snorted.

My mother came over to me and laced her fingers with mine. "You ready to open up your store for the first time?"

I gazed at my beautiful shop, my mother, father, brother, giggling niece, and The Pride at my back.

"Absolutely."

She squeezed my fingers and passed me a key with a golden metal keychain with the club's insignia on it. A roaring lion's head and the words *Hero's Pride* on the top and Oregon under the animal's wild mane. What not everyone knows, but a lot of people probably suspect, is my parents gave me the capital to open my business. I owe them seventy-five grand.

I licked my lips and stared deeply into my mom's icy blue gaze, the same as my own. "I'll pay you back, with interest."

Dad cuddled my mother close, dipped his head, and whispered. "You'll do no such thing. The money we gave you is yours. It was put into an account for you over the years in case you wanted to go to college, buy a house, or whatever you want. This is our gift to you to start your life. We have the same offer for your brother. He's holding onto his for now as he looks for a home for him and Shayna that he can afford."

I couldn't help the tears that fell. "I love you so much, Mom and Dad. I swear I'm going to work hard."

Dad and Mom both smiled huge. "We believe in you. Now hurry up, I want first dibs on those skulls that artist made before Champ gets a look and scores all the good ones." Dad lifted his bearded chin up toward the red painted doors.

I grinned. "You get first dibs on anything, Daddy."

He nudged my mom as she rolled her eyes. "See...my baby, my girl, my biker princess."

Chapter 2

Rex

THE CLUBHOUSE ON THE OUTSKIRTS OF GRANTS PASS, Oregon is huge. Surrounded by nothing but trees with a paved road leading up a long winding road. The building sits on land that includes three hundred acres of forest. Used to be a lodge that out-of-towners, tourists, and hunters would rent. The club President, Riot, an old army buddy of my dad's, bought the lodge for a sweet deal. Word is the lodge was in need of some serious repairs, and the original owners were an older couple with no children between them. The husband died, and the wife tried to keep it up, but with her own failing health, she had to sell it off. She died a year after he did, making it so Riot could buy the place from the bank for a song.

Since then, he and his brothers cleaned it up, refurbished all the wood, gave it a new roof, an overhaul on the inside, and added an enormous warehouse and additional attached rec room. The brothers use the warehouse for storing their bikes, fixing them, and everything else the club does.

I drove up and was met by Riot, Tank, Champ, and Hammer. All four men, large and in charge, were standing shoulder-to-shoulder, arms crossed over their massive chests, feet hip distance apart.

When I made it close enough to stop and turn off my Harley, I noticed Riot's small grin. "Took you long enough, T-Rex. Thought you'd never make it up from California." His voice was a low, commanding rumble. Kind of like rolling thunder.

"You know how it goes. Took my time, old man. Had a lot of thinking to do and nuthin' but the road in front of me and freedom at my back."

"Sounds like heaven, T-Rex," Tank offered.

"Just Rex, guys," I added. My father and his brothers gave me the road name T-Rex. In most circles, I'm the biggest fucker around. The T was a combo for my real name, Taggart, and being as big and mean as a T-Rex. Except here, Tank took the prize for biggest dude. He was massive.

Riot nodded then moved right to the point by lifting his chin and asking, "You make the right choice?"

I rubbed at my overly long beard and mustache. My shoulder length hair was pulled back in a braid one of the club girls back home had plaited for me. She called it my warrior look, whatever the fuck that meant. I just liked the shit out of my eyes when I rode. I wanted nothing messing with the wind against my face.

"Not sure if it's the right choice, but seeing this building, the scent of pine in my nostrils, you men greeting me with utmost respect, I think moving here suits me just fine."

Riot finally grinned, his salt and pepper beard and 'stache a familiar, welcome sight. He walked over to me as I dismounted my ride.

"Welcome home, brother. We still got a vote to take in Church later today, but your rep is known far and wide, and the guys know you or your old man. Don't expect we'll have a problem," Riot said while he locked an arm around me and slapped my back a few times.

I eased away and squeezed his shoulder. "Thanks for having me, brother."

"Any child of my brother-in-arms, and a brother to my club, is always welcome in my home." He confirmed what I already knew. Riot was the real deal. A biker and a leader through and through.

I cleared my throat, wishing I'd had that same respect from my old man back home. "Means a lot."

"You taking on the role of my VP and second-in-command will mean more, Rex. Now come meet some of the new prospects and take a load off. You already know all the brothers, but they're eager to hear how the California chapter of The Pride is doing."

I chuckled and moved to shake the hands of Tank, Champ, and Hammer, the men who held top positions in the club and welcomed me with open arms.

"You know it can't all be bad with nuthin' but sunshine and tanned bodies," I clipped, trying to find humor in a situation back home I knew was not good. That will be for when I have a quiet moment with my new Prez.

Champ whistled loudly. "Shit, I heard that. Need to take a road trip down to Cali. Wrap my dick up in some sweet and sunny California pussy."

I shook my head and followed the Prez inside, my heavy motorcycle boots and my heart leaving behind all that I'd known back in California. I had manned up, taken some responsibility, and got out from under the thumb of my father, Gunner, the California chapter's president. I didn't agree with a lot of the shit he was bringing into the club and don't support it. This was my chance to be part of something I believed in with my entire being.

In any club, if you're a brother, you support your President and take his back no matter what. Unfortunately for me, my father and I had a serious moral difference of opinion. Not to mention, he was pushing me to settle down with one of the club whores. There was one in particular he was fond of dipping his wick into behind my mother's back. Took a liking to her, wanted to keep her around. If she was tied to me legally, he thought it would be cool to have a father-son tag team-type sitch. I was so not down with that. Not to mention, any man that cheated on his wife, the mother of his children, needed to take a flying leap off a short cliff.

I didn't like seeing that side of my dad. 'Cept something in the last few years had changed in him. He got greedy. Started wanting dangerous jobs, the kind you end up doing five to ten for if caught. I was already the VP but couldn't come to terms with what he wanted or the jobs they were starting to take. It wasn't what The Pride was about.

That's when I called on Riot. Asked him if he was looking for another member of his club. As expected, he opened his arms, and much to my surprise, offered me a lateral move. They'd recently lost their Vice President last year to a nasty motorcycle accident. This I knew since most of our club, along with the other Hero's Pride chapters throughout the States, rode up for the funeral.

Turned out, the VP position had not been filled, and none of the men wanted to step into their brother's boots. The guy was beloved and always would be. When I asked to come, Riot offered the role. I jumped at the chance to make a move in the club, even if it was in another chapter, but better yet, in a club two states away from home. From my father.

Now it was my time to prove myself. Be a part of something I believed in again. And hopefully talk to Riot about the shit going down in Cali. Get his thoughts on it. I know that when the club was created, it was about towing that thin line between biker and law-abiding citizen. Bikers liked to live wild and ride free . We didn't do well having anyone put restrictions on us, but since every brother had, or currently, served in either military, law enforcement, or another public service type role, we understood the importance of staying clean. We kept that deep line in the sand between us and full outlaws—the one percenters—without fail.

We had no desire to run drugs, guns, pimp women, or get into gang wars. At least that's how most of the clubs ran. My father's was another story.

However, the goal of any Hero's Pride club is, first and foremost, to protect its own, and second, protect our turf. That meant we kept the county we lived in safe. If we had to break some rules to do that, we would. End of. No shame.

From what I understood, in Grants Pass, there were very few local law enforcement officers. Something about the town's timber and taxes taking a serious hit due to some environmental restrictions. This had a cyclical effect, making it so the budget for cops was cut to the quick, leaving one sheriff and a small handful of deputies to patrol the city of close to forty thousand and the entire county, which made the total population closer to ninety thousand. The club offered relief by doing their own patrol and keeping the streets of the county clear of drugs, whores, and any other wrongdoing they saw.

The sheriff and the club have had an understanding. That understanding has lasted twenty years and has grown over time. Didn't mean the deputies didn't bring in our boys when things got out of hand, it just usually meant they tended to be lenient and let the club deal with their own.

So far it worked, and I was looking forward to being a part of it.

Club voted unanimously last night. I was officially the new Vice President of the Oregon Chapter of Hero's Pride. I thumbed the patch between my fingers as I stared up at the flashing sign and snickered.

Biker Babe. These bitches would come up with anything.

When I got the patch last night, Cricket, an oldie and founding member in the club, informed me that if I didn't sew it myself, I should head into town to his shop after lunch, and he'd take care of it for me.

Not letting any grass grow under my boots, I woke, took an hour long run through the woods, hit the club gym and lifted for another hour, showered, ate, then headed down the mountain. Before I could get off my bike, I saw a brunette enter the shop window. She was tall, tan, and curvy with wild dark hair. She adjusted the vest hanging in the window and placed a series of silver necklaces around the hook to complement the leather. It looked good. Would look better on her, but what she was wearing already had my dick hardening as I straddled my bike in front of the store.

She turned to the side, and I bit down on the inside of my cheek and inhaled deep. All down the side of her skintight leather pants where grommets that left quarter-sized circles of bare skin visible from the ankle all the way up to her hips. If she was wearing underwear, I'd've given my left nut to rip them off with my teeth, but my ultimate guess was she was going commando.

Fucking hell.

The brunette turned around and the back of her was better than the side. Her ass was heart-shaped and cupped to perfection by her pants. The tank top she wore skated up her trim waist and was tied into a knot at the small of her back. She bent over, and I nearly busted a vein in my dick with how tight my jeans became. I palmed my junk and readjusted, watching the sexiest woman alive make that store window even more tricked out.

A scruff of shoes against concrete moved my attention to a man in an ugly suit in front of the store windows. As if I was watching a movie play out, he promptly smashed his fist on the glass to gain the brunette's attention. She turned around, and her eyes met mine not the man's. They were blue but not. Icy blue, like the water over a lake after a heavy freeze. That gaze seared into my chest like a knife to the heart and a punch to the gut at the same time.

She gasped and then her attention was diverted to the fuck face banging on her window.

"Don't you dare ignore me, Shay! I've been calling for months, trying to work shit out with you! Come on! Get out here and deal with your man!" The insufferable pig continued banging on the windows, ramping up my irritation.

A slice of fear flashed across my girl's face, and I growled. Lifting my leg over my bike, I stomped over to the man who was walking to the entrance and put myself between him and the door.

"Got a problem, buddy?" I attempted to cool my rage before I let loose. I didn't know the situation, but I didn't like the guy's tone or him pounding on the windows.

My girl opened the door and appeared just behind me. I glanced over my shoulder and noticed her eyes flash to my cut.

Her shoulders sagged as if in relief when she caught that I was a brother with the local club.

Not good. Her initial response meant this was an unwanted caller. She was less afraid of me, a stranger to her, than she was of the suit.

"I'm her boyfriend, man. It's cool." The fuck face lifted his hands in surrender. He was at least a half a foot shorter than me, which didn't say much because I was unusually tall at six five.

"Ex-boyfriend," she sneered. "As in six months ex. We've been broken up longer than we were dating…"

"Baby, you know I love you…" the wuss pleaded.

"Love me! You smacked me…in the face, Gary! No man puts his hands on me. You're lucky I didn't tell the club!" she fired off.

The only club in the area was The Pride. The one I was now an officer of. "Too late," I snarled low, my hands closing into fists, eyes lasered on the pipsqueak in front of me. "You just did."

Without a second's thought, I pulled my arm back and punched the guy right in the face. He tumbled onto his ass, grabbing for his nose. Blood gushed out his nostrils like a faucet turned on high.

"That's your warning, motherfucker. You don't mess with what's mine; you sure as fuck don't hit a woman, and from what I'm gathering, you don't touch club property."

The woman came up against my back, her hands at my waist as she peered over my shoulder. "Yeah! You better leave me alone, Gary. No more calls. No more stopping at my complex. No more coming to my work or my friends' houses."

"I'm bleeding over here. I think you broke my nose, man," Gary whined.

Hearing how much this fucker was harassing her, I wanted to do more. "You're lucky that's all I broke. Again, warning. She does not exist to you."

"Shay, but I love you, baby," the suit groaned.

I rolled my eyes as Shay made a gagging sound. Then she squeezed my sides with her small hands and rested her forehead on my back. "Please make him stop," she whispered, digging her nails into my cut to emphasize her fear.

That was it. That's all it took. That small pleading voice, her warmth at my back, and I knew I was changed forever. Gone for a girl I didn't even know but would protect with my life.

"I got this, pussycat." I moved her hands from my waist reluctantly. "Retract your claws...*for now*." I walked forward a few feet as the man, Gary, crab-walked backward along the dirty sidewalk.

"No, no, no." He shook his head as if I were a mirage he could make disappear.

I bent down and picked the fucker up by his neck, twisted and held him against the concrete wall. "You see her, you even *think* about her, you remember my face." I plastered my nose to his bleeding one and hissed, my teeth together in a mighty sneer. "She. Does. Not. Exist. To. You. Say it! Now!" I barked.

The man was shaking and attempted to speak through my hold, blood pouring down over his mouth and chin, dripping along his neck and rumpled suit. "D-doesn't e-ex-exist."

I grinned maniacally and dropped him to his feet. He immediately bent over and grabbed for his throat. "Fuck your damn family! Bunch of stupid ass, good for nuthin, bikers!"

What Gary said didn't bother me. It's the talk of a man who just got his ass whipped and is trying to save face. My girl, however, didn't accept it.

As I turned around, she screeched, "Take that back!" and attempted to make a flying leap toward the crumbled man. Before she got there, I caught her mid-air around the waist and swung her around my body. She immediately tried to wiggle out of my hold, but I did a similar move to her as I did to Gary, putting her body against the concrete wall. Except this time, my arms were a protective band around her back with one hand to her head, cupping her cheek. I pressed my thumb over her plump pink lips.

"Still, pussycat. *Still.* I got you." I stared into her porcelain white face and icy gaze until the fire simmered, not completely going out. No, not this woman. She banked those embers and took a full breath in.

Fuck, she was beautiful. Beautiful in the kind of way a man never gets over, would bleed for in a heartbeat. The kind of woman a man regrets leaving in his bed before going to work but doing so, knowing he has a reason to come home at night. A fucking damn good one.

Her gaze searched mine for a couple of moments before she nodded, and I let her go. When I stepped back and glanced to the side, Gary was gone, hightailed it out of there fast. Smartest decision that schmuck ever made.

"He's never going to be a problem again," I promised. And I would make sure of it.

She huffed. "You don't know Gary."

"No, but I'm going to know you. Personally. *Intimately.*" It was one of the first promises I'd ever made to a woman.

My girl licked her lips in a seductive as fuck manner that made me want to kiss that smile away and replace it with a moan.

"I don't date bikers." She cocked an eyebrow, offering up some serious sass that made my dick twitch inside my leathers.

"That's just fine, pussycat, because we're not dating."

That time both her eyebrows rose in question. "Oh?"

I dipped my head closer to hers and caught the scent of sunshine and wildflowers. My new favorite perfume. "No. We're gonna be *fucking*. A lot."

She split into laughter. "You're so full of yourself."

I grinned and ran my hand from her side down to her rounded ass, squeezing tightly, hiking her against my lower half so she could feel the heavy weight of my cock against her body. "Soon, *you'll* be full of me."

She swallowed slowly. "You think I'm easy?" Her head slanted to the side, her eyes narrowing.

I rubbed my hard dick against her center and listened as she gasped and mewled, telling me everything I needed to know.

"No, sweetheart. I think you're going to be a challenge. A challenge I'm entirely ready for."

And on the last word, I pressed my lips to her neck, inhaled her fragrance deep, and ran my tongue along the tender column. She sighed and tipped her head to the side in offering. I nipped and sucked the flesh until a purplish mark appeared at the space just above where neck and shoulder met.

When I pulled my mouth away, her eyes opened and blazed with a white-hot fire. "Did you just mark me?"

I slowly grinned. "Just making sure everyone knows you're taken."

Her chest lifted high, her round breasts pushing against my cut in the most delightful way until her hands came up to my chest, and she pushed off with all her might, forcing me back a couple steps. On a normal day, no one would be able to get the lock on me like she just did, but since I wasn't expecting it, she got the advantage. Usually, women tugged me closer, not pushed me back.

"You're a dick!" Her voice was strangled and filled to the brim with her ire.

"No. Correction. I'm *your* dick. The only dick you'll be fucking from here on out." Again, spoken as a promise, not a request.

She made a pissed off sound between her lips and flung her long, dark hair over her shoulder, maneuvering her sweet ass to the door. "Not happening. Definitely not after you so rudely marked me when I don't even know your name."

"Rex. I'm the new VP of Hero's Pride."

She gasped, her eyes narrowing, and her entire body went perfectly straight before she spun on a kick ass heel to face me. "No fuckin' way."

"Won't ever lie to you, pussycat. Not ever." I dug into my back pocket and pulled out my new patch. "Came here to get this sewn on by Cricket. He in?"

She closed her eyes, seemed to take a deep breath, and shook her head, which contradicted her next response.

"Yeah, he's in the back. But now I have even more reason not to date you, and better yet, you'll never ever touch me again."

"'Fraid nuthin's gonna to stop me from winning you over. When I see something I want, I get it. And babe, you're in my sights."

"That will change." She smirked as if she knew the punchline to a joke I hadn't yet heard.

"Why's that?"

"Because I'm a biker princess." She blinked prettily as if that explained everything.

I looked her body up and down from tip to toe, noting the killer high-heeled boots, leather pants, Harley tank, wild hair, and silver at her fingers, neck, and wrists. "Got that from lookin' at you, babe, and the picture I'm taking in is all I want in my life and in my bed."

"I don't think you understand," she taunted, waving a finger as if I'd been a bad boy and she was about to reprimand me. Again, a twitch to the dick.

"Why don't you tell me what you're going on about?"

"I'm *the* biker princess. My father is your President, Riot."

The blood in my veins went stone cold. "You're Shay O'Donnell?"

She smiled as though she'd just let the cat out of the bag. "Yep. Come on in, *brother*. Take a load off, and we'll get that newly minted patch sewn on."

"Fuck." I clenched my teeth together, looking at everything I could ever want in a woman but wasn't allowed to have. The President's fuckin' daughter. Nothing in the club is more sacred than the President's daughter.

"Not in this lifetime." She shrugged, whipping her heart-shaped ass around in a move that made my dick throb to the beat of my own heart.

How the hell was I going to get around this?

Shay O'Donnell was off limits.

Chapter 3

Shay

REX CRAWFORD.

The new Vice President of the Hero's Pride MC. I closed my eyes and remembered the way Rex lifted Gary by the neck and pressed him into the wall, a foot of space between Gary's feet and the ground.

I trembled at the memory. God, he was magnificent in that moment. I mean, all the brothers are good looking in their own way, but I'd never thought of any of them in a romantic context. Brothers have always been *off limits*. Not only because they answer to my father, but because they're my family. I grew up with the older ones as uncles, the younger ones as something akin to siblings. To them, I'm the club princess. The baby. Someone who is sacred, to be protected.

It's an issue I've fought my entire life. Proving my independence, my worth, has always been difficult, but I earned their respect as a woman who could take care of herself, the day I opened my own business. I moved into my own place, and I'm finally paying bills, surviving on what I provide for myself. I'm twenty-freakin'-five. It's time I climbed out from under my father's thumb. Was my own woman. And I'm finally doing it.

Then, in walks Rex Crawford.

Stunningly handsome. A damn giant compared to most men. Incredible brute strength. It was obvious he worked out. A lot. The first man in a long, *long* time that made my teeth ache with the desire to take a bite out of him. When he walked into my shop after the Gary debacle yesterday, I wanted to put my hands and my mouth all over him. Even if I was breaking my no-dating-bikers rule.

Rex was the exception to any rule.

Built, and with a rugged façade so manly he looked like he could rip trees right out of the ground with his bare hands. And oh, how I wanted those hands on me. Or to run my fingers through that hair. When he arrived, it was down past his shoulders, and the sun glinted off the golden light brown messy waves. He needed to trim his beard and mustache, but I wouldn't kick him out of bed for a little whisker burn. Hell, I'd relish in having his marks on my chin, my breasts, between *my thighs* the same way I sported the new purple mark at my neck.

I clenched my teeth and thighs, trying to stave off the desire that thoughts of Rex have been pounding through my body all damn night and day.

There was no way my father would allow one of his brothers to date his daughter. It didn't matter who he was. His princess was off limits to his brethren.

Besides, Rex was bossy, handsy, and forceful. I usually dated guys where I was the one in control. Hence car salesman Gary, who I thought was sweet, but he had hidden a dark side, brought to the surface with a mean backhand against my cheek when he drank. And he tended to drink when he didn't bring home a sale. When I visited on those nights, I'd spend the entire time trying to get his mind off his job. Until the time I suggested that, if he hated it so much, why didn't he quit. That's when he backhanded me and told me to—quote— "shut the fuck up."

I walked right out of his apartment and his life. Made it clear that we were done. Two days later, he started in with the texts, the calls, the pop-in visits to my friends' places, and the old job I had before I opened Biker Babe.

I grinned, thinking back to Rex punching him in the face, Gary's blood gushing out of his nose, ruining his best suit. I ought to thank Rex for that. At the very least, it sent a powerful message. I don't think he'll be too keen to mess with me anymore. And if he keeps it up, I'll just have to tell Dad. I was trying to solve my problems on my own, without involving the club, but in the end, Gary taught me a powerful lesson.

Family is family.

If you need them, they're there. Especially to lay out those physical lessons to sniveling little insecure asswipes who think it's okay to hit women and stalk their every move once they've broken up with them.

"What's on your brain, Princess?" Cricket asked while tooling a leather purse. This one was so kickass I might end up having to make it mine and not part of the new store inventory.

I sighed heavily and ran my hand over some leather fringe dangling from a bomber jacket.

"This about the new VP taking out your ex?" he speculated correctly.

I narrowed my gaze at the old man sitting in his small space, head bent over the table, his ZZ Top-inspired beard of white blond hair resting on the table. The sides of his hair matched the beard, but the top was bald as a babe's bare bottom. Just as smooth too. Cricket was not a young guy, but I don't think anyone knew his actual age. He'd just always been around. He'd served in the military with my grandfather and stood by my dad when he decided to start Hero's Pride over twenty years ago. He'd always been like a father to all of the brothers. So much so, my store has been a revolving door of brothers coming and going to bend his ear.

"How did you know about that?"

Cricket snuffled and laughed. "First thing Rex did was take your man's issue to the club at Church last night. Made it clear he handled it but wanted everyone to be vigilant."

I rolled my eyes and shook my head, my hot temper getting the best of me. "Is that why Dad and Mom have been checking on me every hour on the hour?" Speaking of which, my cell phone rang.

Cricket simply smirked and continued working.

"I can handle myself," I insisted.

"Sure you can, but why would you need to when you got a man like Rex and every brother in the club willing to lay down his life for you?" Cricket raised his head, his light eyed gaze coming to rest on my face.

My entire body felt heavy, like a 600 hundred-pound Harley had landed on my chest and pinned me to the floor where I stood. "I'm trying to do my own thing. Take care of myself for once." I bit my lip while the emotions flooded my system, shame being the predominant emotion.

"Princess, you're beautiful," he said—as though this answered all the questions of the universe.

I let my shoulders slump. "Thanks, Cricket."

He shook his head. "No, you misunderstand. You're *beautiful*. No woman looks like you. Acts like you. Talks like you. From your head to your baby toe, sweetheart, you're one of a kind. A lot of men will try to catch hold of that, try and hurt it, take it away from us. Drown out that beauty you got. You need a man whose gonna let you bloom in all that you do. A man who isn't afraid of your light. The kind of man who sees a beauty like yours and will break his back to earn it. Feed it, water it, protect it with his entire being. Not someone who is threatened by it."

"Cricket…what kind of man is going to do all of that? He doesn't exist."

He laid down his tools, leaned back in his chair, and put his hand over his not so small beer belly. Hell, the man could almost pass for Santa Claus if he wasn't such a shit stirrer and dirty scoundrel. "Sure, there are. I've met many 'em."

I laughed and ran my hand through the long waves of my dark hair. "Yeah? Where are they all hiding?"

"Right in front of your face, darlin'." He glanced at the Hero's Pride logo t-shirts I had printed and hanging in my shop for the guys and their babes to buy if they needed fresh duds.

"The brothers?" I said sarcastically.

His lips quirked. "One brother in particular. I believe he saved your ass yesterday and made it clear he'd like to own that ass."

I leaned against the glass display of rings and stared Cricket down. "Even if I was interested—and I'm not saying I am—Dad would never allow it. A brother? That's suicide for any man, and you know it."

He shrugged and pressed his lips together. "I don't know. If the right guy was willing to step up, the safest person in the world for you to settle down with would be one of us. A brother would never do you wrong. Not only because it goes against what our club believes regarding women, but because your father and the rest of the brothers would kill him. Simple as that, Princess."

I licked my lips and ran the concept through my mind. Every way I looked at it, every scenario I considered had Dad and his band of brothers destroying Rex in a bloodbath of epic proportions.

"No." I shook my head. "It's not worth it."

"Love is always worth it, darlin'."

I snickered. "Who's talking love?"

Cricket grinned a knowing smile. "We'll just have to see. I look forward to watching the show play out."

The sun had just fallen past the tree line as I walked up the wooden steps to the clubhouse. Loud music was blaring from the workshop, mingling with the sound of metal clanking against metal, echoing through the forest from the open rec room doors where the guys worked out in the homemade gym.

I didn't bother knocking. Club Princess gave me a lot of privileges. Once I was old enough to know and understand the way of things, it was no longer hidden from me. Everything from a bunch of drunk brothers to pot smoking and full-scale public fucking between them and the club girls. Nothing was off limits to me except Church. No woman was allowed where the boys did their club business. Besides, my parents were very free and lived life loud. They didn't shelter Shane and me from much, which meant I didn't hide a lot from them.

Entering the game room, I walked past Tank and Champ playing a game of pool. One of the club girls, Trixie, was rubbing her hand up and down Tank's chest, slipping the other into the front of his pants to cup his package.

He smiled at her and smashed his lips down over hers while

pushing her leather mini skirt up and over her bare ass so he could return the gesture and cop his own feel.

Tank was a big fella. Nice as hell, but frisky. He liked to fuck. One time, he drunkenly told me that being between a woman's thighs made the demons fly away. Seeing as he had a club girl or a one-night stand from the bar on his dick every night, I figured he must have a lot of demons. The only thing I knew for certain about Tank was that he'd literally driven a tank in Afghanistan. It's how he got his road name, but that's about all I knew of his time serving his country. Dad encouraged me not to ask. Didn't want me tainted by the bad shit of the world. Since I liked being a pretty, yet sassy, princess, I took that advice to heart and just snuggled him when he wanted a cuddle from someone he thought of as his baby sister. It worked.

"Come on, man, I do not want to see your dick tonight. I want to see a shiny twenty-dollar bill in my pocket from kicking your ass at pool. Lay off Trixie and take your shot, bro," Champ semi-whined, as much as a burly, supremely cut, biker badass could.

I smiled and waved at them as I passed through to the bar, hoping to find Rex. I'd picked out a present for him from my shop that my local jewelry designer, Sonia, made. One I hadn't even put out. When it came in, I kept it. I didn't know why at the time, but now I do.

Jay, one of the club prospects, was wiping down the long countertop. Being a prospect, he didn't have a road name yet. The club would determine that name when the time was right or the name presented itself.

"Hi Jay, you seen Rex?"

He lifted his chin toward the stairs that led to the brothers' rooms. The brothers were on the third floor. The second was the club girls and extra bedrooms for out of town bikers or guests of the brothers. The fourth, the top floor, was kept open for the President and his family. My father believed in being close to the club at all times. Full immersion.

My mother, a biker babe to the bone, agreed with this. Which meant my brother and I still had a room on the fourth floor. Dad also believed that his kids could always come home, no matter what age. This helped Shane a lot when his daughter, only days old at the time, was dumped into my father's arms by a wacked out baby mama, saying my brother, at the time serving his country in the Army, was the father, and left their daughter to the club and never came back.

A paternity test that I took on my brother's behalf proved that Shayna was his. My brother named her by phone, only having seen a snapshot by text message, and let my parents raise Shayna the first two months of her life until he finished his four-year enlistment and could leave to come home and be a father. Something he'd had no plans for at the ripe age of twenty-one. The entire club kicked in, and Shayna's now the light in our lives. And as for Shane, four years later, he's the second-best Daddy I know. At the time, it was rough, but now he sees it as the best thing that ever happened to him. We all do.

I just wished my brother could settle down, find a good woman who wanted to be a mother. Shayna deserved that in her life.

I took the stairs two at a time until I got to the brothers' floor and the big corner room at the end designated for the VP.

A growling rumble filtered through the walls. "Bitch, I said, get your ass out of here, right now, or I'll toss you out. Believe me, it will not feel good when I do."

I held my breath and pressed my ear closer to the door.

Lacey's voice came through the door loud and clear, forcing me to grind my teeth. "But, Rex...the club girls are here to please the brothers. And you're new. It's my honor to break you in."

That fucking skank.

Just the thought of her nasty ass all over Rex made my heart race. She's the only club girl I couldn't stand. Thought she was God's gift to men with her fake tits and long legs and boney ass.

"I'll say it once and only once. I'm *taken*. Besides, a man like me doesn't want to fuck a stick. You need some meat on your fucking bones, woman. Go eat a goddamned sandwich and leave my room. NOW!" Rex roared.

Her whiney voice kept going. "Rex, baby...just let me suck you off. I'm amazing at head..."

That was it. I lost my patience. I wouldn't listen to this shit for one more minute.

Instead of knocking, I turned the knob and slammed the door open.

Rex's gaze flew up to mine from where he stood in the center of his large room. In nothing but a towel, water droplets ran down his chest from his wet hair. Sweet Harley, he was a wet dream incarnate.

"Lacey, I could hear Rex blowing you off from downstairs. If he doesn't want your skanky ass, get gone." I pointed to the door and down the stairs.

She narrowed her gaze at me, her anger so fiery I could almost feel the burn against my torso. "What would you know about it? You're a walking, talking, cock tease. Everyone thinks so. All the brothers want to do is split you open and fuck you raw, but daddy dearest won't allow it..." After the pause, she started to speak again but didn't get another word out because a big, beefy hand had tunneled into her bottle blonde hair at the roots and gripped so tight the hobag screamed.

Rex didn't seem affected. Instead, he shuffled Lacey toward the door so fast that she had to hustle on her ridiculously high stripper heels to keep up, or he might rip out a huge chunk of her hair extensions.

"Don't you ever..." He gripped Lacey's head and tugged it back so she was forced to look in his eyes. "...ever, talk about Shay like that again, or your ass will be out of the club, your stuff in the street."

Her eyes flashed with defiance. "You can't do that. I've been here for two years!"

"Get a clue," he spat in her face. "I'm the fucking Vice President of the club, bitch. Aside from Riot, what I say goes. That means, if I kick your ass out, you're gone. Now get the fuck out of my room, and stay gone!" He tossed her out into the hallway, none too gently, before slamming the door in her face and locking it. "Fuck!" he roared, using both hands to sweep the long, wet strands of his hair back.

I stood with my arms crossed over my chest. "Do the brothers really think that?"

Rex's dark brown eyes went soft as he shook his head.

"Seriously? I deserve to know. Am I nuthin' but a piece of untouchable ass?" My throat got tight, and I had to clench my jaw in order not to cry.

Lesson number one about being a biker babe. Tough girls do not cry. At least not in front of anyone. In the shower, sure. At night when you're alone...definitely. Never in front of a brother or all hell would break loose, and you'd lose some of your street cred.

"Fuck no. And believe me, in the last two days, I've asked about you. *A lot*. The brothers love you. Every last one of 'em.

31

They're your family. A couple prospects want to tag you, but I cut those thoughts off immediately. They didn't know better. Not then anyway."

I sucked my bottom lip into my mouth and swallowed the rest of my fear and anxiety down. "And what about you? What do you think about me?" I lifted my chin proudly.

His brown-eyed gaze swirled a dark caramel color that I could have gotten lost in. "I think you're nuthin' but beauty."

A flash of heat exploded in my chest so fast I had to clutch at my heart to hold back the desire to bum rush him and wrap my arms around his naked skin. Instead, I dug into my jeans pocket for the soft velvet bag I'd hidden there. "I got you a present." With shaking fingers, I held out the black bag.

Rex reached out and dangled the small bag between his fingers. "What's this for?" He held the bag in front of him but didn't open it to see what was inside.

"You saved my ass. Besides, you're new. Taking the place of a well-loved man. That can't be easy, so I figured I'd commemorate that by giving you a little something. It was made by a local artist, my friend Sonia. It's one of a kind; there are no others like it."

His lips tipped up into a small smile, but I couldn't help letting my gaze skate over his bare torso. The man was muscle on top of lean muscle. He reminded me of that actor Jason Momoa right up to the tribal tats coasting up his left arm. He was ridiculously hot, and I had to grip my hands into fists so that I wouldn't touch him.

He cocked a dark slash of a brow my direction in what I could only assume was a question.

"Just open it," I huffed, and he grinned.

He pulled on the small string holding the little pouch closed and tipped it so the handmade silver ring fell into his palm. He set the velvet bag on his dresser behind him and fingered the ring. It was a wide silver band that had a phoenix rising from fire and ashes on the front, its talons curled around an icy moonstone. The entire thing was large and would sit base to knuckle on a man's finger. It was intricate, detailed, and something only a badass biker could pull off.

He moved the ring to his index finger on his left hand and slid it on. It fit perfectly and looked smokin' hot on him.

I smiled and waited a long time for him to say something while he stared at it on his finger so long I swore I could hear the crickets outside singing "Unchained Melody".

Just when I thought he wasn't going to speak, and I'd given up and decided to leave him alone, he reached out, cupped my neck with one hand, my hip with the other, and crushed our bodies together. He tipped my head up, and his lips came down over mine like a hurricane. Wet, forceful, and all consuming.

He took from my mouth as though he could drink for days. As though it was his right.

I gave him everything. My lips, my tongue, my heart…in a single fucking kiss.

We kissed for ages, our tongues dancing, teeth nipping, lips demanding, until we couldn't continue any longer.

Rex pulled away first, gasping for air, but kept his forehead pressed to mine.

"That's it," he grated breathlessly, his mouth so close I could smell the mint from his toothpaste.

"That's what?" I breathed against his lips, my arms wrapped around his bare shoulders, my hands exploring his smooth, muscular back.

"That's the end." He rubbed his forehead along mine and palmed my ass.

I mewled into the feeling of his hand on my bottom, but more so, against the hard rod of steel pressing against my belly through the flimsy towel he had around his hips.

Then his words penetrated my kiss-muddled brain, and I stilled. "The end?"

He nodded. "Yeah, the end of all women who came before you. You're it. My beginning and end. I'm claiming you."

Chapter 4

Rex

"CLAIMING ME?" SHAY SCOFFED AND ATTEMPTED TO push away, but I held fast.

"Yep."

She shook her head vigorously. "No, uh, Rex, as amazing as that kiss was, and my word..." She took a deep breath. "...it was damn sweet; we *cannot* do that again."

I frowned and eased back enough so I could get lost in her icy gaze. "Woman, what're you talkin' about? That kiss was the *beginning*. Next, I'm going to peel away every thread of clothing you're wearing, then I'm going to kiss you somewhere else. When I've had enough of tasting what I know is going to be a world class cunt, I'm going fuck you so hard you'll have trouble lifting your leg over the back of my bike. The place you're going to sit for the rest of your goddamned life. You hear?"

Shay whimpered, and her nails digging into the naked skin of my back sent a pleasant shiver racing down my spine. I grinned and dragged one hand away from her ass and up her chest until I circled her delicate throat with my hand. Her neck was slender, and with my thumb on her pulse, I could feel her heart pounding like a butterfly's wings in flight. She was scared or excited.

I'd not have my woman scared. Not of me. Not of that fucker Gary and not of blowback from the club.

I dipped my face toward hers. "Pussycat, I can tell from the way your nipples are diamond hard against my chest, even through your sexy as fuck tank, and the way your body is rubbing along my dick, you like the idea of me taking all that's *you* and making it mine. All mine. And I'm gonna do it."

"Rex, baby…" she said on a small mewl as I gripped her ass harder, rubbing my length against her delectable body. Jesus Christ, she was perfection.

"I also know you're scared, and I'm here to tell you right now, that shit ends. With me, you fear nuthin' and no one. Got it?"

"But the club…" She tried to protest but lost her train of thought when I moved my hand from around her neck down to her plump tit and gave it a squeeze. The flesh fit perfectly in the palm of my hand, big enough to spill over, giving a man more than a mouthful. I couldn't wait to get her tank and bra off so I could worship it until she lost her mind.

"Club is my problem," I promised, squeezing her tit one last time, moving both of my hands to the hem of her tank and lifting it up and over her head.

Best part, she didn't fight me on it. Within a second, I had the latch at the back of her bra undone and the red lace falling to the floor at my feet.

I dipped my head down as I palmed and lifted both of her luscious breasts up to my mouth. I took the one I'd been teasing into the heat of my mouth and sucked hard as I could until her knees started to quake. Her fingers dove into my hair, and she arched her back as I went to town on her tits.

"God, Rex…" she cried, her eyes closed, chin pointed at the ceiling. I thumbed her nipples, tweaked, pinched, and plucked the pink little berries until they were a dark plum color and erect as fuck.

"Hot damn, your tits are as succulent as the rest of you. Now baby, it's time I had all of you." I undid the buttons on her pants, bent over, and shoved them down to her ankles. When they were around her feet, I lifted my hand and pushed at her belly until she fell back against my bed. Once there, I tugged off her boots, socks and jeans, leaving her in a tiny speck of red lace.

My dick throbbed as I took in my woman, lying against my red comforter. Her hair was a dark halo, body pearl-like and shimmering in the low light, while her nipples stood erect, waiting for my next touch. She was a goddess. I stood before her and fingered the towel wrapped at my waist, then pulled it off, finally letting my cock free.

Her eyes widened as she took in my length, pointing straight up at my stomach just past my belly button.

"Jesus, Rex, you are so…so…" She licked her lips and lifted up to a sitting position. She placed her hands at my hips and stared face to face with my dick. No prettier picture could ever be had. Mentally, I snapshotted that image for future spank bank material. Not that I'd need it now that I had the real deal panting in front of me.

"Baby, you're *huge*." Her little pink tongue came out and flicked at the mushroom shaped tip. I closed my eyes and groaned as she stretched her mouth around the large, broad, knobbed head. Almost immediately, she gagged, only taking about an inch of my girth inside.

Nowhere near enough. But my girl would learn, and I was a patient man when it came to my woman giving me head.

I locked one hand around the nape of her neck and grinned down at her while I brought my other hand up and petted her bottom lip. "Don't worry, your mouth will get used to stretching wider. You're just gonna have to practice, pussycat." I gripped her hair tight, and her eyes bugged out a bit while I retreated until just the tip of my cock was in her mouth. She swirled her tongue around the head as I thrust inside, using the lubrication from her saliva to go another inch deeper.

Without warning, she swallowed around my length, and I jerked forward, shoving in another inch until I hit the back of her throat, and she gagged hard, her eyes watering.

I pulled back and out instantly, letting her breathe and get herself back together. One of her hands wrapped around the base of my cock and squeezed, the tips of her fingers not even touching, but the effort still felt good as hell.

"Baby, I'm not sure I'm ever going to fit this mammoth thing in my mouth. Frankly, I'm a little scared about how it's going to fit *anywhere* inside me."

I chuckled and pushed at her shoulders until her body was flat on the bed again. This time, I hooked my arm under her back and hauled her up the bed until her head lay against the soft pillows. There, I straddled her body.

"Don't worry, woman." I kissed her softly, then dragged my lips down her neck, working her there, before taking both of her tits one at a time into my mouth and worrying them for a couple minutes each. Once I'd gotten them as ripe as possible, I slid down her belly, kissing, nipping, and tasting her velvet soft skin as I went. "It's my experience that a woman's body can do amazing things, especially with the right type of encouragement."

She reached for my head as I nibbled on the string of her

panties at her hip, yanked the elastic, and let it snap against her skin the same way a guy twists up a wet towel and whips someone with it in jest.

"Ouch!" she called out and followed it with a moan when I kissed the little pinch better. I gripped her curvy hips lovingly while inserting my big body between her thighs and getting more comfortable.

"So this is your encouragement? Snapping my panties like a schoolboy?" she half moaned, half teased.

I grinned and placed both of my hands on her thighs, butterflying them open, the red triangle of lace stretched across the heart of her. Like my own fucking buried treasure. I dipped low and used both of my thumbs to swipe along the damp fabric covering her heat. She trembled at my touch.

"No, pussycat, it's about making you so fucking wet your cunt will be a slip and slide for my dick in about five minutes. Now, shut up, lie back, and enjoy the ride of your life." I finished my promise with my mouth over her cunt, panties and all. I soaked the lace even more, enjoying abrading her sensitive flesh and my tongue with the texture of the lace as I worked her.

"Oh my god!" she screamed, one hand holding my head to her pussy, the other reaching for a rung on the headboard so she could work her hips. And work her hips she did. Magnificently.

My woman was a wildcat in the sheets. She lost all sense of reason, bucking her hips, holding my head down against her lace-covered flesh in a firm grip I liked a fuckuva lot. I let her ride out her first orgasm, humping my face as though she might never get the chance again. I loved every second.

When she finished keening through her first one, I lifted up, pulled off her soaked underwear, spread her wide again, and devoured her cunt. Orgasm number one tasted like honey-dipped fruit, and I wanted more. So much more that I knew, with my tongue as far inside her as I could get, I'd never get enough of this woman. Not ever.

She howled, shaking her head back and forth as I pinched her clit between my thumb and forefinger and fucked her hole with my tongue.

Shay gasped as she spoke. "Never had two...not ever."

I smiled, getting her honey all over my face. Lifting my chin, I pressed my beard against her clit and rubbed it back and forth over the hard knot. She bucked like a feisty bronco, screaming through her pleasure.

Her body shook as I ate up her second release, memorizing the taste of her on my tongue. If her cunt was as good around my cock as it was on my tongue, I'd never need another woman.

As her body rocked through the throes of ecstasy, I inserted myself between her thighs, rested a fist on the bed to hold me above her, slicked the head of my cock through her sugary cunt, centered, and eased home, wedging inside my woman until there was nothing left but a complete connection of our bodies.

She started to cry out, her mouth open in a silent scream as her limbs locked around me.

I held her in my arms, holding my breath, my body in a Shay vise lock.

Shay closed her eyes, took a deep breath, and purred like a happy kitten, while I swirled my hips in small circles, getting her used to my size.

I dipped my head and took her mouth in a series of small kisses. "You okay, baby?" I kissed her down her neck, holding my cock deep but not moving.

"I'll never be okay again," she said in a soft whimper, then wrapped her ankles at my lower back, her arms more fully around my back, and lifted her hips once. Hard. Impaling herself on my cock to the root.

Her neck stretched out, her nails dug in, and she hissed through what I could see was both pleasure and pain. I had a feeling a lot of our lovemaking was going to be a combination of the two.

"Pussycat…" I tried to reach her again, my dick throbbing, my body needing to move. Now.

"Never going to be okay again after this. Nothing will ever be good enough." Her lips dragged along the side of my face, her tongue poking out to taste what she wanted.

I smiled against her neck, eased my hips back, and thrust home.

She moaned and then whispered, "No man…"

"That's right, baby." I thrust a few more times, setting up a slow rhythm. "No other man but me."

"No better cock…" She dipped her head and laid her forehead to mine.

"That's it. Only my cock. You're mine now, Shay. Say it for me while I ride you."

She cried out as I fucked her harder, grasping her hip, my fingers digging in to get more leverage.

"Yours." Shay nodded and licked her lips.

That was all the admission I needed to hear. With that, I wrapped a hand around one of her knees, pressed it up toward her shoulder and got so deep, my pelvic bone ground against her wet clit.

I knew I had the right position when my woman chanted my road name over and over.

"Rex, Rex, Rex…"

"Name's Taggart, pussycat." I thrust as deep as I could go. "In our bed, you call me by my name. Only you, Shay." I dipped down and pressed my lips to hers.

"Now admit it while I fuck you till you come all over my dick. Taggart "Rex" Crawford, Vice President of the Hero's Pride just claimed his old lady." I lifted up, slamming home while watching my cock pierce her pink, wet flesh, over and over again. "Who's my old lady?" I roared, spinning my thumb around the tight little bundle of nerves peeking out of its hood, nestled pretty and pink between her thighs.

Shay's entire body rocked into each thrust. "Me! I'm your old lady, Taggart. You own me."

I grinned and fucked my woman until her cunt locked me up in my own personal heaven where I shot deep in her heat. Claiming her inside and outside, in word and deed.

Shay O'Donnell was my old lady.

Chapter 5

Shay

A FEATHER LIGHT TINGLE SWIRLED AROUND MY NIPPLE, WENT up and across my clavicle, and then down and around my other nipple. I opened my eyes, blinked, and turned my head.

Rex, no *Taggart*, was up on one elbow, head in his left hand, his right tracing patterns along my naked chest.

"Mmm," I hummed when he circled my nipple again, the flesh tightening and stinging with need. His golden brown gaze swept over to meet mine. He smiled a bright, pearly white grin, then eased forward and flicked the aching tip with his tongue.

I sighed and pushed my hands over my head, arching into his touch as well as getting a good morning stretch in.

"You're so responsive. Even in your sleep, you reacted to my touch." He sucked on my nipple, working the tip inside the heat of his mouth with his tongue before worrying the very edge with his teeth. The zing of electricity zipped through my body and slapped my clit to attention. My body bowed up, and he grinned. "Love it, pussycat. Like that my old lady loses her mind the moment my mouth is on her."

I rolled my eyes and cupped his cheek and jaw, preventing his mouth from taking my other breast. "We need to talk about this old lady business." I arched an eyebrow in warning.

In a second flat, Taggart's body was straddling mine, his massive thighs locked against my hips. He eased over me with both of his muscled arms resting on either side of my head so he could dip down and be face-to-face but still hover over my naked body.

"No talk necessary. We fucked all night long, and in that process, you gave me you. That means you're my property. My old lady. And I'm your man. No one talks to you the way you don't like. No one gets in your face. No one touches what's mine. And that includes fuckwads like Gary, a random man in your shop, or the brothers."

I sucked in a full breath, filling my lungs with as much air as I could take in. "I understand what an old lady is, Taggart. I've been a biker princess my entire life." I blew out a frustrated breath. "You need to listen to me. The Pride is the least of your problems, and they're formidable. You know this. My brother, Shane, is another story. My father, your Prez, is going to fucking explode."

Taggart lowered his lips to mine and sucked on my bottom one. I got into the kiss, licking his top lip, running my tongue over his, biting down on that flesh until he groaned. He shimmied a hand under my back and forced me to latch on to his shoulders.

"You hold on to me, pussycat. I'll take care of everything."

I wrapped my legs around his waist until he lifted up and sat at the side of the bed. "Much as I'd like to fuck you all day and night, I've got Church in an hour and then a ride-along to The Pride businesses, and a meet-and-greet with the Sheriff."

Naked as a jay bird, I slumped in his lap. "This is going to be hard. You and me…"

He smiled and shifted his hips so I could feel his cock lengthen. "Did you say hard, pussycat?"

I groaned and shook my head. "You need to be serious. I can't be your old lady."

He lifted my hips, centered his now fully erect cock and teetered me on the tip. "Ride that while you talk to your old man. Turns out I still got a taste for my woman's pussy this morning...Fuck!" He hissed as I slammed down on him to the root. My entire body jolted as his width pierced me in this new angle and stole my breath.

"Jesus fuck, you're a goddamn enchantress." He lifted me up and slammed me back down over him.

I'd let my head fall back, the ends of my hair tickling my ass and his thighs. Before I could fully comprehend what was happening or remember what we were talking about, one of his beefy hands tunneled through my hair, gripping it like a rope. He spun it around his wrist as he arched me so severely he had full control over my body. With his other hand on my hip, he sawed in and out of me, dragging his massive length along every beautiful nerve ending until I could feel nothing but him. I kept my arms at his shoulders and used my thighs and calves to move with his powerful thrusts, crying out with pleasure at each retreat and commanding thrust back in.

"Whose old lady are you, Shay?"

"No." I shook my head, not wanting to get sucked into his sexual manipulation once more, though with every teeth-rattling plunge of his thick length, I got further and further away from true, thoughtful reason.

"Tell me you're mine, pussycat," he murmured next to my ear, his breath a prayer against my fevered skin.

"Mine to kiss." He placed a kiss between my breasts.

"Mine to pleasure." He sucked an erect nipple into his mouth and tugged until I mewled.

"Mine to fuck." He lifted me up and urged me down on his cock, letting go of my hair and wrapping me fully in his arms.

"Mine to protect." He cupped my face and gazed into my eyes while he rubbed a thumb over my kiss-bruised lips.

"All mine. Tell me..." he urged, holding me tight, grinding our bodies together so that his pelvis smashed my hot bundle of nerves with every subtle twirl of his hips.

I gasped and closed my eyes. "Are you mine? Mine to kiss, to pleasure, to fuck, to protect...all mine?" I fired back, using his own words against him.

"Fuck yeah." He fused his mouth to mine, and I went wild, bucking on his lap, digging my knees into the mattress and riding to my heart's content. Heat filled my core and spread out through my chest, my nipples like little fire pokers, burning and sizzling as they dragged across the iron-like slabs of muscle across his chest. I cried out as he fucked me hard, pistoning in as I rode harder than I ever had in my life.

The wave of pleasure overrode my hearing and any rational thought, and the room faded as sparks of color flashed behind my closed eyelids when I went off like a rocket. Rex roared with his climax, pumping his essence deep within me until we were both a bundle of trembling limbs and sweaty skin.

A few minutes later, Rex ran his hands up and down the length of my back, his face plastered against my neck and the mark he'd made on me yesterday. Hell, he'd probably refreshed it.

"There's no stopping this train, pussycat. You've got to get on board because I'm not leaving the station without you."

His words filtered through my brain, and the hilarity of him making a train and station joke hit me so hard my body quaked, and boundless laughter spilled through my chest and out my mouth in loud, quaking guffaws.

Rex palmed my head while I laughed against his naked form, his length softening and slipping from my body with each spasm. Abruptly, he stood, holding my body to his chest, my legs wrapped around his waist as he walked our naked asses over to the en suite bathroom. He flicked on the shower spray, tested its temperature, and walked us both inside.

I had just shoved my socked foot into my sexy as hell boots when a banging sound filtered through the door. "Rex, yo, brother! Come on, Church in ten. Get whoever you're fucking out of here. Time for business." My father's booming voice rang through the flimsy wooden door but dissipated since he must have moved down the hall. Thank God!

"Oh no!" My stomach lurched and adrenaline flooded my veins while Rex's jaw tightened.

"I'm telling him, first chance I get," Rex confirmed and clenched his jaw.

I shook my head and stood up, wobbling on my four-inch heels before righting myself. "No, please. This is new. Let it sink in that you're here to stay. Show them they can trust you as the VP of The Pride, and then"—I shrugged—"we'll see."

He shook his head and pulled a tight black t-shirt over his head, covering the chest I swear could have been chiseled by Rodin himself. The man's body was a work of freakin' art. I felt a blush creep across my chest at the amount of times I'd kissed, sucked, and licked every inch of that chest throughout the night of us becoming a couple.

"I don't like lying to my brothers and most definitely not

my Prez, pussycat. I'm also new to this club. They need to be able to trust me. Starting out with a lie isn't my gig."

I walked over to him and laid my hands on his chest. His heartbeat thumped against my palms. "Just for a little while. Until we figure this out between us, and you have some time with the club." I lifted up on my toes and kissed his mouth, trying to make him understand what I was having trouble getting through his beautiful head. "You better go. I'll leave after you when I know the coast is clear."

He sucked in a rumbly breath and let it out. "I want you in my bed, Shay. Tonight." He pointed to the bed we'd just left.

I shook my head. "No, come to my place. It's…more private." I smiled and bit down on my bottom lip.

Rex smirked, hooked me with a hand to the nape of my neck, and pulled me close enough so he could kiss me. He finished by kissing my nose and then my forehead. "Text me the address."

"I don't have your number."

He smirked. "I have yours. All the brothers do. They all have you listed under Princess."

My shoulders fell forward as I slumped. "Told you. This is not going to be easy."

Rex opened the door, looked me up and down, and winked. "No, but it sure will be fun. See you later, pussycat."

I sighed as he left and finished getting myself together, putting on my silver, pulling my now wet hair into a twisted knot on my head and went about making the bed. As I pulled the sheets in place, the door behind me opened and in strutted Loose Lacey.

She cocked a hip and set her expression to her ultimate resting bitch face. Not hard coming from a skanky bitch like her. "You just wanted him for yourself!" she sneered.

I ran my hand along the dark red comforter, working out all the wrinkles, and tucked in the bottom. I didn't leave my home without my bed made. Besides, seeing his bed made by his woman's hand will make him think of me.

Dammit! Not that I want him thinking of me. Did I?

"Didn't Rex tell you to get to steppin'?" I reminded the festering scab.

She harrumphed loudly and looked at her chipping nail paint. Why bitches bother with nail polish if they're not going to keep it up, I'll never understand. One chip and it instantly looks trashy. Then again, the chick wearing it is a piece of trash. Maybe that was the vibe she was going for.

"I did," she squawked. "I went and blew Champ after seeing how hot Rex's body is. Got all horned up, and since you stole what's one day going to be mine, I had to get me some another way."

I shook my head. "Don't even think of trying your crap with Rex. He doesn't want you. It's never gonna happen. I'd set my sights on something else. Like a brother from another clubhouse would do perfectly."

"You just can't handle the competition." She pursed her lips in a duckface that stupid girls like her thought was pretty.

I grabbed my purse and flung it over my shoulder. "What are you going on about? I forgot you were here."

"Mark my words, *Princess*," she griped with an ugly twist to her overly glossed lips, "that man will be mine."

"Keep dreamin'. Everyone should have one. How's about I show you the door? Or are you going to hang around until it gets dark and wait for one of the brothers to sidle up to in order to get your dinner paid for?"

She gasped and reached for her neck like a proper Southern woman scorned, which she was not. Far from it. "At least the brothers bend over backward to buy me dinner. Whoever does, gets a night they won't soon forget."

I nod. "Uh huh. Sounds like you've got your day and evening all planned out. Good luck with that." I hoofed it down the stairs with biker skank on my heels.

"I'll make sure to tell daddy you spent the night and took care of his VP like a good little biker princess," she clucked.

I stopped in my tracks, having just made it out of the lodge and down the front wooden steps to the asphalt that curves in front of the entrance. Spinning around on my heels, I crossed my arms over my ample chest. "You speak to my father about me or suggest anything about me and Rex, you'll regret it. You think I don't have pull around here. One call to Mags and you're *fucked*. She even hears you shared breath with her old man, especially if it's to talk shit about her daughter, and you'll never see the likes of a biker club again."

Laggy Lacey shivered at the mention of my mother. My mother may be small, but she is queen of the bitches. She hand-picked the club girls. Nothing but the best for her boys. The only reason Leaky Lacey was still around is because the brothers are hooked on her head giving skills and sweet talked my mother into letting her stay, provided, of course, they kept her in line.

The rest of the club girls are awesome. They just like to fuck hot bikers, get free booze, food, and party hardy. Some of them even work the businesses to make some cash. Mags runs a tight ship. It would not do to have one of the club girls gossiping about her daughter. She'd cut the skank off right at the knees.

"Please don't talk to your mother. I'll let it go," she whispered tightly, her eyes flicking from left to right in order to ensure no one was around to hear our conversation, especially my mom.

"Then we have a deal." I lifted my hand and wiggled my fingers at her. "Toodles, bitch." I smiled and headed to my slick little Harley Davidson sportster. Sexy as hell. All black and all mine.

I swung my leg over my pretty baby, revved her engine, and took off like a bat out of hell, Lacey and her bullshit gone the second the wind hit my face. I reached up and tugged out the knot in my hair and let Mother Nature serve as my hair dryer.

Live wild. Ride free. That was our motto, and I'd live it every day until I took my last breath. Which might be soon if my father hears about Rex and me.

I needed to talk to Mags.

Chapter 6

Rex

I HOOFED IT THROUGH THE CHURCH DOORS AND SAT DOWN NEXT
to Riot. The Prez pounded the gavel, and the rest of the
brothers took their positions around the huge ornate
wooden table. The officers sat at the front next to Riot.

The table was made of long wooden boards at least ten across
and cut almost like a picnic style table would be. Only this one
was giant, the size of a decently sized tree. Over twenty huge ass
brothers sat around it, each having a deep leather wheeled chair
that fit their large frames comfortably. It was much nicer than
what we had back in Cali. There, we huddled around a boring ass
conference table with our club insignia on a tablecloth hiding its
tarnished surface. Here, the lion's head and mane were burned
into the wood, its open mouth snarling as though it could pop
out of the table and bite someone's head off at any moment.
Whoever had worked the wood was an artist. HERO'S PRIDE
was engraved above the lion's head and OREGON was below it.

The club's headquarters were in Grants Pass, the only char-
ter in Oregon. And so far, no other bikers in the state wanted to
mess with that.

"All right, men, settle down." Riot waved a hand in the air, and the room went quiet. "We have a lot to get through today, but nothing's more important that what needs to be done about my baby's ex-boyfriend, Gary."

I lifted up from my chill position in my chair. "Already dealt with that fucker," I growled, my hand going into a tight fist. "He'll be breathing through his mouth for the next good while."

Riot nodded, but his lips went flat and turned white. "Not enough. Word is he was heard at the sports bar groaning about how he was going to retaliate against those—and I quote—steroid-injected jocks on two wheels."

I saw red. Stood up, my chair flying against the wall behind me. "I'll fucking kill him!" I roared, and several of the other brothers stood up, banged a fist on their chests, and hollered their own profanities.

"That's my fuckin' sister. I get first dibs!" Shane, also known as Whip to the club crowed, and I had to bite my tongue until I tasted blood in order to let that fly. Yes, she was his sister, and provided she didn't have an old man that they knew about, it would be his right to make that call. Except he doesn't get to make that call, because she's my *old lady,* and it's *my* job to protect her from any threat.

Riot hit the table with his fist. "Sit your asses down. All of you." His gaze met mine, and he squinted, as if he was assessing me for something else. "I also want to know what's going on with the California chapter."

I clenched my jaw and stretched my neck from side to side, trying to leak out some of the tension. This was my chance to spill. As much as I wanted to leave well enough alone for my father and my brothers back home, the shit he was getting into couldn't go on.

"Shit going down with Gunner?" Champ asked, concern plastered across his rugged face.

I ran my hand behind my neck. "Yeah, the club's not good back home. Main reason I wanted out. Find my own path. Which brought me to you."

"And we're happy you chose to come to a sister chapter, but what's going down in California?"

I licked my lips and sighed. "Fuck, guys. It's bad. My father…shit, he's running guns and possibly drugs from Mexico."

Tank slammed his fists on the table. "Goddammit! Stupid fucker could ruin it for all of us. Our club reputation as servants to country and community means everything to us." He shook his head and crossed his arm over his chest.

Whip let fly, his tone seething with anger as his gaze narrowed, and his mouth curled into a twisted snarl. "What the fuck was he thinking?"

"Money. Greed. Power," Cricket, the oldest brother, correctly surmised. I hated to admit it, tried for a long time to let it go, but I couldn't. My father had slipped down a path I couldn't condone and was no longer able to be a part of.

I rubbed my hand down my face and admitted the truth. "He's in deep. Half the club is ready to revolt, the other half likes the money he's bringing in. And it's a lot. Hard to pass on when you're a retired vet or a current civil servant. They don't have the businesses Oregon has to give them the life they want for themselves, their old ladies, or their kids. This was my father's way to make up for that."

"Bullshit move!" Hammer blurted. "They didn't fucking *try* to build them. Everything we have we fought for, bled for, and worked our asses off to have as a family. Not one brother here doesn't earn his take one way or another," Hammer offered angrily.

I nodded but kept quiet. I'd shared what needed to be shared. It was time for the club to determine what to do about it. There was no way a man like Riot would let this kinda shit fly, tarnishing the good name of the Hero's Pride MC.

Riot raised his hand to quiet the room. The man had respect because he gave it. Every brother settled down and awaited their President's words.

"I'll get some more intel and dig deeper. We've got a PI we can turn to for shit like this. We may have to get a vote from all the clubs in order to do anything long lasting, but first, I want the deets, then I want to talk to Gunner. See if I can sway him back to the right side of club business."

I couldn't help the sigh of relief that left my lungs. "I'd appreciate it, Prez." I thanked Riot, but the fire in my gut over my father and the shit with Gary, Shay's douchebag ex, was still burning inside me.

Riot nodded, and then his eyes turned hazy, and his jaw tightened. "Now, back to Gary. How do we get this assclown outta town and away from my baby? I'm livid he took a hand to her. No man touches my daughter in anger, especially not your princess. I'm ready to charge at this piece of shit. Except I want this permanent. He needs to be gone. Out of state gone."

"Done," I growled low and throaty, my hatred coming back full force. I clenched both of my hands into fists on the table, wanting nothing more than to give old Gary another beatdown.

"What's your stake in this?" Riot spun his chair, his knees splayed as he sat back and focused his shrewd gaze on me. "You're pretty pissed off. And sure, I get that you're the new VP and want to back your brothers, but this is more than that."

I licked my lips, wiped my bearded jaw with my hand, and stood up. It was now. It had to be. We'd already talked about my club business. Regardless of what Shay thought, I couldn't keep shit from my brothers and especially not from my President. It's just not done in an MC. Ever. I crossed my arms over my chest, looked at each brother in the eyes, and then back to my President.

With as strong a commitment as I felt deep in my soul, I said the words they all needed to hear.

"I've claimed Shay O'Donnell as my old lady."

Whip flew out of his chair, his brown shaggy hair wild over his brow as his green gaze flared with anger, and he bum rushed me, slamming my two hundred and forty pounds against the concrete wall so hard my head hit. I saw tweety birds flying around in my peripheral vision as my skull throbbed with searing pain.

"You motherfucking bastard! That's my goddamned sister. She's the fucking princess. She. Is. Untouchable!" he screamed in my face, his beefy forearm shoved against my neck so hard I could barely suck in a breath. The man had definitely learned a thing or two during his time in the Army.

Right behind him was a line of brothers ready to back up Whip and defend Shay's honor.

I struggled against Whip's hold, eventually wrapping my fingers around his forearm enough that I could pull in a breath or two. "She's mine!" I growled right in his face, my eyes bulging, my teeth ready to snap and bite into flesh.

He pushed hard against my neck. "Fuck you. Fuck you! You are *nothing*. No one is good enough for her. You're dead meat, brother!" he sneered, shoving his forearm tighter against my windpipe. Before I could do anything, he jerked up a knee and struck me right in the balls.

"Christ!" I howled in pain and fury.

"Let him go," said a stern, stoic voice near us.

My vision had started to darken from lack of oxygen. My

nuts were screaming in agony, but I held strong. Keeping my feet. A man worthy of Shay couldn't falter. I could have fought harder, but her brother deserved his due. I was claiming his sister. His twin. The Pride's princess.

"I said: Let. Him. Go." This time, I was able to see the President's fingers digging into his son's shoulders and tugging him back.

Eventually, he let me go, but not before pushing me against the wall, my head cracking against the concrete again. "Fuck!" I reached for the back of my head. I'd have an egg the size of a baseball, but I'd live.

The rest of the brothers were scowling, ready to jump me at the President's signal.

Riot raised his hand in a stop gesture, his eyes black as night and on me. "It seems we've come to a new situation. One that we've never had to deal with before." His voice was chillingly calm.

"Yeah, the excommunication of a brother!" Whip spit on my boots and snarled like a wild coyote.

The President gripped my shoulder and squeezed painfully. I gritted my teeth and couldn't help but flinch. He shoved me into my seat. "Sit."

I did as ordered.

"Everyone, sit. This is our brother, our VP. He deserves to be heard."

When the brothers finally sat, I coughed and cleared my throat, rubbing at the tender skin that Whip severely bruised. When I spoke, it sounded like I'd run my vocal cords over a cheese grater, such was the damage he'd wrought. I adjusted my now swollen, aching balls and winced.

Whip smirked at my discomfort. "There's more where that came from, motherfucker!" he said snidely.

"I get it. I deserved it. I deserve anything The Pride wants to put me through. But there is nothing and no one that's going to change my mind. Shay is mine. She's my old lady now."

"And how did this come about?" the President said calmly, as if we were just having a Sunday chat while walking through the park like normal, civilized human beings. Though I wouldn't confuse that dark gaze and chilling tone for what it wasn't. The man was simmering like a boiling pot of water under the surface, and he could blow at any time.

"I went to her store to get my patch sewn." I glanced at Cricket, who nodded and was grinning like an old loon, apparently enjoying the shit out of the situation. Still, I continued. "Laid eyes on her once. It's all it took. Fell for her instantly."

"Bullshit! You just want a piece of ass!" Whip griped. "My sister is no piece of ass!"

"No, she isn't, and I'll bloody any man that disrespects her like that." The snarl that left my mouth was unmistakable. My alpha male side was bursting at the seams to rip free, but I was doing my damndest to stay as calm as possible. "She's the most beautiful woman I've ever laid eyes on. She's the fucking sun. The moon. The goddamned Universe. My heart." I slapped my fist over my chest where the thing lay beating for her. "And I'll do anything, suffer any situation you brothers want to put me through to prove it to her and to you. I'm going to bend over backward to make her happy. And no one, not any of you, will get in my way."

Riot's mouth twitched with anger, his nostrils flaring, like a bull ready to charge, but he set his palm out on the table. Each and every brother watched and waited for his next words.

"You want to claim my baby or you already have?" His words were direct, and a lie wouldn't cut it. Not that I'd ever lie about my commitment to her.

"As I said, I claimed her."

His intake of breath was sharp and seemed overly loud when the room went silent. It was so quiet I could easily hear the scrape of one of the brother's boots against the floor as he re-situated himself.

"This means you've also bedded her," he said flatly with zero emotion. It was the most frightening thing I'd ever seen.

"I have." I swallowed but spoke as clear as I could through a bruised windpipe.

His flat palm twisted into a fist; he turned in his chair, pulled his arm back, and clocked me in the jaw so fast and hard my body listed to the side with the blow. It was as if I'd been hit with a sledgehammer to the face, not a man's fist.

"You will take the fist of every brother in this room, any-where they want to show the disrespect you wrought on our princess. If you are still breathing by the end of it, I will person-ally brand my daughter's name across your fucking chest with a hot iron, right over the heart you claim to have given her. You will bleed for her. You will sacrifice for her. You will fucking BURN for her!" His voice rose to a volume so loud my ears throbbed.

Fuck. He's calling for the Gauntlet and Honor Guard.

"And then, if you are still conscious, you will be forgiven. With the expectation that, if you ever, and I mean *ever*, hurt a hair on her head, a fucking pinky toe on my baby, you will regret claiming my girl, The Pride's reigning princess. Do you understand?" He gripped my jaw, and his twisted, angry face hovered right in front of my own.

"So be it." I firmed my jaw and stared him down until the bastard gifted me a wicked smile.

"First, we ride to see Gary. Tomorrow at nightfall, you'll face your brothers' wrath and fight for Shay's honor."

"I'll wear my Sunday best," I joked even though the situation was dire. These men could kill me if they wanted to. Especially men like Champ, who had been a professional prize fighter in his past life or Tank, who was as large as his name suggested.

"It's a date, motherfucker." Riot grinned. "Now we ride together as brothers. No one lays a finger on the VP until tomorrow. All in favor of this ruling?"

Twenty plus "Ayes" rang out over the buzzing that had taken up residence in my head after the head cracking and punch I took to the jaw.

"Motion passed. Let's ride."

Chapter 7

Shay

"WHY DIDN'T YOU TELL YOUR FATHER AND ME about Gary hitting you?" My mother's voice held a thick note of contempt with a side of frustration.

I grabbed the handful of black, red, and white skull and crossbones scarves I'd just finished tagging and took them over to a display that held a bunch of hooks and started placing them strategically, so they'd look best. I sighed. "It really wasn't a big deal. Besides, it was more of a hard, backhanded slap then anything. I bailed immediately. Left his ass where he stood."

"Excellent, Shay-la-la, but that isn't the problem. I'm glad you stuck up for yourself by leaving and didn't take his crap. It's absolutely what your father and I raised you to do. But honey, you were also raised a biker princess. You do not get backhanded by a man and not tell your father, me, or one of the brothers. Your honor is our honor. Now, don't be surprised if this comes to a head…" Mags warned letting her words fade away.

I spun around and placed my hands on my hips. "It's already been dealt with."

Mags shook her head and puttered around my store, adjusting things that had been sifted through by the customers. "It's not how these things work, and you know it as well as you know the sun rises each morning and the moon takes its place each night. Your father"—she winced—"the brothers"—she shrugged—"it's their way."

"Rex already dealt with Gary by breaking his nose and running him up a wall by the neck. I'm pretty sure he learned his lesson, Mom."

My mother smiled and waved her hand as if this were not my concern. "Yes, but your father and The Pride have other ideas."

"Jesus, Mom. Am I going to have to go down there to make sure that they don't kill him?"

Mom put a hand to her chest. "We do not kill people, Shay, and you know better than to suggest otherwise. The Pride protects its own. You are theirs. Gary messed with club property. Consequences are such that he needs to understand the full scope of his transgression."

For a moment, I just breathed, letting air fill my lungs and then releasing it until I counted a full ten seconds and did it again because I was still fuming.

"This is insane!" I gritted my teeth and slapped my hands against my leather clad thighs. "The last thing I need to deal with is my father going apeshit or to jail over my douchebag ex. Someone who's already received his warning."

Mags lifted a shoulder and tipped her head. "This is the life of a biker."

She was not wrong. Someone messed with the club, the club messed back. In this case, it was worse because I'm the President's daughter. I was raised with those men as my family from the day I was born. They were not going to take kindly to hearing about me getting roughed up by a car salesman who's a mean drunk.

Shit. What did I do now? And that didn't even touch the surface of what I called Mags here for.

"Moving on..." I started to speak but my mother interrupted.

"Yes, let's!" Her blue eyes, the exact same shade as mine, sparkled. "What did you think of the new VP? I mean, you've probably met him before at one of the club parties..."

"Actually, I hadn't. Him coming to the store to get his patch sewn on by Cricket was the first time we met."

She fanned herself blatantly. "Isn't he dreamy? All the club girls are in a titter over who's going to have him first."

Instantly, a wave of heat bathed the surface of my skin and tingled like I'd been standing outside on a hundred-degree day in the dead of July.

Mags continued. "I'm betting Trixie. She's sweet, and those big guys tend to like them sweet. Though Lacey will probably try to jump him first shot she has."

That flame on my skin was raging fire alarm red, and I ground down my molars at the thought of any of those club girls getting a taste of my old man.

Shit.

My old man.

And he was. It's the reason I needed to talk to Mags. Get her help with this. Figure out what to do. There was no way that Rex was going to back off no matter what was good for him.

Men like him, *brothers*, didn't claim a woman one second and then suddenly decide they didn't want her anymore. When you were an old lady, you were it. Period. End of. No rolling the dice again. No do overs. Unless you cheated, or did something against the club, or were a screaming bitch, and even then, it might still stick if that was a brother's gig. You were *claimed*. Property of the brother. Wore your patch. Showed your honor to The Pride and the rest of the world with your ass on the back of your old man's bike.

"Lacey better back the fuck off," I grated through clenched teeth.

Mags narrowed her gaze and crossed her arms over her leather clad chest. Her bosom was large and in charge, but she flaunted it because that's the way my father liked it. Instant access to her goods. She teased that she wore tight jeans to show off her ass but make it harder for him to get to her sweet spot, which she claims is half the fun. Most of the time, though, Mom wore flirty little dresses because she wanted his hands on her all the time. I got it. My dad is hot. As a woman, I can totally see his appeal to the opposite sex. Large, dominant, with a tight salt and pepper beard and thick hair the same color, always just barely curling around his collar, and a bright smile that made women swoon.

"You think she's not right for the hunk of burning biker? Maybe Trixie is the way to go." She tapped a bright fuchsia nail against her bottom lip. "I'll give her a heads up to dress smokin' hot tonight, and maybe she'll score first go…"

"Not. Fucking. Happening. Mom." I hissed the venom so severely my mom stepped back in surprise.

Her gaze ran all over my face and she straightened her spine and tipped her head. "Why ever not, Shay-la-la?" She grinned wickedly.

"Because I've already had him. And he's *mine*," I grated through my teeth.

A huge smile broke out across Mom's face. "Is that right?"

"Yeah, I'm the new Vice President's old lady."

My mother's mouth dropped open as if she was about to catch flies. Her eyes practically bulged out of their sockets. She blinked a few times without saying a word. "Old lady? Are you telling me that Rex Crawford claimed you?"

I nodded and flung my thick hair over my shoulder and laid down the law. "Damn straight. Which means no club girls. No hang-arounds. No bitches of any kind. You hear me?"

Mags nodded over and over until she brought her hands in front of her chest and clapped. "Oh my God! My baby has been claimed! This is better than when you became a woman and lost your virginity all rolled into one!" She cheered and continued her fawning. "Oh my, oh my, oh my God, I can't wait to tell your father. He is going to be…" And all of a sudden, her body stopped moving in the middle of her excited rant, and her gaze cut to mine. She gasped, and her voice sounded as though it had been run through a garbage disposal. "He's going to be *so angry*. Sweet Harley on high. He's going to lose his ever-loving mind."

"And therein lies the problem." I lifted my head to the sky and prayed that God could help.

"Yes, indeed. This is going to take some serious schmoozing. A whole lot of booze. And creativity. Yes…definitely creativity," she said cryptically while walking to the beaded-off section where I kept the adults only toys and other paraphernalia in the event that the biker babes brought in their littles to go shopping with them.

I followed my mother to the curtain, and she pulled it aside and walked right up to the sex toys. She immediately grabbed a leather flogger. "Yes, I'll need this. And…" Her voice drifted off until she picked up a mask, like the ones you wear when you want to shut out the sun and get some serious Zs, or in this case, for a little foreplay. "Uh huh, and maybe one of these."

She scooped up a long feather and bit her bottom lip, worrying the surface as her gaze scanned the shelves.

"You think sex is going to fix this with Daddy?"

My mother spun her head around and looked at me as if I'd grown devil horns. "Yes, my darling. The biggest tool in your arsenal as a woman is the treasure between your thighs. Bikers don't take kindly to getting their honey cut off. Ever. Which means you do what you have to do if a situation arises where you need your man to have a kind ear."

"Mom, that's sexual manipulation."

"Exactly!" She patted my back and went back through the beads and set the stuff on the counter. "Let's see what else."

I watched in absolute fascination as she perused the lingerie section and picked out the skankiest slips of lace. A full body jumpsuit that had holes cut out for the nipples and the crotch with a bow that sat on top of the ass like a present. "This will do nicely for round one." Then she chose a royal blue slip of satin that had little black lace edging on the hem and bodice. It was positively sweet in comparison to the slutty getup she'd already chosen. "And then this for round two after I've worked him good, then I'll work him slow and easy while I tell him that he's not allowed to kill his new Vice President who's already claimed his only daughter."

I sucked in a huge lungful of air and let it go slowly. "Mom, this is weird."

"This is the circle of life, child," she tutted.

"No, it isn't."

"Shay-la-la, it is for a biker babe. Now ring me up."

"Mom, you get everything for free. Remember, the early inheritance. And I didn't ask you here for you to plan a twisted sex-a-thon with Dad. By the way, ew and gag me!" My shoulders sank, and I reached out to the counter to hold myself up. The weight of the situation had finally hit home. "I need your help on all this. I don't even know how to be an old lady, let alone the old lady of the club VP. And that's provided my father, brother, and The Pride don't kick Rex out on his sexy ass or kill him! Either would be really bad, Mom!"

My mother pulled me into her arms. "Oh baby, you have nothing to fear. You're going to be an amazing old lady. Because you've learned from the best. And honey, I'm always here to help guide you. Always."

I nodded against my mother's neck and inhaled the rose inspired perfume she wore and the scent of the leather on her back, proclaiming her the property of The Pride and more importantly, the President.

She ran her hands over my hair and back soothingly as I let it all sink in. I have been around the club my whole life. There's nothing I don't really know about them. They love me; I love them. That's half the battle for an old lady. Even the club girls are cool to me, with the exception of Lackluster Lacey. God, that bitch needs to hightail it outta here. She's never going to hook her star to a brother. They don't take home the club girls. They fuck 'em at the club and share them with their brothers and other visitors at parties. I shiver at the thought of Rex partaking.

Would he expect me to be okay with him having club girls and me?

A knot in my gut the size of Texas formed and twisted. A lot of the old ladies looked the other way when it came to club girls. As long as their man was committed to them, came home to them at night, they didn't care. Before now, I'd never considered this an issue. It was their relationship, their terms. Not my concern. Now, with Rex, I was all about beating down some ass if any one of those girls even touched him with one of their glossy coated nails.

"Mom, can I ask you a question?"

"Anything baby. You know that." She pulled back but kept me within arm's length.

"It's pretty personal, and you don't have to answer if you don't want to," I tried to offer even though I really wanted to know.

Her brows furrowed and her gaze turned soft. "What is it?"

I swallowed down the fear and let it fly. "Do you allow Dad to uh...partake of the uh, you know..." I waved my hand in the air, trying to be nonchalant but failing miserably.

"Are you asking if I allow your father to enjoy the club girls?"

I let out the breath of air I was holding. "Yeah."

Her entire face went from stunning woman barely touching fifty to angry hellion in one go. "Fuck no! That dick is mine." Her temper flared a bright red on her cheeks and neck. "Under no circumstances does he dip his wick in any other honey but mine."

"How do you make sure of that?" I asked, feeling shitty for even going there. I mean, this was my father we were talking about, but he was also the Prez, and she was the Queen Old Lady in the club.

Her lips twisted into a sexy sultry smile. "Baby, all you have to do is lay down the law with your man. But you also have to be willing to ensure your man is sat-tis-fied regularly. You get me?"

I nodded.

"I'm also the woman that runs the girls. It's law that they serve my man beer, food, be some awesome eye candy, but never, and I mean *never* touch what they know is mine. Not only would they be kicked out of the club right straight, they might even lose a hand in the process." She shrugged as if what she'd said was no big deal. Just shooting the shit when, in reality, she's scary as all hell.

"Wow. You're kind of my hero, Mom."

She smiled huge. "Don't you worry, my darling; I'll show you the way. No one will touch your man. Especially now that I know he's yours. I'll have a meeting with the club girls directly. No worries."

"Thanks, Mom." I went over to the counter and bagged up her stuff in a black bag with the shiny silver Biker Babe logo on the side.

"You betcha. Now I have a man to sex up and some girls to give a talkin' to."

"I love you."

My mother strutted her sexy self to the door, plopped on a pair of pink aviators, and waved her fingers. "I love you more, Shay-la-la. Toodles, my darling."

"Bye, Mags!" Cricket roared from the back room. One I had no idea he was in.

"Bye, Cricket. See ya later."

"Definitely, hot stuff!"

I walked over to the room where Cricket was working in the dark, only a desk light shining down on a leather vest. Turned out it was my man's cut, and I knew that because he was stitching on the Vice President patch.

"So, you heard all that, eh?" I tapped at my lips, waiting to hear the verdict.

"Princess, I hear all. How do you think I got my road name?"

I shrugged. "Actually, I never knew the story."

He lifted his face, and his long white beard moved with him but still curled on top of the table; it was that long. "I've always been the sounding board. Ever since 'Nam. Your grandfather

69

would bend my ear. Then the other soldiers started doing it. Got the name Cricket. Like Jiminy Cricket from *Pinocchio*. I'm the voice of reason."

Nodding, I slumped into the chair near his desk. "And?"

"And what?"

"What's your verdict?"

"You've already made your bed by sleeping in it with the VP. Now you have to suffer the consequences."

I narrowed my gaze. "That's it. Your big, wise advice. I've made my bed?"

He grinned and waggled his bushy white eyebrows. "Yeah, and since your ass got claimed, I'm guessing you had a lot of fun in that bed."

I lifted my head to the sky and groaned. "You are not helping."

He shook his head. "Can't tell the future, Princess. Though I will say, Rex is gonna have to prove himself to your dad, your brother, and The Pride in order to survive this claiming."

"That's what I'm afraid of."

He reached out a hand and placed his over mine. "Don't be. You're worth it. And any man who's worth his salt, knows that. He'll do what he has to do to keep you and the club, or he wasn't worth the trouble to begin with."

Chapter 8

Rex

LATER THAT EVENING, MY WOMAN WAS IN A FULL SNIT. "WHAT the hell are you talking about! You told them! All of them? Are you insane? Do you have a death wish?" I watched as Shay paced on her bare feet, her long as fuck legs going for days in a pair of the tiniest booty shorts I hoped to hell were pajamas. Seriously, those shorts were a hair above underwear, pink with little skulls and red roses stitched into the pattern. Her tits were encased in a slip of cotton that had next to nothing at her shoulders. The wild mane of dark espresso colored hair I loved running my fingers through was twisted up on top of her head in a funky knot with little wisps poking out in every direction.

Christ, she was beautiful.

Her face was clear of any makeup, and her ice-blue gaze was set at scalding. Eventually, she stopped pacing, slapped her bare thighs, and just glared at me.

As I suspected, my old lady was not fond of the path I'd taken regarding our relationship. Outing us to the club, sharing my intentions about her, and the fact that I had officially claimed her did not go over well. On either front. Instead of spewing some sugary bullshit, I just waited it out and watched her heart-shaped ass strut back and forth across her small kitchen,

"Yep, you're certifiable. That's the only conclusion. The Gauntlet? For real? That's some bullshit if I ever heard it. What are they going to do? String you up by your toes and hang you from a tree? No, let me guess, tie ropes to each of your limbs, attach the ends onto a Harley and rip you to pieces?" She blew a loud breath between the most sumptuous lips I've ever had the pleasure of kissing and pouted. "Baby, they're going to hurt you. I know it."

I nodded. "Yeah, they are. And it will be worth every second to know that I have my woman's honor vindicated and get to keep the respect of my brothers."

Her face twisted up into a pinched expression that was cute as fuck. "I don't want this for you. No man should have to go through this messed up crap in order to be with a woman. My family is so fucked up!" Tears filled her eyes, but she firmed up her chin, compressed her lips into a flat line, and breathed through it.

My strong, beautiful girl.

I walked over to where she stood and saw her shoulders start to slump, all the fight leaving her body shaken. I wrapped my arms around my woman and tilted her jaw up to face mine. "I'll take any hit. Suffer any pain, physical or otherwise, to keep you in my life, Shay."

Her eyes were the prettiest sky-blue, shimmering with tears that didn't fall. "But you shouldn't have to."

I dipped my head and took her mouth in a long, lingering kiss. "Yeah, I do. It's our way, pussycat. I'm claiming a biker princess not some random woman off the street. Not only does that take balls, it takes commitment, strength, and guts. All of which I have. All of which I will prove to you and the club."

She laid her palms on my chest. "You don't have to prove anything to me. I fell for you the moment you defended me against my ex."

I smiled and cupped her jaw, swiping along the rounded apple of her cheek. "And I fell for you the second I saw your sexy as sin body in the window. Then you spoke, and I saw your face up close...shit babe, I'll never forget the first moment I looked into your eyes. Best day of my life."

Her expression contorted into sadness as she laid her forehead against my chest. "What are they going to do to you? I'm assuming they told you."

I shook my head and cupped her nape. "Not for you to worry about."

Her body jerked, and she flung her head back and glared at me. "Tell me right now or...or..."

"Or you'll what?" I chuckled and ran my hand down her back.

Her gaze narrowed, and she gifted me one of her sultry smiles then licked her lips. "I'll take away your honey." She smirked as she leaned away from me and drug her hands over her full tits, down her ribcage, and over her hips. One hand shifted position and moved down toward the treasure between her thighs, and one reached out and cupped my hardening package.

"You wouldn't." I barely got the two words out, my voice raw and scratchy as she palmed my cock over my jeans with more fervor.

She tipped her head and smirked smugly. "Wouldn't I? Remember, baby, we're technically only just getting to know one another. There's a lot you still have to learn about me."

I growled and held her hand to my erection. "You don't keep *you* from *me*."

One of her delicate shoulders rolled up and then down as she shrugged. "Then don't keep things from me. You want unfettered access to my honey pot, you're going to share. All things. No lies. No secrets." She harrumphed, seeming pretty proud of herself.

A growl rolled up my chest and out my lungs as I shoved her hands away from between us and cupped her sex roughly. "This is my cunt." Her intake of breath was fast and surprised.

"And you're my old man. Now, you want all of this…" She waved her hands over her body, but it didn't prevent me from pressing my third finger hard against the fabric of her tiny thin shorts to where I could feel she was already getting hot.

She gasped, and her eyes blazed. "What are they going to do to you?" Even getting turned on she still tried to get me to succumb to her request. No way in hell.

"I'll tell you after I eat my cunt, then fuck my pretty cunt." I gripped the skimpy shorts and shoved them down around her thighs.

She reached for my shoulders to steady herself. "Baby…" The word was laced with desire as a hint of nervous energy filled the space around my woman.

Didn't matter. I was gone. I shook my head. "No. You went too far, woman."

Without any preamble, I lifted her up by the ass cheeks, laid her ass on the open counter, and ripped off her shorts that were dangling around her shins. In seconds, I had her bare assed on the granite, her legs butterflied open, and my mouth on her treasure.

Her hands flew to my hair and twisted around the heavy locks, pressing up her hips and pushing my head down to grind on my face. My woman was not shy about sex. She went for what she wanted, and she went hard.

A perfect fucking old lady, if there ever was one.

"Goddamn, wildcat. Dig your claws in me, baby!" I roared when she sunk her nails into the meat of my shoulders. I growled around her wet flesh and ate hardy. Sucking, licking, blowing cold air, and sinking my tongue deep until her body was squirming all over the counter, legs restless, chest panting, mouth open, and eyes closed tight.

"Baby, please. Taggart, make me come."

I grinned around her soaked flesh. "Don't you ever take my honey away. You hear me, woman! This cunt is mine for the taking."

Proving my point, I wrapped my lips around her clit and sucked so hard my cheeks hollowed out.

Shay screamed and bucked, her heels locking behind my back, her fingers digging into my shoulders so deep she was going to leave crescent shaped marks in my skin. Marks I'd wear with pride.

Once she was boneless, I gripped her legs, and turned her naked ass over on the counter so she was belly down and legs and ass hanging over the edge. Her toes touched the ground right as I released my cock, wedged it between her wet lips, and drove home.

"Taaaaag!! Fuck!" she cried out again. I wrapped my hand around one hip, the other around her shoulder, and went to town on her, punishing her with pleasure for trying to take away what's clearly mine.

"Don't." Ram of my hips.

"Ever." Spoken through clenched teeth.

"Take." Grind of my cock in a circular motion.

"Away." She screamed on a deep thrust.

"My." I moved my hand to her hair and tugged it back, arching her neck until she moaned deep.

"Honey." With a flick of my hand over her cunt, I pinched her clit.

My woman soared once again, her body convulsing, her nails scratching at the granite for purchase but finding none. She was completely at my mercy.

I fucked her hard, long, and so deep she came again before I shot inside her on a roar the likes of which is heard in the animal kingdom.

When I was fully spent and my cock stopped throbbing inside her heat, I pulled out. Her body lay boneless against the counter. I tucked my cock back into my jeans, lifted my girl in a princess hold, and walked her through her apartment until I found her bed. I laid her on the mattress, removed my cut, shirt, and jeans, and laid them on a chair next to her dresser. Then I walked naked into the bathroom, got a wet washcloth, and went back to my woman, who seemed completely dead to the world. Her chest was moving, so I knew I didn't fuck her to actual death, even though I tried.

I opened her legs, and she mewled as I wiped up my mess between her thighs. Then I took it to the bathroom and tossed that fucker in her laundry basket.

I'd never cleaned between a woman's legs. Mostly because I'd never actually come in a woman without a condom. Shay was the first, but this wasn't the first time we fucked without protection.

Fuck, I hoped she was covered, but if she wasn't, it didn't matter.

Shay O'Donnell was it for me.

In my experience, it was that way with most of the bikers in The Pride. All of us having been men of service in one field or another, we knew a good thing when we saw it. Now that didn't account for the douchebags that cheated on their women with the club girls, but that was between them and their women. In my mother's case, she didn't care as long as my father came home to her and paid the bills.

Me? I was not that man.

My President, Riot, was also not that man. Especially when it came to his daughter. He'd accept nothing but the best, and even though I wasn't worthy of her, because no man was, I'd endeavor to be. And that had to count for something.

"Baby…" When Shay spoke, I realized I was just standing naked in front of her bed, looking down at her. "Lie with me."

I smiled in the dark but went around to the other side of the bed, pulled back the covers, and slid in. She lifted up for a moment, tugged off her little top, and tossed it on the floor. Once I got all the way in, I captured my woman around the waist, tugged out her hair tie, and tucked my nose at the base of her skull where her scent was the deepest. Wildflowers and sunshine. I inhaled her essence fully before letting it out in a relieved, sated breath.

"What are they going to do to you?" She ran her hand down my forearm back and forth as if she was soothing me when, in reality, I'm pretty sure she was soothing herself. "Please tell me. I have to know, or I'll worry beyond reason."

My woman was not an idiot. I knew she was going to come back to this eventually, and I'm a man of my word. I ate her. I fucked her. Now I had to be honest with her.

"They each get to punch me once." That was the truth, not necessarily the entire truth, but it wasn't a lie.

"Do you get to punch them back?" She wrapped her hand around where my arm crossed her chest, and my hand cupped her breast protectively.

"Not the way it works, pussycat."

"What else?"

I snuggled against her body, inhaled the scent of her hair, and rubbed my forehead against the back of her head. "Nothing I can't handle. Don't worry. I'm going to take a beating, but baby, it's nothing I didn't see in my three tours with the Marines."

"You were a Marine?"

"Yeah, babe. Served twelve years. Been all over the place. That's how I knew home was here when I rode in."

Her voice stuttered when she spoke next. "How old are you?"

I chuckled against her body. "Thirty. Graduated at seventeen, went right in. Did my twelve years, socked away a shit ton of money since I didn't have to pay for room and board or most of my meals. Was smart. Invested over half of it. Came home, my father offered me the VP position. Pissed off a bunch of the brothers seeing as I didn't earn my position at the time. Proved them wrong, but over time, found I didn't like the culture over there."

Her body went rigid in my arms. "What do you mean? They're a Pride chapter. What's so different about there and here?"

I rolled my girl over to her back and settled in next to her, then cupped her cheek. "Club business, baby. I may tell you a lot since you're my old lady and you're warming my bed, but I won't go against the club by sharing business. That's not how this works, and you know it."

She nodded. "I won't make you, but that's not the same as this gauntlet thing. I need to talk to my dad…"

I cut her off by pressing two fingers to her lips. "You will do no such thing. This is between me, my club prez, and my brothers. As my old lady, you can be pissed, share your drama all you want, but you do not get involved in this. It's my cross to bear and bear it I will."

"But…"

"No buts, pussycat. I will not let your sweet smiles or sexy body distract me from this. And don't pretend I'm stupid and try that shit. There is a lot this body and your beautiful face will weasel out of me, and I look forward to all the ways you attempt to do so, but not with this. Not when it comes to your honor or mine. I've got this. You have to trust me."

She closed her eyes, and I waited a minute. Eventually, she nodded.

"There's one more thing we need to talk about." And I was not looking forward to it.

Her body went stiff in my arms, so I ran my fingers along her shoulder and down to her hand where I picked it up and kissed the center of her palm.

"The club ran Gary out of town today."

She gasped and pushed her body until she was sitting, the sheets falling around her waist, giving me a perfect view of her voluptuous tits.

"What!?"

I pushed up on a forearm and rested my head in my hand. "Yeah. We got him transferred to another dealership out of town. Apparently, the owner owed Riot a favor for some stolen car thief the club tracked down in the past."

"No way."

"Yeah. Then the boys followed Gary to his shit hole apartment and tossed the place, making the furniture useless. He left with his clothes and his car. We followed the fucker out of town. Sheriff was right behind him. We were behind the sheriff."

She covered her mouth as she tried to hold back her laughter as I remarked, "Guess the Sheriff owes the club a lot of favors. So many those IOUs are stacked a mile high."

"Yeah, Dad and the brothers have been backing the Sheriff

and the deputies for the county and most of the state for almost twenty years. They help keep the riff raff out."

"It's an important relationship to the club. And after he found out he'd hit you, he was happy to help us guide Gary out of town."

She shrugged. "Can't say I'm sorry, because the bastard brought it upon himself. He knew who I was when he asked me out. Knew who my family was. The guy has a screw loose to mess with me or talk shit about The Pride."

I cupped the back of her neck. "You don't have to worry about him anymore. Promise."

"Thanks, baby." She leaned forward and pressed her lips to mine. "Now how am I going to thank my big, strong, biker for taking out the trash?"

"I can think of a few things," I said low and leaned back.

She trailed her lips down my neck and kept going along my chest.

"If you stay in that direction, eventually something will pop up for you." I leaned back, opened my legs, and cocked them at the knees so my dick was standing loud and proud for my woman.

"Hmm, seems like I found just the thing," she said right before kissing the tip of my cock.

I leaned my head back and sighed.

"My old lady has the best fucking mouth…" I groaned when she took me as deep as she could.

"And don't you forget it," she said and then went back to work.

"Not a chance," I murmured, running my hands through her long hair while I let my woman thank me in the best way possible.

Chapter 9

Shay

THE NEXT EVENING, I CLOSED DOWN MY SHOP EARLY. BIKER babes did whatever the hell they wanted regardless of the store hours I posted. Besides, Cricket had left hours before to go to the clubhouse, and I wanted to get there before all hell broke loose. My nerves were electric, sizzling with fear and anxiety. I knew the club concept of a gauntlet was not unusual; it just wasn't put in play often.

If my memory served, the last time the club had to deal with something "honor" related was when one of the brothers lied about a protective custody job. Turned out the club was protecting a criminal, and when that little detail came out, the club was none too happy. They beat the shit out of the brother and kicked his ass to the curb, excommunicating him from the club.

Hero's Pride was just that. About heroes. Men who served the community, the state, the country in whatever capacity that meant to them past or present. We had every military branch represented, and a handful of ex-cops. A few previous government employees, one practicing physician, an active duty firefighter, and so on. The guys in the club might kick some ass when warranted, and scare the fuck out of someone who wronged The Pride, such as Gary the douche, but they did not harbor criminals or accept criminal activity within their ranks. It's just wasn't done.

In this situation, where the President's daughter's honor was involved, I could only imagine how bad it would be. Most of these guys have known me since I took my first breath. They truly are the only family I've ever known. This meant the level of freak out that was working through me right then was intense and justified.

I parked my baby in the large circular front entrance. The guys' bikes were lined up by the warehouse where they communed. Right then, the line of bikes was almost thirty deep. Every man was there. That niggle of fear skipped its way up every bump in my spine as I firmed my jaw and threw my leg over the seat. Only one place I needed to go. I had a plan and was putting that plan into action right now. I strutted to the place where the guys were hanging out.

My guy was standing at the bar, shooting the shit with a few of his brothers as though nothing was going on. I knew better. All was going to be fine until the moment my father decided it was time. The sun would set, and they'd get on with doling out their bullshit punishment.

Rex's brown gaze shot to mine. At first, it was filled with surprise, then his eyes narrowed as though he knew what I was about to do. Instead of letting him in on my plan, I walked directly to my man, wrapped my arms around his strong shoulders, lifted up on my toes, and kissed him long and very deep. In front of the entire club. This was how an old lady staked her claim.

There were some grunts, some catcalls from the younger

guys that probably didn't have a problem with Rex and me being an item, and some seriously growly animalistic sounds that came with my action.

"Hey, baby," I leaned back and stared up into his handsome face.

He grinned, dipped down, and gave me a peck on the lips as he squeezed one of my ass cheeks in greeting.

Bikers were usually very affectionate men who didn't shy away from PDA as a matter of course. They did what they wanted when they wanted to do it. That meant a lot of grab-ass with their women and the club girls. Usually, if the old ladies were around, the club girls kept their distance and only got involved if there were visitors or lonely brothers hanging around. Mags made sure the respect for the old ladies was always given first and foremost.

Speaking of Mags, she rounded the corner where the huge industrial sized kitchen was and came out holding a bowl of chips and dips; a couple club girls followed her with more food. She set it on the table they used as a food buffet for the brothers, and then she lasered her gaze on me, noticing my arms wrapped around Rex.

Her lips twitched, but she kept on doing her thing, making sure everything was just so as the queen bee would do for her boys.

"What are you doing here, pussycat?" Rex nuzzled my neck and laid a sloppy kiss there.

I grinned and locked eyes with my guy. "Just saying hi, checking in on my man and my favorite people in the entire world. The people that wouldn't hurt me by hurting someone else I cared about," I said loud enough so that at least ten or so brothers could hear my statement, and hopefully, have it hit home.

Rex gripped my hips and focused on my face. "Shay, you shouldn't be here. And I don't want you getting involved or making a scene. Got me?"

I nodded like a good little old lady and then kissed him deeply again before letting him go and saddling up to the bar. "Jay, beer me."

Obviously stunned, the prospect recovered in seconds, nodded, and got to work getting me an ice-cold beer from the fridge, removing the cap, and setting it in front of me.

"Rex, a minute?" my father said, and Rex left my side to talk to Daddy.

I grinned and spun around on my chair and surveyed all the guys. Perfect timing for my man to leave my side. I slipped off the stool and went over to Tank, the Sergeant-at-Arms of the club.

"Hiya, *Uncle* Tank." I emphasized his status with me as I approached. Even though he was only in his early thirties, I still pushed the Uncle business. The club girl who was attached to his hip immediately let go and moved around me, saying something about getting him a beer. Like I said, respect for the old ladies was paramount, and this one knew her place.

"Hey, Princess." Tank pulled me into his arms and gave me a big hug. "You know, you shouldn't be here," he warned solemnly.

I nodded and looked up at him while batting my eyelashes. "I know, but I couldn't stay away. Not when the club is going to hurt the man I chose just because I happen to be the President's daughter. It's not really fair to me or Rex."

"Sweetheart, you know how much we all love you? You're family. No man disrespects you…"

"How did he disrespect me? By choosing me? Caring about me enough to make me his old lady and lay claim to me even knowing his brothers weren't going to be happy? That sounds like a pretty stand-up kind of man to me. Someone I'd thought the brothers would want me to have."

Tank frowned and rubbed at the back of his neck. "You got a point there, Princess."

I pouted and nodded even though I wanted to smile wickedly. "Just promise me you'll go easy on him. For me." I batted my lashes again. "Please, Uncle Tank?"

He cupped my cheek and pressed a kiss to my forehead. "Anything for you, sweetheart."

"Love you." I hugged him and grinned at Mags over my shoulder.

"Love you too, girl." He patted my back and let me go.

I saw Champ walk by and head over to the food table. "Excuse me," I told Tank and shimmied my way to one of the other large-fisted brothers' in the group. Champ was a boxer and used his fists to keep the streets clean of drug dealers, which was his "service" to the community. He wasn't paid for this, and it was vigilante, but at least it helped keep the drug dealers out of our county. The Sheriff and his deputies looked the other way if they happened upon him exacting justice for the community.

In the past though, Champ was a true champion in the boxing ring. He'd gone pro right out of high school, made bucket-loads of cash, then abruptly left the business, joined The Pride, and is now running the local boxing gym and fitness center the club owns. No one knows why he left the circuit, only that, when he did, it shocked the fighting world. It's still a mystery to this day, and Daddy's always warned me not to talk to Champ about it, so I never did. With his contribution to the club—running the gym and boxing league—he's a big part of the brothers' work and business profits that go into the kitty for the club.

Regardless of what the club guys contribute individually, everyone gets their cut.

My concern, however, was that Champ had fists of steel and next to Tank, him hitting Rex scared the bejesus out of me.

I looped an arm around Champ's shoulders. "Hi, Uncle Champ," I pulled the same card I did with Tank.

"Hey, baby girl. How you doin'?" His dark eyes scanned over me from top to toe, taking in my tight jeans, Pride tank, and sexy booties. I'd left my hair wild and free the way I knew Rex preferred. "Looking beautiful as usual, but what's up with your face?"

I worked hard to put as much sadness into my expression as possible, even trying my damndest to rustle up some tears, though all I accomplished were wet eyes, but that would do. Champ was a straight up sucker for a woman in distress.

He cupped my cheeks with both hands. "Did Rex do this to you? I'll fucking kill him now. To hell with the Gauntlet."

I shook my head emphatically. "N-n-no. I'm j-j-just so sc-scar-ed for him. He's my man, Uncle Champ. I don't want him hurt."

Champ pulled me into his arms and held me tight. "He'll be okay, baby girl. Promise." He leaned his jaw against my ear. "I'll go easy on him, yeah?"

Once again, I held back my happiness and nodded into his shoulder, then whispered in his ear. "Thanks, Uncle, Champ. Love you."

"Love you too, baby girl."

I let him go and scanned the room looking for my next victim. Shadow was leaning against the wall, watching two club girls fumble with playing pool. Mostly they were bending over in their short skirts and low tops to try and get his attention. They had it; that's for sure. His eyes were currently on Lana's ass, one of the new sexy little brunettes. Thought the girl had it going on. All curves and legs. I couldn't blame him. She did have it going on.

While he was distracted, I went over to him, leaned against the wall, and sighed loudly. I couldn't pull the Uncle card with Shadow because he wasn't much older than me. Only three years.

"What's up, Princess?" Shadow asked but didn't take his gaze off the women in front of him.

I shrugged and sighed again, crossing my ankles and my arms.

With that, Shadow turned to the side and faced me. "You upset about the Gauntlet?"

"Wouldn't you be?"

He shrugged. "Not really. Goes with the territory, don't you think?"

"Oh, so every brother had to go through this when they claimed their old lady?"

"Nah, but Shay, honey, you're you."

I pushed off the wall, placed my hands on my hips, and offered up some serious sass. "So, the other old ladies don't mean as much, is that what I'm hearing? Only the VP's choice comes with a vicious beatdown?" There was such ire in my tone the two club girls at the pool table stood up straight and exited the area fast.

Damn. Mags ran a tight ship. I definitely needed to take lessons on being the Queen.

He watched as the girls left and rubbed at his chin, then licked his lips. "You know, I get what you're sayin', but the guys don't see it that way. You're the Princess. Untouchable."

"Shadow, I'm twenty-five years old. I picked a respectable man who claimed me in the most honorable way known to mankind. He chose me as his old lady. The highest honor to a biker. Out of all the women he could have had, especially with his rank in the club, he chose me."

Shadow chuckled. "Yeah, and he chose wrong."

I snapped my head back. "Because I'm not good enough?"

He shook his head and lifted a hand to place it on the ball of my shoulder. "Nah, Shay. It's because you're too good."

"Oh, so I'm too good for the VP of The Pride. I think that says more about how you feel about your brothers and The Pride at large than it does about me and respecting my honor, don't you?"

And on that parting note, I spun on my heel and headed to another brother for a talking to. Once I'd hit up at least fifteen or so of the brothers, I caught sight of my father and beat feet to him before he could get caught up in a conversation with someone else.

"Daddy, a word?" I said when I passed right by him and headed straight for his office. He followed me and shut the door when we were both inside the small space. His office didn't have much. Two large black safes against the far wall, a metal desk, a laptop, landline, a rolling chair, and a couple chairs in front for guests. On the walls were pictures of motorcycles. Hanging directly on the wall above his desk was a full-size American flag. It was the one the military gave my father when granddad passed away. He didn't put it in one of those triangles for safe keeping. No, he hung that flag with pride where he could admire it every day, just like my granddad would have wanted.

My father groaned, leaned his back against the closed door, and crossed his arms over his chest. My dad was not a small man by any sense of the word. He had a striking amount of dark hair on his head, a beard that was just now showing the salt and pepper of his age, stunning eyes, and a muscular physique he worked on. His voice was one that I adored more than any other. As a true daddy's girl, his voice usually soothed and calmed me. This moment was not one of them.

"Now, Shay, you cannot change my mind about this. Rex fucked up by putting his claim on my little girl..."

I held up my hand. "Save it, Daddy. I'm not here to get you to take it back. That would undermine your authority and make my man look weak. Which. He. Is. Not. What I want is simple." I set my fiery gaze on my father's green ones, the same dark green my brother shared.

"Anything for my Princess."

"Good to hear. This should be easy as pie then." I cocked a brow, readying for battle if needed.

"Okay, lay it on me."

I smiled sweetly and played with a lock of my hair, buttering him up like I used to when I was a teenager and wanted something that he didn't want to give me, but usually ended up caving in on.

"I want you to offer the brothers the opportunity to abstain from their shot against Rex. It shouldn't be required to punish a man when they personally don't agree with the charge against him. Am I right?"

Dad firmed his jaw and placed both of his hands on his jean-clad hips. My father was fit as a fiddle at fifty-three and looked amazing for his age, but today I could see the lines around his eyes and mouth that proved the decision to put forth this gauntlet was wearing on him.

"Honey..."

"Daddy, please, this is important to me. He's my old man." I gulped and took a big breath as my chin actually trembled. This time the emotion was real and not to lay a guilt trip on the brothers. "He's everything to me and my future, and I..."

My father shifted, moved toward where I stood a few feet away from him, pulled me into his arms, and hugged me tight. "Princess, you barely know him. He's only been here a few days. How can you possibly care that much for him? To be claimed by him."

I sniffed and pressed back. "How long did it take for you to fall in love with my mother?"

Dad's arms tightened around me. I knew the story. Everyone did. Dad met Mom when he was on a weeklong ride. She was waitressing in a biker bar in Vegas. He bought a shot for himself and one for her. Then he looked into her eyes; she looked into his, and he asked her if she wanted to leave Vegas with him. She set her tray down, locked her arms around him, and laid a big fat wet one on him. Right there in front of all his brethren. Thirty minutes later, she was on the back of his bike, headed to her house to pick up the essentials. That night, she left with him, married him a month later, and never went back home. Much to her mother's happiness. My grandmother was a first-generation biker babe through and through.

"Thirty minutes after we met, had a couple drinks, and she slung her leg over the back of my bike and wrapped her body around mine. Love. Instantly."

I nodded. "Yeah, and I fell in love with Rex the second he broke the nose of the man who was harassing me. He says he fell for me the second he saw me in the store window. Every man in this club who has an old lady found her in a story like that. Every. Single. One. It's Pride lore. When you find the one you're meant for, it's instantaneous. No screwing around. It's just right."

"Shay…"

"It is, and you know it. Mom's been telling me I'd find the man for me without even trying. And she knew it would be a biker, as much as I tried to avoid it. All because I knew how you and the brothers would be. I knew you wouldn't be able to handle your baby girl growing up, but Dad, I have grown up. And now I own my own shop, and I'm making a way for myself. Don't I deserve a man at my side, someone who would love and protect me until his very last breath? A man like you. A man worthy of The Pride cut?"

"Fine," my dad growled. "I'll give the option to the brothers to abstain without any recourse or judgment."

I smiled, jumped up and down, and hugged my father, then kissed his entire face. "Thanks, Daddy. I love you!"

"Love you too, Princess. Now get out of my office. We need to do what needs to be done."

Knowing what that meant, the fear of Rex getting seriously hurt pressed down over me like a two-ton weight. I left my father's office and knotted my fingers together, hoping I'd done a good enough job protecting my man as best I could.

Looked like I'd be finding out soon enough.

Chapter 10

Rex

GAUNTLET. FUCKING HELL. A YEAR AGO I'D HAVE NEVER believed I would be the recipient of the wrath and disdain of my club. Figured that would be my father's cross to bear one day, not mine. Didn't matter though. Shay O'Donnell was worth any amount of pain my brothers could inflict. I'd bear each fist with pride as it meant she'd be mine; her honor would be avenged, and my brothers, and the President, her father, would accept me as being worthy.

The guys walked me out to the back of the warehouse and clubhouse where we had a huge lawn area, a fire pit, the grills, and several picnic tables and seats scattered around. I still couldn't believe I lived in this beautiful oasis in the Pacific Northwest. Nevertheless, the stunning nature surrounding us couldn't distract me from what was about to happen.

Thirty men walked right out to the center of the open grass and formed a circle, although five of them were prospects and wouldn't get to participate. Small favor to not have five additional fists. They broke off and stood outside the circle from the patched men.

Shay stood off to the side, her arms crossed over her chest and an intense glare centered on every single brother here, but most specifically, her father. Mags was by her side as were two prospects who appeared to stand casually behind her. My guess, they were there to hold her back if she let out her wildcat. I noticed another prospect was lighting the fire pit and another was walking the perimeter and lighting the tiki torches. The warm glow those lights gave the back area where the club members came to chill out usually had a peaceful and serene affect. At that moment, it was ominous and foreboding.

I stood in the center, inhaled long and deep, removed my cut, and stretched out my arm toward Shay. She hustled over, and instead of holding the cut, she slipped her arms through and settled it around her body. A statement if there ever was one. One I liked a fuck of a lot. I wrapped my hand around her neck, pulled her close, and kissed the daylights out of her for all to see. She would be mine in word, deed, and body. The club needed to see that for themselves.

"Thanks, baby. Keep it safe. Now go. I'll be fine, I promise." I pecked her lips once more and smacked her tight ass.

She nodded, cinched my cut around her chest, and shot daggers with her icy gaze once again to each man surrounding us, before pushing her way past a couple of them, making it very clear that she was pissed way the hell off.

Riot entered the circle of men and everyone went dead silent.

"We're here today to avenge the honor of one of our own, my daughter, Shay O'Donnell."

"Who doesn't want to be avenged! I make my own fucking choices about who I love and who I want in my life!" Shay crowed.

I lifted my hand palm out toward my woman and shook

my head. "Enough. Quiet." I firmed my jaw and stared into her beautiful face until she finally nodded, knowing this wasn't her place; it was mine. I smiled and blew her a kiss, then turned back to my President.

"Do you have anything to say for yourself?" Riot asked.

With a nod, I turned in a slow circle, meeting each brother straight in the eyes before I spoke. "I'm not sorry I claimed Shay O'Donnell as my old lady. She was meant for me and me for her. I knew it the second I laid eyes on her. No amount of damage you do to me, fists or otherwise, will change this outcome. I accept your need to take action and welcome each of my brothers' fists with pride."

All the men cheered and grunted in approval. Some were smacking their firsts into their hands, warming up for what was to come.

"As this is only the second time we've had to implement the Gauntlet, and never to avenge one of our own, I'm going to offer the brothers an out." A few of the men gasped and grumbled but didn't dare speak. "If any brother does not feel the punishment fits the crime or doesn't believe there was a crime, you may abstain from your free throw. There will be no discussion or reason needed as to why you are abstaining. No fault will come to you. No judgment. Each brother may act in accordance with his own conscience."

Utter shock went through my body at the President's words as the men around me started whispering to one another. In an unbelievable turn of events, Riot was allowing the brothers to give me a get out of jail free card. This was unheard of, never done. Usually the club acted as one; however, this particular set of circumstances had never come into play as far as I knew either.

"That's bullshit!" Shane hollered. "He fucked and disrespected my sister!"

I clenched my teeth, wanting to pop the motherfucker in the jaw where he stood. Not only for speaking against my President but for talking about my woman the way he was. If he wasn't her brother, he'd be on the floor bleeding from the gums, possibly having lost some teeth. With everything I had, I held my anger back. It defeated the purpose of the Gauntlet and my ability to prove to every man here that I'd do anything to claim Shay O'Donnell.

"Not true. He claimed her as his own. There is no greater honor given a woman from a biker," Mags insisted, her gaze narrowed at her son.

"Enough, both of you. No more is to be spoken. There is a decision to be made. It will, however, not affect the final outcome. If any patched brother does not want to participate in dispensing punishment, take two steps back, outside of the circle."

I stood still, my chest puffed up and ready to take on every brother here.

To my complete disbelief, more than half the men stepped back. Only ten brothers stood in the now broken up circle around me. True, those ten were no small guys. Tank, Champ, Whip, Riot, Hammer, and Whisper, the longer running club members, stayed still, along with a few of the others who had only been in the club a few years.

"I'll be first and last," Riot growled, his expression one of intense focus and determination. This was his daughter. The club princess. I'd take anything he could dish out to prove myself worthy of Shay.

I licked my lips, took a breath, and stood tall.

Riot got close to me, his face only two inches from my own. His jaw was rock hard when he spoke through clenched teeth. "You better love her more than your next breath because that's what it's going to take to hold onto my baby girl."

"Done," I stated instantly.

"She's wild and out of control," he snarled with a devilish smile, as though he was proud that his daughter would put any man that earned her through the ringer.

I looked right into his harsh green eyes. "Just the way I like her."

Riot's nostrils flared, his face pinched tight and his lips flattened into a thin white line. Before I knew it, he'd pulled his arm back and clocked me right in the jaw.

Pain blasted across my face as stars swirled in my peripheral vision, but I didn't react. I cupped my jaw, opened and closed my mouth, and cranked my neck from side to side to work out the new kinks.

"Who's next?" I grinned.

Champ walked up and glared. "You love her?"

"More than my motorcycle."

Champ's lips twisted in an evil smile. "Good answer," he said before twisting his body and punching me straight in the gut. Even though I'd braced, the air flew out of me, and I bowed over to clutch at my abdomen. I hissed through my teeth but knew the man had held back. On a good day, he had fists of steel. He definitely socked me good, but nowhere near the pain or damage he could have inflicted had he wanted to truly hurt me. I lifted my head, and he winked at me before turning back around and getting into position, arms crossed over his chest, feet wide apart, enjoying the show.

Next up was Tank.

Fuck me. His arms were the size of missiles found on military jets.

I inhaled as best as I could through the gut punch I'd just sustained and stood back at attention, readying for more.

"You going to treat her like the princess she is?" He tipped his head to the side to assess me, his blue eyes lit with an intensity I wouldn't wish on my worst enemy.

Still, I had something to prove, and prove it I would.

"Abso-fuckin-lutely. Except she'll be my fucking queen." I clenched my teeth and lifted my chin.

His lips twitched. "Let this be a reminder of what will happen if those feelings ever change," he said before he socked me so hard in the right pectoral, he knocked me back a few steps. I knew I'd have a black and blue Tank-sized bruise there for at least a week. I expected him to knock me out by hitting me in the face. Both he and Champ were known far and wide to be the absolute best fighters we had, yet they'd gone easy on me.

The light flicked on in my brain, and it finally dawned on me while biting back the pain that they were on my side. It was obvious they felt I needed to be warned to do right by their family, but their responses were nowhere near vengeance induced.

After I'd taken a fist in a variety of locations, which again, seemed sporadic instead of hell bent on truly hurting me, I watched as Whip, Shay's twin, adjusted his shoulders and bounced from foot to foot. He was the last man up, aside from Riot.

"This time, I want you to fight back, you piece of shit!" Whip roared angrily.

"That's not how this works, son," Riot reminded him.

"Fuck that! He screwed over my sister just like that douchebag we ran out of town."

My temperature rose to an uncomfortable degree as I lost all sight of what we were accomplishing. I stomped toward Whip, forgetting about the punishment I was supposed to endure. I shoved his chest with both hands, palms out like I was a defensive linebacker playing football. He stumbled back a few feet.

"How dare you compare me"—I pounded my own chest—"to a dickwad abuser! That man hit your sister. I'd never touch her in anger. Ever!" I barked right into his face. "Don't you ever put me in the same category as a disgusting piece of shit who gets his rocks off on trying to hurt and control women."

Whip fisted both hands. "You met her, fucked her, and claimed her in a what? Three days? My sister is no whore, and that's how you treated her."

The second he used the word "whore" in reference to my woman, I saw red. Blood red.

"Take your shot, brother. Now. Then, it's on." My tone was scathing, and I was ready to knock this fucker down a few notches.

Whip shook his head. "Fair fight, you and me, or we'll pick this back up later."

"You will do no such thing, Shane. This has been voted on by the club." Our President's voice rose over the brothers watching the show. "After you've taken your shot, he will burn for Shay. Then it's done. Like it never happened."

"Burn?" Shay said at the same time Mags said, "Shit."

Whip came close me and stood right in front of me, his face only a few inches from mine. "Nothing you will ever do, could ever say, will be good enough for my sister."

Without blinking, I gave him what he needed to hear and understand. "No shit, Sherlock. Shay O'Donnell will never be good enough for me. Just like Riot will never be good enough for Mags. The difference is, we *want* to be. We'll work our asses off every damn day proving our commitment. I'll fucking die trying to be good enough for your sister, man!"

I barely got the last word out when Whip swung his arm and clocked me on the cheek so hard it split, blood pouring down my face. Whip gripped my hair at the back of my head and held me nose to nose. "She is my twin. Shares my blood. My DNA. Is one of only three women in the entire world I would lay down my life for."

"Yeah, brother, and for me, she's the only woman I'll die for until she gives me children of our own. Until then, your sister is all there is for me. My *everything*. Nothing comes before her. Nothing. I swear it."

Whip's lips tightened into a scowl. "I'll be the judge of that. You hurt her, and there will be no hell hot enough, no hole in the ground deep enough for you to hide from my wrath. I'll be your worst living nightmare. Don't. Fuck. This. Up. You get one chance."

"I won't hurt her. I swear it on my patch. My cut. My bike. *My fucking life*."

Whip nodded but pushed me away as if he couldn't even bear to share airspace with me any longer.

"Jay, bring the iron!" Riot called out over the crowd.

"Baby, what's going on? You're done." Shay's beautiful voice cut through the pain that throbbed over what seemed like every inch of my body.

I shook my head, still being braced by the two prospects, and held up a finger. "One more thing, pussycat."

"One more thing? What one more thing?" she screeched, about to charge at the circle of brothers.

"Brandon, James, hold her back," Riot ordered the two men. They each locked a grip around her biceps.

Anger rippled through me like a wave of electricity sizzling and looking for a place to exit. "You bruise her and you boys will answer to me," I warned the two young prospects. Their eyes widened, and one adjusted his grip. "It's okay, baby. No worries, yeah?"

"Mom, what's happening?" Shay's voice was strained and fearful.

Jay brought over the red-hot iron. In block letters, locked in a curve, was the name *SHAY*.

I swallowed, whipped off my black t-shirt, and kneeled down in the grass. Bones came over and washed my sweaty chest with some form of sterilizing solution that smelled of antiseptic. Bones was his road name because he was an orthopedic surgeon at Three Rivers Community Hospital and also the club doctor for obvious reasons. He had his medical bag at the ready, which should have been comforting but wasn't. Regardless, there was no way in hell I was going to back down.

"You're going to brand him? Jesus Christ, Dad! No! It's barbaric...it's..." Shay was flinging her body to and fro, giving the boys an awful time trying to hold on to her.

Damn, my woman was a wildcat.

I grinned while watching her voluptuous body contort and twist under her ire.

"It's part of your claiming, Princess. It's what's done in The Pride. If you take a woman as your old lady, you burn for her. Then the club will officially do anything to protect her as one of our own. A true sister to all the brothers."

Three other men in the club, removed their cuts, and then their shirts. Right over their heart were their old ladies' names burned into their flesh. Riot lifted his shirt and showed Shay her mother's name. Technically, I was getting off pretty easy. Magdalene was nine letters to my woman's four.

"Dad, I thought you got that for Mom because you're a crazy freakin' lunatic who was stupid in love and twenty-one!"

Riot smiled and ran his fingers over the scarred letters that took up a good expanse of the center of his chest because of how long her name was, but also because he'd gotten big block letters. I got to pick the design of Shay's as did any brother who was claiming their woman officially to the club. We had a metal worker brother in the club we called Hammer because he hammered metal like a genius. The iron I had him make was curved because I intended to tattoo the footprints of the children we were going to have down the road one day right under it. And I couldn't freaking wait. Just the thought of getting Shay knocked up with my babies gave me the extra dose of strength I needed to get through this last part.

"Yes, baby girl, I did. I was crazy for your mom. Am still crazy for my Magdalene and always will be. I wear her name with honor, as will your man."

"I love you, baby!" Mags hollered, and her man grinned.

Riot flicked his wrist out toward the prospect, and Jay handed over the glowing branding iron.

"Hold him steady, Tank; this is gonna hurt."

Tank came up behind me and crouched. He placed his chest to my back and held on to my arms in a vise lock. Champ pulled his belt from his jeans and stretched it out in front of my mouth. I welcomed the leather and bit down over it.

"Not a sound. Your honor and hers are at stake," Riot warned.

I nodded curtly and watched the iron come closer, mesmerized by the glowing red of the hot iron. Its radiated warmth had a calming effect on my mood.

Shay's beautiful name in golden red was the last thing I saw before blinding, white hot pain seared through my chest. Riot held the iron there only a couple of seconds, but it was long enough for the smell of burning flesh to enter my nose, making my mouth water and sour as though I could vomit at any second. My entire body jolted and arched forward as he pulled the brand off quickly. Tank held me as I bit down so hard on the leather belt I was sure it left permanent teeth imprints.

It was done.

Instantly, Bones was pushing me to a seated position in the grass. He'd squirted some type of cooling liquid on my chest that was like heavenly angels had placed their healing hands directly to the burn and coated it with love. The heavy weight left my back, and then there was my woman. Her arms surrounded me from behind, her face next to mine, kissing my cheek, my neck, and petting my hair and back with her cool hands. I was panting and dizzy as Bones tended to my wound, slathering it with an antibiotic salve and pushing a prescription bottle of antibiotics into Shay's hand.

"Just in case. Already filled the prescription. Don't like to take any chances. I'll be over first thing in the morning to change the bandage and clean the wound."

I nodded but continued to let him work until he'd bandaged the wound and protected it. Then he looked into my eyes and wiped away the blood pouring from my cheek.

"You stupid, stupid, man!" Shay continued holding me from behind, her lips trailing everywhere she could reach from her position. My shoulder, the back of my neck, my cheek, my temple, the crown of my head.

I inhaled her wildflower scent deeply as Bones butterflied my cheek. When he finally moved away with a squeeze to my shoulder, I turned and scooped my woman into my arms. She straddled my lap and tried to keep her chest off mine.

"No, need you." I locked my arms around her and plastered her to me where I could plant my nose right against the curve of her neck where her scent was the strongest. After a few breaths, I could finally only smell her and not my burned flesh.

"Baby, you're crazy." She ran her hands through my long hair, pushing it behind my back.

"Crazy in love." I cupped her gorgeous face with both hands.

Her blue eyes were bright and shining as she ran her fingers down the side of my face. "I'm crazy in love with you too."

I smiled proudly and kissed her.

Kissed her like the sun would never rise. Like the moon would never shed its light again. Like the entire world was ending. Yet we both knew it had only just begun.

This time, when I kissed my old lady in front of my brothers and her family, the entire club cheered.

Chapter 11

Shay

IT'S BEEN SIX GLORIOUS WEEKS SINCE REX WAS BEAT TO HELL BY the club. For a solid month, I snarled and glared at every club member who had thrown a single punch at my man, honor be damned. Rex, however, strutted around like a proud peacock, his massive arm slung over my shoulder, dragging me from one club event to the next. Normally, I'd welcome this. I'd been going to club events since I could walk. That wasn't the problem. The issue was I was holding onto my ire against all the men that hurt Rex, and that Lusty Lacey had now shifted her interest from Rex to my brother, and I hated it. Hated her. Hated everything about the situation, but there was nothing I could do. As Mags demanded, she left Rex alone and now carried on with her fascination with her newest prey, my freakin' twin brother.

Regardless of Lacking Lacey, there was something else bothering me. Something so huge it could only go one of two ways. Super awesome or straight up devastation.

It wasn't like we hadn't been playing with fire over the past seven weeks, but when it comes to Taggart "T-Rex" Crawford, I

104

lose my ever-loving mind. Every. Single. Time. The second that man's abs come into play I'm a puddle on the floor. And for Rex, it's no better. If I even hint at offering up a sliver of cleavage or skin, he's all over me.

With that type of sexual chemistry, it was bound to happen. Also explained why I've been so moody and craving anything in the protein family. Seriously, I could not eat enough meat lately. It's been so bad that I've gained at least eight pounds, much to my man's elation at the extra curves. He hasn't seemed to notice anything different.

Once we got through the first month and my man had healed completely, I found I was happiest when I got to sleep no less than ten hours a night, there was a pound of meat in my gut every day, and plenty of water.

Thankfully, beer, wine, and cocktails have made me gag. Now I know why.

Good Lord above, how do you tell the man you love, the man you've only been with for seven weeks, that you're pregnant.

I ran my fingertips over the early ultrasound photo the doctor gave me. I went in for my regular womanly annual checkup with the plan to get on birth control.

Um yeah. Little too late. As in seven weeks too late. Rex must have gotten me pregnant the very first time we had sex.

Good news about that is, I was able to see the hearts and hear the heartbeats.

Yep, plural.

Heartbeats.

As in two.

Because there are two babies.

Fuck my life.

When you're a twin, you've got the latent gene. It usually skips a generation, but not for me. Nope. I'm the exception.

The bathroom door opened, and my man entered our bedroom wearing a towel, just like the time that got us into this situation.

My mouth watered as I watched droplets trickle down his muscled torso and disappear against the pale green towel wrapped low around his hips. The muscle ridge just above his hip and down toward his cock was a stark definition on his abdomen. My man had been pumping the iron with his brethren since his arrival. Apparently, they're going to compete in some iron man competition against sister clubs in the future for a charity gig they wanted to support.

I licked my lips as I scanned his entire body and settled on the scarred, pinkened flesh where my name had been burned into the skin. I never thought in a million years that I could get off on something so archaic and barbaric, but every time I saw my name right above his heart, my belly dropped, and my panties got wet.

"Pussycat, you lookin' at me like that means we're going to be late for the club barbecue."

I stood up, placed the square image upside down on the nightstand, curled my fingers into my ribbed tank with a badass bedazzled rose on the front, and tossed it to the floor. I grinned until he grabbed his towel but didn't tug it completely off. I pouted and waited for my prize to be revealed.

"Keep going. I want to see everything you got waiting for me."

I smirked, unbuttoned my jeans, unzipped, and pushed them over my hips and down to the floor to puddle at my ankles. I kicked them away and stood in nothing but a lacy black bra and matching G-string.

"Fuck, woman, every time I see you bare it's like the first time all over again. Beautiful. Jesus Christ." He dropped the towel and was already hard as a rock, his heavy cock lifting up toward his belly button in what I'd like to think was a greeting to me.

"Get over here, woman." He pointed to the floor right in front of him.

I shimmied over to him, wrapped my arms around his waist, and looked up into his toasted brown eyes.

"Before I fuck you stupid, how's about you tell me about your appointment yesterday. You jumped me so fast when you got home you never gave me the deets, but you've been acting weird since I came home last night. Now give."

I bit down into my bottom lip and glanced away, trying to get my wits about me and the bomb I needed to drop.

I attempted to change the subject. "Wouldn't you rather have sex?"

His gaze narrowed while he locked his arms around me. In a complex shuffle step movement, he backed me up until I hit the bed and maneuvered me down to the soft mattress, hooked a hand up higher on my back, and dragged me until my head was on the pillows. Once he had me where he wanted me, he straddled my form, a knee on either side of my hips. He pushed up and wrapped a hand around his thick erection and gave it a couple sexy strokes.

I mewled and squirmed, my gaze zeroed in on his hard flesh, wanting to get at his body.

"You want this?" His voice was low and scratchy.

"God, yes! Taggart, please," I begged. He loved it when I begged.

"Tell me what you've been hiding from me, and I'll give it to you." He ran the blunt head of his cock against my panty-covered sex a few times.

It took a moment to sift through the pleasure haze he'd put me in to really hear what he asked.

"What do you mean, baby?"

He stopped rubbing his tip against me. I frowned and reached for his body, but he took my hands and placed them flat on the bed near my head. I was officially restricted from the ability to move my arms or legs. He hovered over me with an unrelenting look plastered across his handsome face.

"Pussycat, I'm not stupid. I know when something is up with my woman. At first, I thought you were maybe on the rag, but the fact that you're using sex in order to get me off the trail of whatever it is you got going on, something to do with your doctor visit yesterday, has me concerned." He let one of my hands go and cupped my cheek, running his thumb down the side of my hairline, over my cheek, and then to my lips.

"Shay, whatever it is, baby, I'm going to be here for you. All the way. In sickness and in health. We may not have gotten married legally, but a claiming in the club is the same thing to me. Whatever you got messing with your head, give it to me. Let me take it from you. I'll carry the burden, and we'll work through whatever it is together." He pressed his lips to mine and kissed me deeply. Our tongues tangled, and in the excitement of having a naked, just showered Rex hovering over me, I wrapped my legs around his waist and pressed up against him.

He laid against my chest but rolled over completely so that I ended up sitting atop him, hard cock right between my thighs where I wanted it most. I rubbed back and forth over the steely length.

Rex gripped my ass cheeks, and I gasped at the pleasure the move ignited throughout my body.

"Tell me, right now. Just say it fast, and whatever it is, we'll deal with it. I promise. If you're sick, baby, I'm here."

"I'm not sick, Taggart." I rested my hand over his chest

where my name resided. He placed his giant hand over mine, making it so I could feel his heart beating a mile a minute.

"What is it, pussycat? Please, just tell me."

I leaned over and reached for the photo I'd set on the nightstand. I turned it over and showed it to him. In a small voice, barely a whisper, I bared all. "I'm pregnant."

Rex's body went completely still. He took the paper and held it between us while he looked at it. His brow furrowed, and a contemplative look stole across his face.

"You're having my baby?"

I swallowed down the emotion threatening to break free like a giant wave over a sandy shore. Still, it didn't change the fact that inside, I was a total mess. Excitement, fear, trepidation, elation, so many feelings were spiraling out of control within me as he looked at the grainy ultrasound photo.

"Yeah," I barely choked out.

For a full minute, he didn't say anything else just stared at the image. "Pussycat, why are there two white blobs inside of two black blobs inside of another circle?" His nose scrunched as he held it up so I could see the image too.

I inhaled fully and pressed my finger to the paper. "This surrounding circle is my womb. This black circle is the amniotic sac, and the white fuzzy spot is a baby."

He nodded and pet the circle as if he was in complete and utter awe. "My child. *Our child.*"

I wanted to close my eyes but needed to see the moment he made the connection.

All of a sudden, Rex locked one hand on my waist, pushed his massive body back and readjusted us so that I was fully encased in his lap, his knees cocked and up as he leaned against the headboard.

"Then what's this sac and fuzzy white blob." He showed me the paper again, pointing to the other circular shape.

My voice shook when I answered. "That's our other baby."

He nodded as if this was totally normal, and we were talking about the news and what we were going to be doing for the day, not the fact that we are pregnant after only seven weeks of knowing one another and having twins.

Within moments, his entire body went completely rigid. The arm around my waist locked tight, and his fingers dug into the fleshy part of my hip. "Other baby? Pussycat, are you telling me we're having twins?"

"Baby, I'm a twin. Happens sometimes." I worried my bottom lip, awaiting his response.

Rex looked from the image to my stomach, then back to the image and once again to my stomach. He set the picture down on the nightstand, then brought his hands up to cover my midriff. "You've got my babies in there." He rubbed his thumbs down the sides of my still pretty flat stomach, though it was a bit harder than it used to be.

I placed my hand over his. "Taggart," I said, tears in my eyes.

His gaze lifted to mine, and his entire face gentled.

"I-i-is this okay?" I stuttered out, not sure how to proceed since I'd never been pregnant before. I'd never even had a scare in my twenty-five years on this earth.

Rex blinked, pulled me into his arms, and tucked my face against his neck. "Shay, you're having my babies. This is more than okay. This is my entire fucking world. Everything I ever wanted and more, right here in my arms. Fuck, I love you." He kissed the crown of my head as I let the tears fall.

I ran my finger over my name across his chest like I'd done so many times before.

"It really is me and you against it all. No matter what," I confirmed.

His arms held me tighter. "No matter what. And now we've got two perfect little beings to add to our family." His jaw went hard, and his lips flattened into a thin line. "Pussycat, now we gotta get married. Right away."

I lifted my head and wiped the tears off my face. "Didn't you just say that claiming me was the same as marriage?"

He cupped my cheek with one hand and my belly with the other. "Yeah, but now you're having my babies. All three of you need to be Crawfords, pussycat. There's just no other way around it."

I narrowed my gaze and set my hands on my hips. "Is that right? Are you demanding I marry you Taggart Crawford? Instead of asking me like a gentleman?"

He laughed. "Yeah, babe. You're with a biker. You're my pregnant biker princess. What in the world did you expect?"

I tapped my lips and thought of a hundred million things that would have been better. Using a different finger, I ticked off each item I came up with. "Um, dinner out where I get to wear a sexy number that makes you drool all night. You getting on one knee. You wooing me with roses. Chocolates." I lifted my hands in the air and then let them fall dramatically to my sides. "You know, romance for crying out loud!" I frowned and sulked.

Before I knew it, I was on my back. My panties and bra were history and my legs split wide. "How's about you get to pick out whatever ring you want? Money is no object since I've got plenty. We put your ass on the back of my bike and ride to Vegas. We do the penthouse, the tables, the fountains, steak and lobster buffet, the whole shebang. You get a sexy as fuck wedding dress I get to peel off you on our wedding night. Invite anyone in the club who wants to go, and in the interim, we celebrate our babies by me giving you a handful of orgasms right now to make up for my lack of romance."

While he spoke, he used his thumbs to open me farther, and I instantly held my breath, waiting for the first touch of his talented tongue. He flattened it and took one long, luxurious taste.

Shivers raced up my body from between my thighs, over my stomach, up my chest, and out my fingertips. "God, baby," I moaned. He felt so good.

He licked again then swirled the tip around my throbbing, aching clit that was desperate for attention.

"How's about it?" He demanded an answer.

"Sounds heavenly." I placed my hand on his still-damp hair and pressed him toward my center, lifting my hips in invitation. "Fuck me good. There are two babies. Twice the celebration. Twice the pleasure to give. And I want a huge fucking ring!" I demanded in return.

He growled, planted his face between my thighs, and I lost all thought of babies, rings, and Vegas weddings.

We never did make it to the club party. We had our own party in bed planning our wedding and our future children.

Epilogue

Shay

Five weeks later...

"JESUS, REX!" I CRIED OUT, HANDS TIGHTLY GRIPPING MY HUSband's hair as he impaled me against the door of our honeymoon suite.

"Fucking hell, my wife is tight!" He grunted, slamming his cock inside me over and over, pounding into me as if he was trying to brand me with his cock the same way my name was branded on his chest.

My slinky white leather and satin wedding skirt was scrunched up around my waist. I was wearing a sexy as fuck bustier, kick ass pair of white leather studded booties that I'd paired with the skintight pencil skirt and satin number. Currently, those stilettos were sunk into my man's ass. God, I hope they left an imprint for me to admire later.

Tonight was our wedding night. Technically, we'd just gotten married, and now we we're at the consummation part, and I was panting, writhing, and screaming his name as he took me for the first time as husband and wife.

At our ceremony, Rex wore a pitch-black suit. Black dress

shirt and black tie. The second we'd said our vows and were pronounced husband and wife, he removed the suit coat, and Daddy handed him his cut. Then we took the customary photos, received the hugs and handshakes from my parents, and most of the members of the Oregon Pride. His parents had come and acted like nothing was different. Riot knew better and assured Rex he'd have a talk with his dad when the booze was flowing. We left the prospects behind to watch the clubhouse, and a few of the long timers were manning the businesses we couldn't shut down. I had put a sign on my store saying, "Getting Married. See you in two weeks" and left it at that. What was the point of having the life of a biker babe without getting to do whatever the fuck I wanted?

After we'd said our I dos, well, Rex said, "Fuck yeah!" to the hollers and hoots to his brethren. Once the ceremony was over and we'd been congratulated, my man bent over, put his shoulder to my hips, and lifted me up and over his body so my torso fell over his back. He smacked my ass so hard I was sure I now carried my own Rex branding.

"Time to seal the deal, pussycat," he said much to my dad and brother's irritation and scowling faces. Mom, on the other hand, was catcalling and fist pumping the air like a cheerleader. The rest of the brothers were slapping Rex on the shoulder with a bunch of "atta boys" and "go get her, man" as he hauled me through the casino, up the elevator, and to our room without ever letting me go.

He didn't let me down until we were safely behind the closed door, then he slid his hands up my skirt, ripped off my bridal G-String, unbuttoned his pants, pulled out his stiff cock, lifted me back up, and impaled me on his massive dick. He didn't speak until we were connected, and that was to growl four simple words right in my ear.

"I. Love. My. Wife."

Rex slipped a hand between my ass cheeks for leverage, his fingers just grazing where he was fucking me. The other hand he dipped down between us where he circled my clit with two blunt fingers. I cried out, and he stole the sound by covering my mouth with his. He swirled his tongue back and forth, licking deep, sucking hard, and consuming me from head to toe.

I sank my heels deeper into his flesh, and he groaned so loud I felt it resonate through my body in a wave of electricity.

Rex took that moment to get serious. He hammered home, my body jostling against the wooden door.

"You okay?" He licked up my neck and back before biting down, marking me in another way. The fucking savage.

"God, yes!" I tilted my head back so he could get more access.

"Babies okay?" He thrust and added a swirl of his hips, crushing my clit in the process.

"Yes, yes, yes!" left my mouth on a war cry. And that was all she wrote. My husband's dick, a little hip swirl, the concern for our unborn children, and I lost it. My entire body went up in pleasurable flames as we consummated our marriage against the hotel room door.

While I soared to the heavens on my husband's cock, he bit down on the fleshy globes of my breasts that were popping out of the bustier as he rocked into me. He held me close, his face tucked between my tits while he grunted, his hot seed coating me from the inside as he jerked and jolted through his release. Tremors of his heat licked up my spine, and I had another smaller—but no less substantial—orgasm shudder through me.

When his breathing had calmed, he held me close, cradling me around his body, and took me over to the bed.

"Baby, don't you think we should go down and party with our family?" I asked when my back hit the cloudlike comforter.

"Yeah, after I clean you up and eat you. I want the taste of my wife on my tongue mixed with the bourbon I'll be sucking back in celebration of making you mine in every way." He grinned a devilish smile.

I couldn't hold back a chuckle at his antics. With great purpose, I cupped both of his cheeks, appreciating the abrasion from his beard against the palms of my hands. "I'm crazy in love with you, husband of mine."

He turned his head and kissed both of my palms before pulling my shredded underwear out of his pocket, wiping away his mess from between my thighs, and then spreading me once again.

"I crazy love you, Shay Crawford. You and our babies." He put a hand over my stomach that just barely showed a small bump. It wasn't much since I was only eleven weeks, but with two in there, I was definitely sporting a bump. One my husband was absolutely obsessed with. Thank the good Lord.

"Come here." I tugged at my husband's long hair. "Kiss me. I want your taste on my tongue too."

For the next hour we made love, expressing our happiness through touch and taste. When we were done, he put me back in my wedding attire, because he wanted to enjoy me in it for the rest of the night around all the people who loved us.

And as everyone knew, when it comes to bikers and their babes, we partied all night long.

Rex

Seven months later...

The buzzing of the tattoo needle was mesmerizing. Instead of looking down and watching the guy's needlework on me, I was keeping my eyes glued to the man hunched over my wife's naked lower half.

I clenched my teeth and watched him slide his hand over the side of her thigh and ass. My hands locked into fists and I gritted my teeth, emitting a low warning growl like a fucking animal. Hell, I felt like an animal. One that didn't like another man's hands on my goddammed wife.

"Brother, chill the fuck out. First of all, he's just a kid. Barely twenty, man. Not even old enough to drink or rent a fucking car. Second of all, he'd never disrespect an old lady. He wants in the club, not to be ousted before he can ever get his prospect patch," my Hero's Pride brother we all called "Ink" stated in a low voice.

I watched as the man-child focused his attention on the design Shay and I had agreed on. The Pride lion head complete with flowing mane and snarling mouth. Above it, in very legible, sexy as fuck script, it said, "Property of" and below it was my road name, *REX*. I loved my name on her beautiful body. Just thinking about touching it later was making me stiffen in my jeans.

"Baby, stop looking at this poor guy like you're ready to slit his throat. You're going to scare the daylights out of him, and he'll jack up my tat!" Shay scolded.

I checked out my woman with her goddammed pants off, lying on her stomach with her sweet ass hanging out for the world to see. Well, there was a sheet over the other cheek, and I made them move the screen so that walk-ins couldn't see what was happening in that kid's stall. Still, I made him push that table out so I could watch his every move while I got my own tat chiseled into my skin for life.

It had been three months since she'd birthed our children, and her body was still smokin' hot. She'd gained a lot of weight with our son and daughter, but it had been falling off her left and right since my children seemed to be attached to her tits twenty-four/seven, leaving absolutely nothing for me to suck on, greedy fuckers. I didn't mind. Shay insisted on giving our children the best, and her tit milk was it. I knew, because I had tasted that sweet nectar just to see what the fuss was all about. My children were already smart. That shit was like liquid gold, not that she let me have it very often. Soon though, those succulent breasts would be all mine.

At least she didn't make me wait the six weeks to tag her ass. Hell, waiting the month we did was brutal. I'd fucked my woman morning and night since we met a year ago and all through her pregnancy. Which reminded me that she'd be getting a drilling when we got home. I'd have her nurse the twins and then they'd be out. Her milk always knocked them into dreamland.

"Just about done." The man child wiped over her ass cheek again, and I snarled.

"I swear to God, Kidd, you're lucky you're the best at the lion heads, or I'd fucking kill you where you sit," I reminded him.

The kid, aptly named Kidd, raised his hands, the tattoo needle buzzing away. "Maybe you should finish her up, Ink?"

Ink chuckled and pressed his own tattoo needle into my flesh a little harder to distract me. "Nah, you're almost there. Just finish. I'll keep the brute in check."

"Fuck, Shay, your husband is no joke," Kidd grumbled, and I sent him virtual daggers through my gaze.

She giggled, and I moved my glare to her.

"He's a pussycat." She used my endearment for her against me and blew me a kiss.

I shook my head and waited out the rest of my tat. Shay was done before me, and I watched like a hawk while the man covered her up with the sheet faster than lightning after cleaning it and wiping it with petroleum jelly.

Shay being Shay, flung the sheet off and pranced over half-dressed, most of her tanned ass cheek bared while she evaluated the ink in the mirror. "I love it!" she squealed and then swung her arms around Kidd in a big hug.

That was it! I pushed Ink away and stormed over to them. I grabbed the guy by the shoulder, spun him to face me, and grated through my teeth. "Back. The. Fuck. Off."

Obviously terrified, he backed up so fast he hit the main customer counter.

"Jesus, Rex, lay off. Come on. He didn't do nuthin'" Ink got in between the two of us.

"He was hugging my half naked wife!" I roared, none too pleased.

Ink tipped his head to the side and assessed my angry comment. He turned and shrugged at the man child. "Dude, he's got a point. You must know that bikers are scary obsessive about their old ladies. They are untouchable, Kidd. Remember that for future reference."

Kidd looked down and nodded. "Sorry, sir." He swallowed slowly, and I could tell he was scared but ready to take whatever lashing I might dole out.

I moved toward him, but Shay locked her hands around one of my biceps. "Baby, come here and look."

"Just a minute, pussycat." I glanced at her. "Trust me."

She pursed her lips and then nodded.

I placed my hand on the guy's shoulder. "Thank you for taking care of my old lady. I'm man enough to say I'm not sorry I threatened you. I'd do it again in a heartbeat. My only concern is Shay and our children. When you get an old lady, you will understand. She is your world. Your everything. Got it?"

The man child lifted his head and looked me in the eyes. "Can someone else do her tattoos in the future?" he asked.

I smiled wickedly and shook my head. "Nah man. You did right by my woman. She wants more ink; you're going to have to pony up and deal with me."

He sucked in a breath of air sharply and straightened his spine. "I'll do whatever you need, Rex."

I clapped him on the shoulder. "You keep your eyes on the ink and we'll be just fine, yeah?"

"Totally. Never peeked. I swear!" he said, and I believed him. Didn't change that he'd hugged my half naked wife.

"Next time, no hugs until clothes are firmly back on. Feel me?"

"Yes, sir."

I lifted my chin. "Well, all right then. Pussycat, let's see what you got." I went over to my woman who was still standing half-dressed, admiring her tattoo.

I inspected the tat and ran a rough finger over the word "Property" and then over my name. She whimpered and shivered. "It's perfect. I love it. Thank you." I gripped her hair close to the nape of her neck and kissed her until I couldn't breathe.

She came away from the kiss completely dazed. "You like it." She beamed.

"Yeah, baby, I like it." I kissed her much softer and a lot longer before smacking her hard on the opposite ass cheek. "Now get your fuckin' clothes on for Christ's sake."

Shay giggled and grabbed for her yoga pants.

Kidd approached with a bandage and offered it to her. "I'm sure you can manage," he muttered and then jetted away to help another customer.

I went back to Ink and sat my ass in the chair, my shitkickers on the footrest. "Finish me up."

He shook his head and then finished the script on my babies' names.

"Oh my God!" Shay said as she approached fully clothed. Thank God. Tears filled her eyes and leaked down her cheeks. "My babies," she whispered, viewing the two footprints we copied and inked from my children's birth certificates and put in the shape of a heart right under her branded name. The left footprint was for my boy, Trace, who was born first, and the foot on the right was for my little biker princess, Swayze. Each of their names were under their footprint, showing the world that Shay, Trace, and Swayze were my heart and soul.

"Come here, Shay," I hooked my arm around her waist, and she sidled up to me on the big black table. Without comment, she pressed her lips in a feather light kiss over each little foot and then over her name.

"I love you, Taggart Crawford," she whispered against my lips and then kissed me softly.

"I love you too, pussycat. Now how's my biker babe feeling after her first tattoo?"

She bit into her bottom lip and squirmed against me, placing her thigh right over my lap. "Um...pretty good."

I could feel the heat of her thigh working my last nerve. This tat needed to be done. As in now.

"You 'bout done, Ink? I got hot and bothered in my lap, and I need to take care of that."

Ink laughed and placed the gauze over the tattoo to protect it. "You know the drill for upkeep while healing."

"Yep." I shifted to the side with my woman in my arms and let her slide down my body.

I gripped her hips, hauled her up against my body and let her feel how much her excitement got to me. Once I paid Ink and got my shit on, we hoofed it out to my bike. I swung my leg over, handed Shay her helmet, and she did the same. The moment she cradled me between her thighs, I knew we weren't going home.

Just as I started the bike, she leaned over and whispered, "Biker Babe is closer, and we've still got Mags and Daddy watching the twins."

"Then hold on, pussycat. I'm about to take you for one helluva ride."

The End

Acknowledgements

To my husband **Eric** for thinking it's cool that your wife is writing about fictional alpha men who fall in love instantly, that also happen to be bikers. I will forever love you more.

To the world's greatest PA, **Jeananna Goodall**, I have no idea how you put up with me, but I'm so glad you do. We make an incredible team. Let's keep doing this for another twenty years or more. Love you.

To **Amy Tannenbaum** for allowing me to write whatever the heck I want and being not cool about it, but excited. You've helped me build my career into something I'm really proud of. Thank you.

To **Ekatarina Sayanova** with Red Quill Editing, you are my one true editor love. It's crazy to have someone be able to so completely crawl inside my head and help make sense of the fictional characters demanding attention. I adore you and your team. Thanks also to **Rebecca Cartee** and **Tracy Damron-Roelle** for the additional line and proof edit. Team Red Quill definitely makes a sparkling final product.

To my alpha beta team **Tracey Wilson-Vuolo, Tammy Hamilton-Green, Gabby McEachern** I can't tell you what it means to be able to send you a draft chapter every time I write and get immediate feedback. You feed my muse and my soul, giving me the support I need to keep moving forward on my work in progress. This one took a long time. You had to wait months in between installments and never complained. You three are the best. I'm so grateful for your contribution to my stories.

To **Jena Brignola** your graphics are on point! You always come up with the most amazing designs. The covers, teasers, and swag for this series is going to rock because of your talent. Thank you for taking the extra time to make things perfect. Madlove.

To the **Readers**, I couldn't do what I love or pay my bills if it weren't for all of you. Thank you for every review, kind word, like and shares of my work on social media and everything in between. You are what make it possible for me to live my dream.

BIKER Beloved

Tracey Wilson-Vuolo

Some losses can never be measured in words.
This year was hard for us.
The silver lining…
We'll always have each other.

Prologue

New Year's Day 2015

"YOU'RE NEVER GOING TO BELIEVE THIS!" I HOLLERED into the military issue mobile device my Master Sergeant let me use. We each got ten minutes to call home and share the good news with our loved ones.

"Um, sweetheart, it's so good to hear your voice. Incredible really." My mother's words shook with what sounded like relief. "But honey, we…uh…have news to share as well."

I ran my hands through my now longer hair. Finally, after almost four years of service in the Army in the hothouse hell that is Afghanistan, I had a lot more on top than when they first buzz cut us.

"Me first, Mom!" I made the sound of a trumpet blaring an announcement. "They ceased operation. They've closed down the International Security Assistance Force. Means when I re-enlist in a couple months, I'll be sent somewhere awesome. I'm hoping for Germany or France!" I chuckled into the phone and imagined my arms wrapped around a French hottie who whispered nothing but foreign sweet nothings in my ear while I fucked her. Damn straight! I deserved that after all I've done and seen.

Working the International Security Assistance Force was a dream come true. To be chosen right out of boot camp for the role pissed off a shit ton of my army buds, but I was the best shooter, physically fit as a fiddle, picked up Dari, or Afghan Persian as Americans call it, and my temperament worked for the higher ups. Without even blinking, I graduated boot camp and was immediately shipped off to Afghanistan where I ended up spending the bulk of my time training Afghanistan National Security Forces not only in combat techniques, but to help re-build their government. Didn't change that I had seen my fair share of combat. Hell, I watched my best friend in the entire world explode through the scope of a sniper rifle.

A sour taste coated my mouth, and I shook off the memories threatening to destroy the good vibes I was attempting to soak up and focused on the call.

"Honey, that is amazing. Truly great. I'm thrilled you're safe and sound and the government is finally moving our men out of harm's way and hopefully sending you all home, but um…" Her voice changed, and a sob ripped through the line.

Instant dread filled my pores. Mags was a ball buster. The old lady to beat all old ladies in my father's club, *my club*, back home. She ran the show and never shed a tear in front of the men or the club girls. Hearing her tears meant something bad had happened. *Really* bad.

"Mom, what the fuck?"

"Shane, my boy…" Her voice trailed off, and my throat went dry as the Afghan desert.

Before I could ask a question, my father's deep rumbling voice came over the line. "Son." His voice was so tortured, shivers ran up my spine.

My father, Riot O'Donnell, was the President of the Hero's Pride Motorcycle Club back home. He managed over thirty members and prospects alongside my mom, Magdalene, or "Mags" to the guys, and never sounded anything but upbeat. Unless someone had died.

My heart constricted. I held my breath, and my chest went tight. "Is it Shay? Is my fucking sister okay?" I roared into the phone. There was only one person on this Earth I could not live without and that was my twin sister, Shay. "Christ, Dad! What happened?" Tears burned the back of my eyes instantly at the mere suggestion that something could have happened to my sister.

"No, no, son! It's not Shay. Get that shit outta your head right now."

All the breath I'd been holding raced out of my lungs in a burst of anger. "What the hell, Dad? What is going on?"

"Son, Jess paid us a surprise visit the day after Christmas..."

"Jess? The new club girl?" I dipped back into my memory of the last time I was home. It was about nine or ten months ago, and we had been given a couple weeks before the next round of training started. I flew my ass home and spent those two weeks hanging with the brothers and Mom and Dad, gave Shay shit about some douche she was dating, and rode my bike. Of course, I'd ridden a few of the club girls a time or two, Jess being a stellar lay. Tall, big blonde hair, and pretty blue eyes. Spent two days straight fucking her but scraped her off when I had to go. She started getting clingy and asking for money. I scraped her off and headed back to my station in Afghanistan to finish out my tour.

"Son, I don't know how to tell you this, but she showed up on our doorstep with a screaming brand new baby girl. So brand new, she was only a day old. No name, no birth certificate. Jess looked like shit. Hollow eyes, all skin and bones with fresh track marks up her arms."

I slumped against the wall of the building where I was

taking my call in private. "What does this have to do with me? Just call social services..."

"Whip, she says the baby's yours." My father's tone was harsh and straight to the point.

"Bullshit! I banged her a handful of times, Dad, and I always use a rubber!" I growled into the phone, holding the thing so damned tight my fingers hurt.

My father sighed heavily. "That was our thought too. Except there's no denying this child, Shane. We took her straight to the hospital when Jess left her in my arms and ran off. We pulled your sister in and had them do a DNA test on the baby and her. We got immediate temporary custody as fosters because of our links with the sheriff. They had to pull a lot of strings to allow the baby to be with your mom and me while we waited for the test results."

I pressed a hand against the scalding hot concrete wall, needing the burn to sink in so my mind could focus. I ran the numbers through my head, and if the baby was only days old, it's possible she could be mine.

Fuck!

"Dad...did you get the results?"

"Son...she's...Christ, boy, she's yours. It was confirmed today. Just got the call before you rang through."

Silence.

Everything around me ceased to exist.

The choppers nearby...gone.

The men laughing and carousing, waiting for their turn on the phone...gone.

My life as I knew it...gone.

I swallowed and sucked in a deep breath. "You're telling me I'm a father to a week-old baby girl, and I'm stuck in the fucking desert half a world away?"

"We've got her. We'll take care of her until you come back. Mags is already in love with her. She and your sister fight over how much love they have to give the baby. She's being filled to the brim with attention by us and the club."

"I'm her father! She's been alive a week, and I haven't even set eyes to her. Dad, this is so fucked up!"

He cleared his throat. "It is, but we've got this. I overheard Mags say your mission is complete, and you should be coming home?"

"I was gonna re-enlist." I let those words fall off my tongue like poison.

"And now?" His words were truly a question not a judgment.

"Now, I need to find the quickest way to get the fuck out of the desert and to my little girl. Jesus! What's her name?"

"She doesn't have one."

"The fucking bitch didn't name our daughter?" I ground my teeth so hard I could have cracked a molar.

"Son, Jess did the right thing bringing the baby to us. She was wacked out to the max on something she stuck in her veins. My guess, heroin since the guys mentioned it was her drug of choice. It was the reason Mags kicked her out of the club not long after you left. She spiraled out of control. Trying to get all the guys to give her money, and then turned around and used it for drugs."

I started to pace along the building wall. "I cannot believe this."

"The doctors said the baby wasn't addicted to anything, which means she probably quit when she found out she was pregnant, but likely not the whole time, and started right back up when she had her. Doc said the baby should be just fine, but we need to make sure she has her regular checkups with the pediatrician.

The problem now is the hospital wants us to submit her birth certificate. We have your information and Jessica's...but your daughter needs a name, and Mags and I didn't feel it was right to give her one."

"I haven't even seen a picture of what she looks like, how am I supposed to give her a name?"

My body was too heavy to hold up any longer, I leaned my back against the concrete wall and slid down to the dirt on my ass. My camo-covered legs and boots were stretched out in front of me.

"I just sent one to the phone you called on."

With a shaking hand, I hit the speaker button, clicked over to the messages, and pressed on the text. I'd talk to my sergeant about the message since it would probably cost him, and it was his unit's work phone. On the screen was the most precious little human being. Bright, big blue eyes stared into the camera. Wisps of blonde hair, a perfect pouty pink set of lips and chubby cheeks. She was gorgeous.

She was mine.

My entire life changed the second I took in her face. Suddenly I couldn't wait to meet this little human I'd made.

My dad's voice came through the speaker. "Son..."

"Yeah." I choked back the emotion and coughed. "She's perfect, Dad."

"She is. A really good baby too. Doesn't sleep through the night, but Mags and Shay take turns every other night."

"My mother and sister should not have to take care of my daughter. I should be there..." I banged the back of my head against the wall, hating where I was every second.

"Then come home when you can. Until then, we have your back. We'll take the best care of her. You know that."

I nodded even though my father couldn't see it. Still I couldn't take my eyes off her beautiful little angelic face.

"Shayna," I said decisively. "After my sister and me. Marie, the same as Mom's middle name. I want my daughter to know her name was chosen based on people who will always love her and be there for her. Unlike her junkie mother."

"Mags, he's named her Shayna Marie O'Donnell." I heard my mother's sobs get louder through the phone. Then Dad spoke to my mom, who must have been hovering close and listening in to the call. "Go ahead, Mag Pie, fill out the paperwork, and we'll submit it today." My father's voice was full of emotion. "Perfect name, son. We'll get this done, and we'll take care of your girl."

"I want regular fucking emails and Skype time so I can see her myself," I growled. "And get the brothers to hunt down Jess. I want to know where the bitch is the second I come home."

"Home?"

"Dad, I'm not gonna re-enlist when I have a brand-new baby to take care of. You, Mom, and Shay are already doing too much as it is. I won't be able to go on terminal leave for two months. Two months of her life I'm going to miss. Fuck!" I let my head fall between my now cocked knees as I cursed the desert, the fucking war, and Jessica. I'd already lost my best friend to this war, and now I would lose two months of my daughters' life.

No more.

Right then and there, I promised myself and my daughter that I'd be there for her. As long as it was within my power, I'd be there. Always. I wouldn't abandon her like her mother did. Not my flesh and blood. No way.

"I'll be sure Mags and Shay are on task in sending updates regularly. Keep us posted on your dates, and we'll pick you up at the airport. Not a second more will go by without you meeting your little girl. I promise, son."

I closed my eyes and let the tears fall down my cheeks. "Dad...thanks. Tell Mom and Shay too. I love you all. I don't even know what to think about all of this, but I couldn't imagine having to go through this without you."

"Never, son. Family is everything."

Those words seared straight through my heart as I stared at the picture of my daughter's face.

"Yes. Family is everything," I agreed. "Kiss my little Sunflower, and tell her Daddy already loves her and will be home soon."

Chapter 1

Anya

"ANYA, POPPET, GET UP OFF THE COUCH," HOLLY hollered from our shared bathroom. "Put some real clothes on, and when I say *real*, I mean no leotards, leg warmers, or anything pink. We're going out, no matter what you say!"

I frowned and looked at my steaming cup of chamomile tea, the new romance novel I'd picked up today at the library where my roommate and best friend Holly worked, and the stack of three sugar cookies I'd planned to stare at but wouldn't ever touch. Sugar and ballerinas were not best friends. More like sworn enemies since the day ballet was invented.

"And that also includes putting your hair in a bun! I swear to the Queen Mother, if you so much as tie those golden locks back I'm ripping the tie right out of your hair!"

As quick as a snake slithering in the grass, I yanked out the perfect roll I put my hair into daily.

On tired feet, I stood and winced as the familiar pain resonated through my knee. After a long day of teaching ballet and contemporary dance to children, including private dance lessons, the last thing I wanted to do was go out. Unfortunately, I'd promised Holly. At least once a week, I'd force myself to live a little. Even when all I wanted to do was curl up into a little ball, with self-pity as my only company, and wither the hours away until I had to do it all again the next morning.

That's what my life was now. A series of steps. Movements. A to B. Ever since my injury last year, I just wanted to hide away and sulk for the rest of my days. My dream of being a prima ballerina with the American Ballet Theatre was over, and I'd only had it for two years. At twenty-three years old, I was retired. From the time I was four years old, I'd wanted nothing but to dance. To travel the world, dancing my way through countless productions across the globe. And I had. For two years. Until the night it was all taken away.

"Are you even listening to me?" Holly stood in front of the couch, one pale hand on her hip and her petite body dressed in a pair of perfectly fitting jeans that accentuated her curvy form, a dark purple leather blazer with a white satin camisole underneath. My best friend, Holly, was a tiny stick of dynamite. Wild red hair, a sprinkling of freckles, big blue eyes, and curves for days. Me? I looked like a praying mantis next to her. All long legs, high cheekbones, whiter than white skin, and very little boobs to speak of. My very sweet friend called my form "athletic" and "trim" when in reality she meant skinny and gaunt.

I sighed and cringed when I made my way to my bedroom. "Sorry, Holls. I'll throw some clothes on real quick. It won't take but a minute," I promised, not wanting to disappoint her. I hated disappointing people. I'd already ruined all my mother's hopes and dreams alongside of my own; I couldn't bear to have one more person I loved be disappointed.

Holly followed me into my room. I picked out a pair of black leggings and a long sweater dress. I grabbed a chunky black belt that would cinch in the heavy fabric but also make my waist compared to my hips look a little curvier instead of straight up and down.

"Anya, are you okay? You seemed like you were limping. Did you see the doctor today? Do you have any news?"

Doing what I do best, I swallowed down the instant flood of emotion threatening to crush me where I stood, leaving me nothing but a pile of skin and bones.

"No news, and yes, I had a checkup. Same response as two weeks ago. Healing takes time, and when you've torn your ACL clean through in your knee, it's not something you can bounce back from. The doctors think I'm healing really well, and that I can even put weight on it, teach ballet and dance four days a week is astonishing."

She sat on the bed as I pulled the leggings up and over my simple cotton panties and reached for the sweater dress.

"Well, that's good news. You're healing better than expected and are able to work…"

"But I'll never be a ballerina again. That part of my life is over." My voice shook, but I clenched my teeth so hard my jaw hurt, relieving my need to cry.

Holly pursed her lips and glanced down at the floor. It's what everyone does when they hear I'm a ballerina who can no longer dance. Pity. Sidelong glances away.

"You're an amazing teacher. I've been promoting you to the women who come to the library to sign up their little ones, and some have. They say your dance studio is the best thing to hit Grants Pass in a long time. The kids are eating it up, and the mommies are loving the much needed break!" She got up and ran her hand up and down my bicep in a soothing gesture. "Besides, you're teaching little girls who look up to you. Hell, poppet, they want to *be* you."

Sadness flowed over my soul as I remembered back to when I was in my first dance class. I wanted so badly to be exactly like my teacher. Over the years, I was better than her. In my teens, Mom had to hire me private lessons from the best Anchorage, Alaska, where I grew up, had to offer.

Tears pricked at my eyes, and Holly frowned, then pulled me into a hug. "You were the best of your time, Anya. Maybe you'll dance again. I mean…"

I shook my head. "No. I won't. Ask any orthopedic doctor, any choreographer in the business. You can fix almost anything with today's modern medicine…except the knee."

Holly's head shot back, and she squinted. "I could kill that man for dropping you. Then I'd spit on his grave."

I chuckled. "You're a good friend. The best. He feels as bad as I do."

"Yeah, if he did, he wouldn't be able to dance any longer; but while you're going through surgeries and losing your dream, he's off jet setting the world with a new prima ballerina to break in."

I had a lot of patience. Dancers had to. We did the same things over and over and over again until our feet bled, and we'd gotten something right. Then we did it again for good measure. Now, with every ounce of patience I possessed, I breathed deeply, allowing the memories of that night to fizzle away into a dirty bad dream. When I had a hold of my bearings, I shoved my head and arms through the sweater and locked the belt around my waist, leaving it loose a good inch to make it look like I had more weight on me, and then grabbed my flat leather ankle boots and sat on the bed.

"It's fine. I'm fine. Everything will be fine. Just let me figure out something with my hair, and I'll be ready.

Holly went over to my vanity and pulled out a tube of red

lipstick. "Wear this tonight! You'll look hot. Sexy and mysterious hot!"

I shook my head but did as she requested, painting my lips a bold red. I added a black cat eye dose of kohl liquid liner and mascara. This was more makeup than I did on a regular basis, but I knew Holly would nag me all night if I didn't give her a little bit of effort. My good-natured friend might be a strict, professional librarian by day, but she took no prisoners at night. Especially when she decided it was girls' night out.

She moved to leave my room while I reached for my brush.

"Hair down, Poppet. I want to see golden waves for days!"

I rolled my eyes, brushed my hair, and let it fall down just past my shoulders. Not too long, not too short. Nice and boring. Though I had to admit, wearing it in a bun all day definitely gave it some big waves I didn't have to manufacture by using a curling or flat iron.

Without taking a second glance at myself in the mirror—because honestly, who cared—I grabbed my dark red pashmina, wrapped it around my shoulders, crossed it back over one side, and flicked off my light switch.

"Where to?" I asked, picking up my simple black leather purse.

"Tonight, you brave O'Donnell's!" She smiled wickedly.

O'Donnell's was a biker bar. Well, technically it wasn't exactly a biker's bar from what Holly said, but a lot of men who rode bikes drank here, if the sheer number of Harleys lined up out front was any indication.

In the small town of Grants Pass, Oregon, there was either O'Donnell's bar with the interesting motorcycle wheel as the

"O" on the sign logo, the sleazy stripper club way outside on the edge of town, or Grants Pass Bar & Grill. We usually went to the grill or met up with some of Holly's friends for drinks at their houses.

At this time of night, the bar and grill would be packed, filled with families finishing up their late-night dinners. Since it was only nine o'clock on a Thursday, O'Donnell's was pretty much the place to be.

The interior was put together well. Everything inside was of the wood and log cabin variety, giving the space a cozy, comforting appeal. The bar sat along the right wall with a shiny mahogany top and a bullnose edge. The seats in front of the bar were cushy red leather with gold grommets outlining the back. On the back wall of the bar was a glass mirror with the bar's logo stretched out dead center in script letters. Under the logo, it said, "Owned and operated by The Pride."

I'd seen that phrase a few times throughout the town. There was even a gym down the way from my studio that had those words under the logo. I'd heard a little about Hero's Pride Motorcycle Club but not enough to form an opinion one way or another about it. In my early experience, bikers were big, badass, law-breaking guys who wanted no part of normal society. However, recently, I'd had cause to meet with a biker or two when one of my students was being picked up or dropped off. So far, the ones I'd met, especially the female biker women, or "biker beauties" as I've heard them called, were really nice.

"Come on, let's get a drink," Holly said, hooking my elbow with her arm and dragging me to one side of the very busy bar. A huge man in a leather vest was sitting at the corner, motorcycle boots on the rung of the tall chair, ginormous muscles protruding from his too tight t-shirt. He had hair as long as mine, if not longer, which was hanging loose down the sides of his face. A stunning curvaceous woman with really dark hair was standing between his thighs and chatting animatedly at the man tending bar.

I blinked a few times as I took in the white t-shirt and jeans wearing hunk who had his head tipped back, laughing heartily at something the brunette had leaned over to tell him, her bodacious ass right in her man's face.

My mouth dropped open as I took in the display. The big guy had amazing pointed triangle shaped eyebrows and a sinful grin as he placed his hands on her hips and winked at me. Winked! At another woman while groping the one in his lap.

The man kissed the woman on the spine in the space where her shirt had risen up in back. "Pussycat, you've got an audience. Wanna take it down a notch?" he said loud enough for the woman and the bartender to hear. A set of similar faces took me and Holly in.

"Holly Berry! Girl, I never see you here! You finally escaped the clutches of the library and made it out on the town! Drinks are in order!" The brunette shimmied back onto her feet with her man's help and pulled my friend into a hug. I've been so busy with the twins and the store, I haven't seen you in forever!"

"Shay, you look brilliant! How old are the wee ones now? It seems like a minute ago you were about ready to pop! Now look at you. Leather pants, tight tank, body for days? What? Did you push out the babies and then bounce right back in thirty days? Bloody hell!"

The large man grinned an all-white smile and wrapped a beefy tatted arm around his woman's waist. "If she'd let me get her pregnant again, she'd be back to packin' on the pounds, and I'd be free of threatening every motherfucker who has his filthy gaze on my wife."

Shay's face took on an annoyed expression as she spun in

his arms, her long tresses flowing out behind her. "Bullshit! You were more of a caveman when I was pregnant with the twins than you are now, and I told you, you need to give me until the twins are out of diapers. No way I'm changing three children's diapers several times a day. No way. No how.

"Holly girl, who's your friend?" The muscled man held out his hand to me. "Rex." He tilted his head toward the beautiful brunette. "My old lady, Shay."

I shook his hand and was happy he didn't squeeze the bones to the point of pain. Big guys tended not to know how much strength they had. Though this man didn't seem the type to be unaware.

"Oh, so sorry. This is my best friend, Anya. She moved here three months ago. We're roomies."

Rex lifted his chin in recognition.

Shay wiggled her fingers but didn't leave her man's hold. "Nice to meet you. Let's get you guys some drinks."

Rex let out a sharp, quick whistle. The handsome man with the white t-shirt and jeans made his way back over to this side.

"Whip, drinks for Shay's friends," he requested in a deep grumble.

The bartender, who answered to the odd name of "Whip", finally took in Holly and then his gaze landed on mine.

I sucked in a breath and couldn't let it out. I was stunned. A pair of the most beautiful green eyes sucked me into a warm pond-colored abyss. I leaned a hand on the bar and moved closer, not able to look away. Were they green? Maybe blue? No. As he grinned and dipped his head my way, I noted they were hazel, definitely hazel. A perfect mix of yellow, blue, green, and brown. The likes of which I've never seen before. His square jaw was shaded with at least a days' worth of scruff, and when he smiled directly at me, I nearly drooled.

"What's your poison, Bella?" he asked, the low vibration of his deep voice sinking deep into my chest and making my heart pound.

"Um…" I blinked and shook my head. "Poison?"

He smirked. "Your drink of choice."

"Well, I don't know. I've never drank much. Only the rare occasional glass of champagne…"

Holly slapped her purse down on the bar next to my side, making me jump back like a frightened cat. "Shots! Tequila. Beer chasers," Holly demanded and pressed her black-rimmed glasses higher up on her nose.

Mr. Whip, or whatever his name was, chuckled at her dramatics. Me, I felt my cheeks heat, and the skin under my sweater got unbearably hot. I tried to push away from the bar, but the hunk grabbed my wrist, encircling my forearm light enough to hold on but not hard enough to bruise.

"Don't rush off now, Bella. What's your name?"

"Anya."

"Anya. Pretty name for a pretty woman." He let my hand go, and I snapped it back to my side.

"Uh, that's nice of you to say." I looked down and to the side where I could see Shay and Rex smiling like crazy people who were in on the same joke. The joke was likely me. I didn't do well with a lot of people. I was much better on stage away from people speaking to me or with children. Little ones were easy. Everything they said was direct and honest. Brutally so. Though I preferred that over the more mature alternative of not knowing what people thought of me and worrying about it endlessly.

My hands got sweaty, and I clutched them into fists, wishing I'd made some excuse to avoid coming out tonight. These kinds of meet and greets usually meant fact finding missions between strangers. Who are you? Where did you come from? What do you do? My life was over the second I was dropped and then landed on the last time I took to the stage. Not exactly a stellar conversation starter.

The gorgeous man with the incredible eyes kept speaking. "I'm Shane, but everybody calls me Whip."

I frowned at the mention of the odd name. "Whip, like whipped cream?" I blurted and then wished I could shove the words right back into my stupid mouth.

Those stunning eyes of his darkened, and his mouth clamped shut as he stared at me. An intense connection built in the space between us. Electricity sizzled and popped like bacon on an open flame. I stepped closer to the bar. So close the edge pressed deep into my midsection. He lifted his hand and moved to touch my face. I inhaled sharply, and the moment before I felt his touch, I was jostled to the side.

"The shots aren't going to pour themselves, and Anya will still be here when you bring them back." My spitfire bestie hooked an arm around my shoulders and shook me from side to side.

Whip didn't speak; he just stared into my eyes.

"Whatever this is," Shane said, pointing between our bodies, "we're gonna continue it. Later. Preferably somewhere else more private." His gaze narrowed on Holly. "Where others can't interrupt."

My stomach dropped. I hadn't been with a man alone aside from the other dancers in the company since I left Anchorage for New York at eighteen to join the American Ballet Theatre. I'd even lost my virginity there to my handsy partner who mercilessly courted me for months until I finally gave in.

Once I had, he said I was a lousy fuck and, from then on,

could barely look at me during our rehearsals, though his eyes would light for the stage when it came performance time. Turned out, he'd taken a lot of innocent young women over the years, promising them good words to the instructors and help securing higher level positions. One of his conquests was the choreographer's daughter. He was kicked out of the company shortly after for issues with ethical conduct. Thank god.

After him, I never opened myself up to a man. Couldn't. Didn't want anything getting between me and my goal of being the world's greatest prima ballerina. Now I was nothing. Not even good enough for the handsome man behind the bar with a great smile and an even better body. He could have any woman in here and probably did.

I cleared my throat and lifted my chin. "I don't think so."

He frowned, and his jaw seemed to harden. Without another word, he spun around and got the beers and shots Holly ordered. I stepped back and to the side of Holly so I wouldn't have to look at the man who I wasn't worthy enough to have.

Over the course of a couple hours, I sipped the rather bitter beer and only consumed one tequila shot. When the liquor burned my throat like fire and left my mouth a bit numb so that I couldn't speak right away, I decided against any more. Holly, on the other hand, was going for the gusto. Once she'd had three shots and two beers, I took her car keys and tucked them into my small purse.

We spent the evening chatting up Shay and Rex. They were really nice. I found out Shay owned the Biker Babe boutique I walked past on the way to my studio. Rex was her "old man" and Vice President of the Hero's Pride Motorcycle Club. Her father was the president, and Shane, or Whip, was her twin brother. He was also a member of the club. I avoided additional mention of Shane and changed the topic when she started to speak of him or include him in conversation while he served up drinks to a steady stream of people all night.

Rex gave me the low-down regarding the motorcycle club and explained each of the members were either active or retired or former civil servants and military. From cops, CIA, doctors, and fireman all the way to the seriously secret type agencies, all of the men in the motorcycle club had served the country in some way. They were a pride because a pride takes care of its own. It's a family. He said they have several businesses they run in town such as O'Donnell's and the gym, as well as a few others, not to mention the club fixes up and restores motorcycles. Then, of course, there was Shay's boutique. I was still uncertain how they were involved in that.

As the night wore on, I saw a lot of different men in leather vests with the Hero's Pride logo of a snarling lion's head in the center and the word Oregon on bottom. Rex told us there were a few high level positions in the club such as his as VP and the President, but they also had an Enforcer and even a club Secretary. Turns out they did a lot for the city of Grants Pass, keeping drugs off the streets, helping the sheriff's deputies when needed, and rode in a large number of charity fundraising rides. Whatever that entailed, I had yet to find out.

Still, the most surprising part of the night, besides my unwavering attraction to Shane, who didn't hide that he was checking me out all evening, was when I met Shay's mother, Magdalene, or "Mags" as they called her. She was quite possibly the most interesting woman I'd ever met in my life. When she entered the bar, the men called out to her with appreciative hoots and hollers, to which she hefted her large bosom and shimmied them for the catcallers who went wild for it. She also had a trail of scantily clad women following her every move as though she was their Queen Bee.

The woman was supposedly in her fifties, but I wouldn't have pegged her past thirty-five. She looked so much like Shay, though a more petite version who dressed a bit riskier than her daughter.

"Shay-la-la, how's my baby girl," she cooed and hugged her daughter. "Looking mighty fine, I see." She ran her gaze over her daughter who danced around in a happy tequila-induced circle.

"Mom, this is Anya, and you remember Holly, our librarian?" The woman nodded, and her vast amount of hair bounced with her.

"Sure thing, though I haven't had cause to step into the library in a long while. How are you, sugar?"

Holly and Mags caught up while I sat back and listened. The trail of women who had followed Mags turned out to be club girls. Basically, women who hung around the bikers, spent time, shared meals, and apparently slept around with them at their leisure. I found this outrageous and totally outside of my comfort zone, but my *babushka* taught me never to judge unless I wanted to be judged. This lesson had sunk deep within me. Although, I was having trouble with the club girls concept because it seemed a trendy name for a hooker or easy girl. I guess it depended on if these were paid roles in the club or not. I was too afraid to ask, and didn't feel I had the right to in the first place. Still, the woman Rex called "*The* Old Lady" and Shay referred to as "The Queen" was beyond interesting. And when she walked up to the bar, Shane or Whip or whatever his name was—I liked to think of him as eternally handsome—placed three shots of some clear colored liquid in front of her.

Mags grabbed a glass, shot it back, and proceeded to do all three in a row. Without something to drink after to settle the burn. She made a satisfied "Ahh" sound and then turned to me.

"Cat caught your tongue, Twinkle Toes?" she asked me even though she knew my name was Anya.

I frowned. "Twinkle Toes?"

Mags lips shifted into a cat-that-ate-the-canary smile as she pointed a long, red tipped nail up and down in front of me. "You look like a ballerina."

I clenched my teeth and stuck out my chin, preparing for the onslaught of questions upon answering with, "I used to be."

It never came. She just nodded, so I proceeded to change the subject. "I'm happy to meet you." Once more, she didn't respond, just cocked a knowing brow, making me spill my guts with one look. "I mean, I just think you're incredibly beautiful and so unique looking. The entire place seems to love you as much as your daughter does, and well, you seem to have acquired your own harem of beautiful scantily dressed women. I've...I've never seen anything like it."

She smiled so big, the lines at the corners of her eyes became visible. Then she tilted her head and scanned my form. "Absolutely beautiful." She placed a curled finger to her chin. "But you don't even know it."

I swallowed down the instant flutter of happiness her assessment added to my belly. "I-I-um, thank you."

She pursed her lips. "You're just my son's type. Legs that could wrap around a man twice. Blonde. You're very slight, but we could fix that with a few of our hog roasts and club parties." She nudged Rex. "Couldn't we, son?"

Rex looped an arm around Mag's waist and kissed her cheek sloppily.

Shay grabbed her man's head and forced him to look at her. Drunkenly, she blurted, "Hey, you only get one O'Donnell woman to kiss, and that's me!" She pointed to her chest but missed and stabbed her own boob with her thumb. "Ouch!"

150

Immediately, Rex was on it, kissing her breast over her shirt until she was giggling herself silly. "Woman, you jealous of your own mother?" He touched his nose to hers.

"Have you *seen* my mother? She's fuckin' hot! Of course I'm jealous." She play-fought with him, which I imagined was a weird form of foreplay for the married couple with small children at home.

"That's why I'm here, baby. Shane called and said you two were tying one on. Riot has an eye on the twins at your house. Told the girls I was coming down for a drink; a few of them followed."

Shay frowned and pouted. "I thought you were keeping them overnight?"

"Works for me." Rex piped in.

She smacked his leather clad chest. "Because you always want your babies with you under the same roof. Your Pussycat wanted private time with her old man."

Mags shook her head. "Sorry, sweetheart. Boys started getting a little wild. Wanted Swayze and Trace to have a good night's sleep, so we took them back home. Now come on, let's get you into the 'Stang before your dad turns into a pumpkin." Mags tossed her keys to a tall lengthy young man of maybe twenty or so. He also wore a leather vest, but his had a patch that said "Prospect" on it. "You're driving, Brandon."

"Got you, Mags."

Looked like Mags drove a car she called a 'Stang, which I gathered must have been short for Mustang. Those cars were way cool, making her the ultimate biker mama.

"Good seeing you again, Holly *Berry*," Shay teased my friend. "And meeting you, Twinkle Toes." She picked up her mother's nickname for me.

"You too." I gave a small wave.

She smiled and looped her arms around her man. He stood with her straddling him, legs wrapped around his waist. He gripped her ass tight and ground against her in front of every single person there, and neither one of them seemed to care. "I'm gonna fuck you until you forget you used to be an O'Donnell and are forever and always going to be a Crawford."

Shay reached her arms up to the sky like a cheerleader and screamed "Woohoo!"

He didn't let her fall or even dip back with the move. Her husband was all about her.

I wished for that one day, but in the end, I really didn't have enough to offer a good man like Rex. Like Shane. I turned my head and watched as Shane's eyes followed his mother, sister, and brother-in-law until they left out the door. Then his beautiful gaze met mine.

Quick as a flash, I grabbed a few twenties out my purse, tossed them on the bar and took hold of Holly, who was singing to the jukebox and dancing in her own little square of space with not a care in the world. I led her toward the same door her friends had left out of.

Before I left, I couldn't help but glance over my shoulder at the most handsome man—with deeply soul-searching eyes—I'd seen.

Those eyes were right on me, but it was his mouth I paid attention to as he smirked and mouthed one word that sent chills skittering down my spine.

"Soon."

Chapter 2

Whip

"**S**UNFLOWER, IF YOU DON'T GET YOUR BOOTY OUT HERE right now, we're going to be late for your rehearsal!" I hollered from the living room while putting Shayna's ballet slippers in my backpack along with a package of goldfish, a box of apple juice, a couple waters, and a change of clothes, just in case. Learned that shit early on caring for a kid. They always messed up their clothes. If there was an opportunity to spill, smudge, or jack up an outfit, it'd happen. And my girl did not do dirty. She was my perfect little biker princess.

"Daddy, I can't get my hair done wike Misses M's, and I want Misses M's hair." She entered in a black leotard, pale pink tights and a matching pink tutu around her waist. Tonight was the rehearsal for her first ever ballet recital. She'd only been training for six weeks, but I was fuckin' psyched. My little girl on a stage. I couldn't wait. I took off the entire weekend at O'Donnell's to be there for the rehearsal tonight and the show tomorrow. My girl was going to know I'd always be there for the important things.

Unfortunately, being a single dad, I had to rely on my family and "The Pride", my extended family of brothers to help with the day-to-day things my almost five-year-old daughter needed. Usually my father, Riot, took her to and from ballet class because Mags had to prep and feed the men at the clubhouse. And if he couldn't, one of the brothers or the club girls took her. Usually Lacey ponied up for that job, and I hated it more than anything. Made me feel beholden to the bitch. I'd already pity fucked her a couple times in thanks, but I knew the girl wanted more. My sister, Shay, couldn't take and pick her up because it was prime hours at her boutique, Biker Babe. Eventually I'd find the right woman for me and Shayna, and maybe then, I'd have a woman steadily in her life and mine to help carry the load.

Not that my daughter was a weight. She was the light of my fucking life. My world revolved around my girl. Though in order to take care of her and give her what she wanted and needed in life, I had to work the bar. I made good money—hell, all the brothers did—but it didn't change the time I was away.

My baby girl stomped her little feet, and her mouth twisted in a scowl. She pointed at her wonky ponytail. "It's messed up."

"I can fix it, baby, come here." She came over and spun around.

"But Daddy, I want it wike a bawawina. In a circwe wike my teacher. She's so pwetty. I wanna be her, Daddy!"

"You mean in a bun like a donut?"

Her little blonde head bobbed up and down. "Yeah! Wike a donut! Wike pwetty Misses M."

"Misses M is pretty, eh?" I tugged out the rubber band and slicked my daughter's hair into a long rope. Then I spun the hair around and around until it made a circular shape Shay'd taught me how to do a couple times before. Once I had it in the smallest little bun on top of her head, I wrapped the rubber band around the entire thing twice. My daughter held up her arm and on her wrist was a big pink fluffy type rubber band. I encircled the entire thing with the frilly rubber band, and damn if it didn't look pretty good.

"Misses M is the pwettiest wady in the whole wide world, Daddy! I want to be her when I get bigger!"

I chuckled and turned her around to face me. Her bright blue eyes seemed bottomless. Sky blue. Just like another blonde's eyes I'd seen recently. The same woman who'd haunted my every waking and sleeping fantasy since I saw her a few nights ago at O'Donnell's with her friend Holly. I didn't know anything about Anya. Her last name. Where she lived. I only knew she was friends with Holly, and I hadn't had a chance to stop at the library to get more information.

Soon though.

I'd find the blonde beauty if it took weeks. My dick stirred at the mere thought of the stunning woman. Yeah, I'd be hunting her down very soon.

Shayna cupped both of my cheeks. "You not wistening to me, Daddy."

"I'm sorry, baby. We gotta go, though, or you'll be late. Slip into your tennis shoes for now so you don't get your slippers all dirty."

"Okay, Daddy. Can we take the bike?"

I shook my head with a grin. My baby girl loved riding the motorcycle with her dad and papa. I didn't let anyone else take my daughter on their bike—no fuckin' way—but she loved when we took her. Shay says she's a biker babe in training. I figured there could be worse things than her settling down with a biker who would make her his old lady one day. Treasure her like my father does my mom. Hell, even my sister's husband,

Rex, practically worships the ground his old lady walks on. I want something like that for my girl one day. As in thirty years from now.

"Sweetheart, we're not going to mess up your hair with a bike helmet or risk getting your outfit dirty. Daddy will take you for a ride this weekend."

She pats my cheeks. "Okay, Daddy. You pwamise?"

"I promise, Sunflower. Now let's get outta here."

We rode down the main street in town, my daughter chatting a mile a minute about how excited she was to be on stage tomorrow. I honked the horn a couple times when we passed Champ's Gym, which my brother Champ ran, along with the boxing league, for the club. The club put up most of the capital in the beginning, which meant we each got a piece of it, so a lot of the brothers worked there in alternating shifts, same as the bar. Kept profits going, and we did some charity fight nights that raised a lot of money for the community. Though since my family put up the capital on setting up O'Donnell's and the club helped build it, we make fifty percent of the profit. I make a wage since I run it, same as Champ does for his gym, but the additional profits get parceled out to all the brothers in equal shares. The system worked, and all of the brotherhood lived well. We weren't rich by any means, but we got what we needed and a lot of what we wanted. Really, I didn't see a better life plan. Aside from finding a woman to share it all with. Except I had to be choosy, real choosy, because I had more than myself or my dick to think about. I had a four-year-old girl who needed to have the right kind of woman in her life since her mother was a junkie piece of shit. Still couldn't find Jess even after all these years. Good riddance, I say.

"Right there, Daddy!" Shayna screeched when we passed the dance studio simply named *On Pointe* with the words "Ballet and Contemporary Dance" in smaller script under it.

"Don't worry, Sunflower. I'm going to park up here."

I found a spot a little ways down the road and got out. My daughter knew not to so much as touch the handle on the door when in the truck with me. I made sure my baby was safe getting in and out of the high vehicle. I opened the door, and she flung herself into my arms and kissed my cheek. I hooked her around the butt and hiked her up on my hip while grabbing my pack.

"I so excited!" She kicked her little legs against me, and I chuckled as we walked to the entrance of the studio. Once inside, I found it was much larger than I'd expected. There was a seating area with about twenty or so chairs, all occupied.

Shayna kicked her legs to get down, and I set her down. She grabbed my hand. "This way, Daddy!"

I followed my girl through the throngs of parents milling around. Several of the men stepped aside when they saw my cut. Each of them nodded in what I felt was respect. Many of the women started whispering conspiratorially to their friends or husbands.

The Pride got two forms of attention. Positive or negative. There was no in-between. Either people knew we were a club that helped out law enforcement, ran healthy tax contributing businesses in the town, and did a shit ton for local charities, or they thought we were bad guys who would cause a ruckus and put a stain on their town. I ignored the latter.

Shayna slipped between several people and went into a hallway that opened to a huge dance studio. The floors were a high gloss wood you'd see in most dance studios. All three walls were floor to ceiling mirrors. Each wall had a different height wooden barre running down it. Large square speakers were set up at each corner. Overall the room was plain. Not much to it.

And then a few sets of parents milling in the center moved off to the side where at least forty fold-up seats were set out, and there she was.

My Anya.

She wore a short, black, skintight leotard with a little ruffle across the middle that fell to the middle of her thighs. Her legs were encased in a pair of light pink tights just like my daughter's, though on Anya, they were the sexiest fucking thing I'd ever seen. She was wearing a pair of pink satin ballet shoes. Not like my daughter's; hers were soft and flexible. What Anya had on looked elegant and so incredibly feminine.

"Daddy, Daddy, you hafta meet Misses M." Shayna tugged on my arm, but I was stunned to the spot where I stood.

Anya was facing a couple, her hands moving in a musical gesture that may have referenced something about the dance tonight. Then she smiled softly and dipped her head. The couple moved away toward the chairs. Anya turned around, scanning the room. Our gazes met and *whammo*! It was like I'd just taken a gut punch by my brother Champ in the practice ring at the gym. I rubbed at the spot and stood there like an idiot, staring at the most beautiful woman I'd ever seen. Even better now in a tiny, flirty dance dress, her hair pulled up in a perfect bun, little tendrils hanging down and framing her oval shaped face. Her neck seemed so long and elegant I wanted to run my lips down its pearly white length and sink my teeth into where her shoulder and neck met. Leave my mark for all to see.

Like a goddamned Neanderthal.

Anya's gaze turned smoldering, and her cheeks flushed a

pretty rosy color. Then her gaze shifted down, and her entire being lit up when she saw my daughter.

Shayna broke away from me and ran to Anya. The woman kneeled down and encircled her in a loving hug.

I hustled over and heard Anya say, "Now, how is my prima ballerina this evening?"

"So good! And my daddy is here!" Shayna lifted her arm out to me.

I held her hand and put my hand around the ball of her shoulder.

"Daughter?" Anya's voice cracked in what I could imagine was surprise.

Shayna nodded happily. "Yep. And he's gonna be here to-night and tomorrow."

Anya smiled and held her hand out to me. "Mr. O'Donnell, I presume."

I took her hand and held it, allowing my thumb to rub along the top of her hand in a sweeping caress. "Yeah. Ms. M?"

"Markova. Anya Markova. This is my dance studio."

I lifted her hand up to my lips and kissed each of her knuck-les. "Had I known you'd be here; I would have worked harder to find a way to drop off or pick up my daughter myself. Most of the time, it's my father."

"Riot," she said flatly. "I should have put the two together last Thursday."

Shayna giggled. "See, Daddy, I towd you Misses M was the pwettiest bawawina in the world."

"She is definitely the most beautiful thing I've ever laid my eyes on." I allowed my gaze to run up and down her long and lean frame.

Anya's cheeks got redder, and the blush ran down her neck onto her chest. Made me wonder what other places turned such a delectable shade of pink when complimented. Anya snapped her hand from my hold, and I frowned, not nearly done with my lips against her skin. Nowhere near done.

"I gonna be you when I grow up, Misses M."

Anya cupped my daughter's cheek and spoke directly to her, cutting off the connection we just had. "You can be anything you want to be, my darling girl."

Fuck.

My daughter beamed up at her teacher as though the sun rose and set on her. Hell, if I didn't feel the fuckin' same spell overtaking my mind and body.

"Now, if you'd like to take a seat, Mr. O'Donnell…" She gestured to the seats filling up across the room.

"Whip," I corrected.

Her lips twitched. "Whip. If you could take a seat with the other parents, we have a rehearsal to get started, don't we, Shayna?"

"Oh yes! Daddy, I need my shoes!" She plucked off her tennis shoes right where she stood.

I grinned and shook my head but dropped the backpack to the floor and helped her put on her slippers. She got up and ran over to the other dancers waiting along the opposite wall. I placed her tennis shoes back in the bag and stood.

When I eased up, I turned my head and noticed Anya's gaze was on my ass. When she realized she'd been caught, her eyes widened in shock, and one of her hands flattened over her heart. "Oh my, I'm sorry. How horribly unprofessional of me…"

"Shut it," I growled.

Her lips clamped shut immediately.

"I like you looking at me. Besides, my eyes, and hopefully *my hands and mouth*, will be all over you, very soon."

She stood there blinking prettily as if glued to the spot. Served her right. That's how I felt when I first saw her too.

Eventually, she shook off her haze and rubbed her hands together. "If you'd go sit down, I'd like to get the rehearsal started."

I smirked. "Sure, if you promise to go out to dinner with me and Shayna after the show tomorrow."

She opened and closed her mouth. "Um, I don't know. Uh, I don't think that's such a good idea."

"It's a fuckin' perfect idea."

"Mr. O'Donnell, I shouldn't date my students' parents. It sets a bad example." She lifted her chin in defiance.

"Don't give a fuck if it's professional. You're gonna find out one important thing when it comes to a biker."

Her hand shook as she placed the tendril of hair by her cheek behind her ear. "And that would be?"

"We don't give up, and we get what we want. And since I want you, and the fact that you want me is written all over your fuckin' body, it would be a whole helluva lot easier if you just agreed to have dinner with me and my daughter tomorrow."

"You curse a lot."

I smiled wide. "Yeah, babe. Maybe I need a posh prima ballerina to help cure me of my nasty habit."

Her entire face changed in a flash. Gone was the uncertain pretty blonde who was at war with her desires over dating the bad boy biker father of one of her students. In its place stood a cold, stoic woman who'd been broken down by something far deeper than we had time to get into.

"I'm not a prima ballerina. At least not anymore. Please, take your seat, now, Mr. O'Donnell." Her voice was stern and direct.

Without another word, she clapped her hands loudly, then

spoke above the din of the chattering families here to watch their child's rehearsal. "We'll be starting in a couple minutes. Everyone please take your seats."

"You win, this time, Anya. Tomorrow, all bets are off."

She inhaled and let out a long sigh. "This isn't a game, Mr. O'Donnell. This is my life and the life of your daughter. It is my job to teach her, and she's a very gifted student. Far more advanced in her study than her peers, as I've no doubt you will see shortly...if you'd kindly *take your seat.*" She spoke the last through her teeth.

I grinned and gave her a mini salute. The woman was too wound up to goad her any further. What's funnier is that she probably thought I was turned off by the proper and professional distance she'd tried to use to dampen the fire burning between us. What she didn't know was that I loved a good challenge, and that sexy getup, her long legs, golden hair, and pouty lips, along with that attitude, made my dick harder than it had ever been.

Anya Markova would be mine.

I thought about this while the boys and girls lined up. I was surprised to see the little boys wearing all black leggings and tight t-shirts. Turned out, the boys were necessary as they helped lift some of the girls into the air as they kicked their legs into what looked like air splits.

As the music progressed and more of the little ones were twirling wildly, some leaning to one side or the others on unsteady feet, my daughter walked right into the center of the group, got up on her tip toes, and as she did, I noticed Anya on the side of the production, balancing on the flattened top of her ballet slippers, her long leg coming out and matching the movements my daughter made, though my daughter was hyper focused and only glanced at the teacher periodically. She brought her leg out and in, lifted her hands above her head and spun in a perfect circle on the toes of her little feet. Anya, mimicked the move looking like a perfect double of my daughter, only womanlier and more mouthwatering.

One of the little boys came up behind Shayna and put his hands on her waist. He was a good foot taller than her, probably a few years older too. I had to clench my hands into fists. I didn't want any boy touching my daughter even in dance class. And while I ground my molars down to dust, the boy lifted my daughter into the air.

"The fuck!" I roared and stood up in my chair in front of the other parents, ready to beat the shit out of the little twerp or maybe his dad. Before I could move, I watched in abject horror but ended up with my mouth hanging wide open as the older boy spun my daughter in a circle a couple times while she held her pose, then brought her down perfectly.

Anya came over to me and hooked my arm, pulling me to the side as the other children continued with the piece, and my daughter bowed and danced her way to the side of the class.

"Do not interfere or yell profanities to my students." Her words were coated in anger as was her expression. Her lips were compressed into a flat white line, her blue eyes blazing with white-hot fire as she spoke agitatedly. "I would never allow a child to be harmed in one of my pieces. They've been practicing that move three times a week for three weeks. They have it perfected, and he's absolutely capable of lifting your much *smaller* daughter. He's six years her senior and has been in training many years before coming to my studio."

"I'm, hell, Bella, I'm sorry." I ran my hand through my shaggy brown hair. "She's my whole fuckin' world. If anything happened to her, I don't know what I'd do."

Her lips pursed, and she huffed. "Well, don't do that. You

can stay here." She pointed to the spot on the ground where we stood. "Where I can see you for the rest of the rehearsal."

I grinned. "Shit, if I knew you were going to get all demanding on my ass, I would have misbehaved more often."

She let out a long, irritated groan before moving away from me and toward the children. The music changed, and suddenly, she pranced across the space to the center of the children where my daughter was waiting.

Then magic happened.

Both females bent into a wide legged move and started skip leaping around the other dancers in the center. Shayna was magnificent, following along with her teacher as if she'd been born with a pair of dancer's legs.

Together Anya and Shayna danced, wooing the crowd in what looked like a mother-daughter dance. At the end, Shayna ran across the space and leaped into Anya's arms where she lifted her above her head at the ribs. Shayna stretched her legs out in the most perfect split, and Anya lifted onto her toes and cocked one of her legs, balancing herself and my daughter on one leg. Hell, it was basically on her big toes. I'd never seen anything like it, and I doubted I ever would again.

I knew right then and there, I needed this woman in my life, but more importantly, she needed to be in Shayna's. After years of waiting for the right woman to come along, she'd appeared out of nowhere.

For now, I enjoyed the show of my daughter and the woman I would make mine bonding over dance. Because as soon as I could swing it, I was gonna make Anya Markova my old lady.

Chapter 3

Anya

"WHAT WAS I THINKING, PUTTING ON A PRODUC-tion of this scale for children four to eighteen?" I rushed through the community college's backstage like a fire had been lit under my feet. I had a handful of tutus and extra hair fasteners.

Holly raced behind me with both arms out, holding the teenagers' borrowed costumes. This show had two costume changes for the teenagers who not only supported the smaller dancers, but also had a contemporary performance on top of the ballet piece I'd choreographed for the smaller children.

"It's going to be brilliant! Though I definitely think you need more help, Twinkle Toes," she joked.

"Stop calling me that," I spat, maneuvering through the contemporary group practicing their skit in the hallway.

Holly laughed. "Why-ever not? It fits. You're the quintessential ballerina. If it's good enough for Mags and Shay, it's bloody good enough for me!"

I sighed loudly as I made my way to the second ballet group with the tutus. "Here you go, my sweets. They were

165

hiding in an unpacked box!" I held up the tutus as though they were trophies.

The kids screeched with glee, and each grabbed a tutu and promptly put it on. I had them going on first because they were a bit older. Then I'd have a contemporary piece, followed by the little ones, and then end the show with the teenagers.

Holly was right; I needed help. There was a lot going on for a beginning recital, but I was determined to make my first one something to remember. For everyone involved. Besides, the kids had been working so hard, I really wanted their families to see what they'd accomplished in such a short time.

Holly and I met up with the teenagers, and she offloaded the costumes they were to wear in the second piece onto the standup racks with their names labeled on the hooks. The girls rushed over and oohed and ahhed at the sparkly outfits, which made my heart pound and my chest fill with a spark of pride. I was making a difference—a small but hopefully important difference—in these kids' lives. I might not be a prima ballerina, traveling to exotic locations and wooing audiences across the globe, but for now, I had this. And it would have to be enough.

Once we ensured each group was set, the two of us made our way over to the small kids. Several of the girls were crowded around someone.

"What is the meaning of this?" I stood with my hands to my hips.

Several of the children scattered, and I noted Shayna was sitting on top of a crate, tears pouring down her face.

"My goodness me," I rushed over. "Whatever is the matter, Shayna?" I kneeled in front of her hand placed my hand on her knee.

She hiccuped through her sobs. "I-I-I can't dance. Too scawed," she cried.

"Oh, my darling girl, you just have a case of stage fright, that's all. Every prima ballerina gets nervous before a performance. It's completely normal."

She shook her head and cried louder. "I-I-wanna go h-hooome. Want my Da-Da-Daddieeee." She sniffled, and the tears poured over her cheeks.

"Oh, sod all, this isn't good," Holly whispered from behind me. "Isn't she the star of the show?"

I swallowed heavily and nodded. "Just sit here, sweetheart. Just breathe and I'll figure something out." My heart kicked up a rapid beat against my chest. "We need to get her father."

"Okay, I'll stay here, you go find him."

"I can't leave backstage. There are too many children here. Anything could happen."

"Just go use the mic up front," she suggested.

I nodded. "Okay, yeah."

With quick feet, I raced to the side of the stage and waited for the music to end and the dancers to rush off the stage. The crowd whistled and hollered at the positive performance.

I held up my hand and each of the dancers smacked me five as they passed, all of them a jumble of excitement and glee.

As they finished exiting, I took a deep breath, grabbed the mic sitting on a podium and slowly walked out into the front of the stage. Immediately, a spotlight flashed on me. Guess letting the lighting man's daughter have free lessons really worked in my favor. He was the reason we got the community college theatre free of charge too.

I made my way to the front and waited while the audience calmed down.

"What a great performance from our ten to fourteen-year-olds." I mock clapped, and the crowd once again applauded. "I want to take a moment between shows to thank you all for being here tonight. The children have all worked extremely hard to get to this point, and I'm thrilled beyond measure to have so many of you here to support them."

The audience clapped again, and I waited for it to quiet once more. "As we wait for our next act to start, I need to see the family of Shayna O'Donnell. Would you please stand?"

I was not expecting what occurred next. When I lifted my hand over my eyes to block the light in order for me to see the audience, and find Shane, I was shocked to see a horde of at least twenty or so men in black leather vests standing tall and proud, many of them next to a beautiful woman. I squinted, attempting to find who I was looking for.

"Oh my, how about her immediate family?"

None of them sat.

"Okay, I need Shane or Riot O'Donnell," I specified, thinking at least I knew those two well enough.

All of a sudden both men were running down the center aisle.

"The show will continue in approximately five minutes with the contemporary group." I smiled and rushed to the side of the stage where both Shane and Riot were taking the steps two at a time, stony faced with fiery gazes.

"What's wrong with my daughter?" Shane demanded at the same time Riot grumbled, "Where's my grandbaby?" in what I thought was the most menacing tone I'd heard. I couldn't help the corresponding shiver that raced down my spine.

"Nothing, nothing. I mean, well something. She's got stage fright. Wants to go home," I explained.

Shane spoke low and direct. "Take me to her."

I nodded and looked at Riot. "I don't think we need both of you," I attempted.

Riot crossed his massive arms over one another and glared at me.

"Or maybe we do. Whatever's best for Shayna."

"That's what I fuckin' thought," Riot rumbled.

I brought them both backstage, and they followed, not missing a step, going around props and kids practicing their moves and getting ready for their piece.

When we got to Shayna, both of them pushed their way through the throngs of kids trying to calm her down.

"Sunflower, come here," Shane stated, and Shayna's tear-stained face lifted, and hope filled her entire face. Like the sun coming out on a cold, dark day. She darted into her father's arms and burst into another bout of tears against his chest.

"Baby girl." Riot rubbed a beefy hand down her back, giving her his presence and his strength.

Shane let her cry for a minute or two until he reached for her head and eased her back far enough that he could see her face. "What's the matter? Tell Daddy everything, and I swear I'll make it all better."

She sniffed and put her hands to her father's cheeks. "I scawed, Daddy. I so so so scawed to dance and mess up. Everybody will see me."

He cupped the back of her head and rubbed his thumb across her cheeks. "Hey, everyone's scared. Doing something important like dancing on stage is a very big girl thing to do. There are a lot of people, and the music is loud, and you have to remember your steps. But honey, you've been practicing this for weeks and weeks. Right?"

She nodded and sniffed again. He wiped the other side of her cheek free of tears.

"And you know every step?"

"By heart. I know it, Daddy."

"Then shouldn't you try your very best? No one is going to think you look silly or care if you mess up a little when you are trying your very best."

My heart melted at the way he spoke to his daughter. All the other kids were jumping around, and the other group's music was playing in the background, but there was nothing for him but his child and making her feel better.

"I would try my bestest. I would." She nodded.

"And don't you think it would be pretty sad for the other dancers to not have their prima ballerina in the center dancing for them, so they know where their steps are supposed to be?"

Her little face scrunched up as she thought about it. "That would be kinda mean, huh, Daddy."

"I think it would be disappointing, baby girl," Riot added, still rubbing her back soothingly. "Wouldn't it disappoint you if Anya couldn't do the dance tonight that you've been practicing? And I watched you two. You're amazing. And Grandmom and the brothers are so excited to see you."

"They are?" She puffed out her bottom lip. "I don't want them sad, Papa."

Shane hiked her up, so they were even closer. "Shayna, I believe in you. Your Papa believes in you. Your Grandmom. Auntie Shay, Uncle Rex, and Champ and Tank, and Whisper and all the other guys believe in you."

"And I believe in you," I found myself adding.

Shayna glanced at me.

"And we can't wait to see you shine, sweetheart. Do you think you could shine for us tonight?" her father added.

She swallowed and looked at her father, then her grandfather, and finally me. "I wanna dance wif you and wook pwetty. Do you reawwy fink I can?" Her words were a fast jumble, proving how emotional she'd gotten over the course of waiting for her group to go on.

I ran my hand along her silky, soft cheek. "I believe you can do anything, my darling."

Her dad jostled her playfully. "So, how's about this: If you promise to go up there and try your very best, we'll have the beautiful Misses M come out to have pizza with us and the club? How's that sound?"

Her eyes got so round I could practically swim in those shimmery blue orbs. She lifted her arms into the air and crowed, "Woohoo!" the same way her aunt did drunkenly the other night at the bar. Seemed to me this family was incredibly close.

Shane grinned and winked at me. Riot chuckled and rubbed at his scratchy looking salt and pepper facial hair.

"Will you come wif us, Misses M? Pwease, pwetty pweeease." She layered on the charm so thick there was no way I could decline.

"Of course, I will," I said a bit tightly. "I'd, um, love to spend time with you and your family."

"Woohoo!" She lifted her arms and cheered again before she started to kick her legs. "Put me down, Daddy, I hafta practice with Logan."

I shook my head and smiled.

Shane let his daughter down and smacked her bum as she sprang over to her friends. All of them hugged and clapped at her willingness to try the routine.

Riot smiled and placed a hand on my shoulder. "Looking forward to getting to know you at dinner, pretty lady." He continued to chuckle. "I'll find my way back to my seat."

I watched as Riot left, and before I could lay into Shane for conniving his way into getting a dinner date, I was tugged by the hand and dragged to a dark corner where the wall and the extra set of curtains met.

Shane plastered me with my back to the wall, using his big body, his chest flat against mine.

"What are you... Let me go, you big brute!" I smacked my hand against his sides, but he didn't let go.

He chuckled low and so deep I could feel his laughter ripple through my body from my breasts all the way down until it landed hotly between my thighs.

I mewled on instinct at the feeling of having such a hunk of a male specimen so close. He smelled of winter pine, leather from his vest, and something darker, richer. A scent that made my legs feel weak and my panties damp with desire. A wholly unfamiliar sensation; I hadn't felt anything near this rush of adrenaline since I'd first lost my virginity five years ago.

"Back away." I swallowed down the lump of emotion threatening to overwhelm me.

"Nuh uh. Now that I have you cornered, there's no escaping." His voice was so close to my ear, I could feel the warmth of his breath against my skin.

"Please," I said, not knowing what I was asking for. Was it to be let go or to have him do something, anything to quench this fire running like lava through my veins?

He rubbed his cheek along mine, and I closed my eyes.

"This is how this is gonna go, Bella. You're gonna let me get a small taste of you so that I have something to get me through this show, and then dinner with my family. After that, I'll take a much bigger taste. You're gonna participate, and you're gonna like it. Do you hear me?"

All thought left my brain aside from the fact that he wanted to taste me. I wanted that. So damn bad I could already imagine his mouth on mine.

"I can't hear you, Anya. Use your words."

"Uh, yeah. I understand."

"Are you gonna let me have my taste, beautiful?"

I nodded. It's all I could do. Lust was pooling in my gut and between my thighs. I wanted him to kiss me, to devour me until I couldn't remember my own name. It had been far too long since I'd had anything remotely this exciting, this…life changing.

"Fuck yeah," he said as he dragged his lips across my cheek. He used one of his hands to cup my nape and tip my head back.

Then he placed his lips on mine.

It wasn't one of those tender little shy kisses. No. Not with Shane. He went right in, pressing hard, sliding his tongue along the seam of my lips, pushing them apart so I'd open for him. And I did. Instantly. His tongue went deep, and he drank from me, our tongues lashing, lips pressing, teeth nipping one another's until the roar of nothing but white noise surrounded us…and there was just us.

His mouth on mine.

His tongue against mine.

His body plastered to mine.

I wrapped my arms around him and lifted a leg, wantonly rubbing against his form. He ran a hand down from my waist to cup my bum and grind against me. Ribbons of heat licked up my spine, and I moaned down his throat. He growled deeply.

And then the kiss went wild.

There was no other way to explain it. He tilted his head one way; I tipped mine the other. We sucked, licked, and consumed each other's mouths until I couldn't feel my legs. Eventually, he ripped his mouth away, and we finally took large inhalations of life sustaining air. With our bodies smashed against one another we panted, taking in as much air as we needed while our gazes locked.

"Christ, woman, you're everything I ever hoped for and more."

I blinked away the lust and heard the music fall away as the audience clapped. I pushed him with all my might, and he stepped away so I could finagle out of his arms.

"Shayna's number is next, and I'm on with them!" I pressed my hands to my hair and hoped it didn't look affright.

He grinned and licked his lips. "See you after the show, Bella. Can't wait." He winked and then swaggered around the corner to the side where he came from.

The little girls and the few boys in the next routine all rushed up to me, jumping up and down, their little bodies positively sizzling with excited energy. Several of them spoke at once. "We're on next!" "Our turn." "So excited, Misses M!"

I, on the other hand, continued to breathe and find my bearings in the few moments I had before we went on.

Shayna made her way through the group and grabbed my hand. "Are you okay, Misses M? You wook different," she asked.

I patted her cheek and lifted her chin to look at me. "I'm perfect. And you?"

She squeezed my hand. "I still scawed, but I'm gonna try my bestest. Then we can have dinner wif my family."

I took in my own huge breath. "Yes, my darling. Dinner with your family."

"You're gonna wuv my daddy. He's the bestest daddy in the whole world."

I smiled as flashes of her daddy pressing me against a wall, kissing me hard, cupping my bum, and grinding me into oblivion raced across my mind.

"Yes, I do believe I'm going to love your Daddy."

She gifted me a toothy smile.

Though I'm not worthy of him, dear one, I added silently to myself.

The music started, and each child pranced out onto the stage. I followed them in my perfectly practiced stage walk, leaving Shane, our kiss, and the upcoming dinner backstage where I would deal with it later. In front of me was nothing but an adoring and silent audience.

Showtime.

Chapter 4

Whip

"DADDY, DADDY, DADDY! DID YOU SEE ME? HUH? Huh?" Shayna squealed as she plowed into my open arms. I hefted my baby girl and swung her around in a bear hug.

"Of course, I did. You were magnificent, Sunflower. Truly amazing!"

She kissed my cheek and then kicked her legs to accept her hugs from Mom and Dad and the rest of our motley crew.

Behind the brawny biker bodies, I saw a halo of golden blonde hair. I pushed through the guys and my dad and mom to greet Anya. She was wearing a pink cardigan over her black leotard and a pair of jeans I assumed she'd slipped on right after the performance.

The family had waited a while for the rest of the patrons to leave and for Anya and Shayna to come out. Anya had been stopped on the way up the center aisle of the theatre several times by happy parents, but my people were content to wait. Good things always came to those who waited.

And there she stood, a shy smile gracing her lips as her blue eyes darted from left to right and down. Basically, anywhere but on me.

I got close and cupped the back of her neck and lifted her chin with my thumb. She swallowed as her gaze finally met mine.

"You were incredible out there, too, you know." I brought her close and kissed her temple, allowing myself the time to soak in her essence and the fresh mint scent of her skin. "Watching you dance is like watching an artist paint in sweeping colors. Every move is a brush stroke, each color bolder than the next."

"T-thank you. It's my passion," she murmured.

I hummed against the skin of her cheek. "I can't wait to find out what other passions you possess."

She backed away and looked off to the side and bit down on her lush bottom lip. "I don't have any other passions."

Running my hand down her arm to her hand, I interlaced our fingers. "Then it will be fun finding new ones together."

Her cheeks pinked a dusty rose color while she tried to pull her hand away, but I held fast, keeping her to my side. "Shane…"

"Well, look at you two. Cozy as a pair of kittens in a blanket," my mother said, her icy blue gaze assessing and not missing a single thing. Her lips twitched. "Good to see you, Twinkle Toes."

"Um, my name is Anya."

"Oh, I know what your name is, sweetheart, but everyone in our family gets a road name." She shifted to the side and extended her arm. "Let me introduce you to everyone."

Anya's hand started to sweat, so I let it go and wrapped my arm around her shoulders. She was obviously nervous, but I couldn't for the life of me fathom why. The brothers might be an intimidating bunch, but I'd never let anyone harm her.

"Hey, guys, this is Anya, Whip's woman. Goes by Twinkle Toes," my mother announced.

Anya attempted once again to move out of my hold, but there was no way in hell I was letting her loose to be picked over by the brothers. Any man with a dick and within a mile radius of her would try to make their play, and I needed to cut that off at the knees right from the start.

"I'm not, um, Shane's…"

"She's my woman," I piped up and tugged her even closer to my chest, flat against my cut, making it known in no uncertain terms this woman was off limits.

A few men whistled and catcalled like the randy bastards they were.

"You claiming her, Whip?" Tank rubbed his hands together and looked at Anya from her beautiful face down her long form.

I glared and scowled at my brother. "Yeah, I am. What's it to you?"

Tank grinned wickedly, put his hands up in the air in a gesture of peace. "Nothin' man. Just testing the waters."

"Yeah, well, swim somewhere else, brother," I stated directly, warning in my tone as I stared each man down.

"All right gentleman, enough already," Riot called out above the din of our crew. "We've got the party room at *Pizza & Brews* down on 7th. Let's hit it. You can all meet Whip's woman there. My grandbaby, the star of this whole fucking show, needs to eat! Don't you, baby girl?" He nuzzled his beard against her cheek as she giggled wildly.

"Papa, no cussing! 'Member. It's not nice! My teacher said so," Shayna chastised. She was always trying to get the guys to mind their mouths ever since she started pre-school.

My father grinned at my girl and kissed her neck until she laughed herself out of breath.

"Fair enough. Let's ride!" He lifted his chin toward the theatre exit and the crowd moved.

I nuzzled Anya's temple and said, "You drive here?"

She shook her head but didn't speak. It was as though she was stunned mute around the group. I could dig it. We were a lot to take in, but she'd get past it with time under her belt.

"Did a friend bring you?"

"No, I, uh, walked. I don't have a car. Never learned to drive."

"No shit?"

She shook her head. "No need. I went from high school straight into dance school, then into the ballet company, and now here."

"Interesting. I'm looking forward to getting more into that story, but for now, I want you on the back of my bike," I said while dragging her out of the theatre, down the steps, and across the sidewalks to the parking area. The line of motorcycles was over twenty deep. My father got on his, Mags behind him, and then she reached down and put Shayna between them. My father had already pulled her helmet from my ride.

"Be careful with my girl. She's the whole world," I reiterated.

"Always, son. Precious cargo." He patted her hands that came around his belly.

Shayna squealed when my father revved the engine. Mom wrapped her arms around Dad and my daughter. "We've got her, baby. See you there." She winked, and they were off.

"Oh, my word. You let them take your daughter on a motorcycle!" Anya screeched, pointing at Shayna. "Make them stop!" She started to move toward the other bikes. I looped and arm around her waist and tugged her to my chest, wrapping my arm around her small waist.

"Shhhh, Bella, relax. She's been on a bike since she was a year old. Hell, maybe even before. This is her life. She's the daughter of a biker. The youngest family member of our club. Nothing is going to happen to her. My father, my mother"—I pointed to all the men firing up their bikes and heading out who just attended a four-year-old's ballet recital because that's what family did—"all my brothers would cut off their own arms before allowing anything to harm my girl. She's safer with them on that bike than she would be on a school bus full of kids. I promise you that."

"But…it's so dangerous." Her words left her on a gasp.

I smiled and shuffle walked her over to the lone bike left in the lot. "It can be, if the wrong person is driving or they're impaired. We're vigilant. My father won't so much as have a sip of beer if he's going to have Shayna on his bike. I trust him with my life and the life of my daughter. Come on, you'll see."

Then, it dawned on her *she'd* be getting on the back of a bike.

Her entire body froze until she shook her head repeatedly and tore out of my arms. "I am *not* riding on the back of…of… that." She pointed at my Harley.

I walked over to the bike and hooked a leg over and settled into the worn leather. "Babe, you are." I turned to the side and patted the seat behind me.

"Mmm, pretty sure I'm not," she stated plain and simple, crossing her arms over her chest.

"You afraid?"

A concerned yet prideful expression flitted across her face. "No. I just don't think it's safe."

"Promise, it's perfectly safe. Been riding since I was sixteen and could get my license, just about ten years, Bella. Besides, been on a bike since I was a baby just like Shayna." I jerked my chin toward the seat. "Come on. *I dare you* to take a chance."

She scoffed. "You dare me? What, you think I won't?" Her voice rose with her desire to prove her lack of fear.

I shrugged. "Unless you're too scared…"

"Pssshtt." She huffed and marched over to the bike. I handed her the extra helmet I had tucked inside my saddlebags.

"Put this on first."

She attempted to place it on her head, but her hair got in the way. I watched in avid fascination as she uncoiled her golden hair and it let it fall down the sides of her face in pretty waves to just past her shoulders.

"Christ, you're gorgeous, woman."

I enjoyed the fact that she couldn't hold back the small smile that slipped across her lips before she hid it away along with her pretend ire. She pulled the helmet on and looked at me and then at the bike.

"How do I get on?"

I grinned slyly. "You know the thing you did in the performance where you lifted your leg out and around then back?"

She nodded curtly.

"Do that and you'll be set."

She did as instructed, and her lithe form slid along the leather and right against my back. "Ooophf!"

Heaven.

Anya pushed off my back and tried to lean her body as far away as she could get.

Uh yeah, that's a hard no.

"Babe, lean forward and wrap your arms around my middle."

"But…"

"No buts, Bella. Hold on to me. That's how you stay safe. You move when I move. Just imagine me as your big ass teddy bear."

She snorted. "Teddy bear? Hardly."

I reached to the sides, grabbed her hands, and yanked them around my gut. Her body lay against mine from tits to crotch.

Warm, comforting, like a puzzle slotting right into place. I closed my eyes and pulled in a deep breath, catching a hint of the minty scent that surrounded her. This was what it was all about. Leaving the army, having my woman on the back of my seat, her scent in my nose, the wind in my face, the road under me, on our way to meet up with my daughter.

Fucking perfection.

When we rolled up to the pizza parlor and stopped, Anya jumped off the bike, ripped off her helmet, hair flying everywhere, grabbed my face, and kissed me hard.

I hooked an arm around her waist and went for the gusto, slicking my tongue over her lips and taking the kiss even deeper.

She mewled as she kissed me wildly, her face turning, her lips catching mine in heated presses. She sucked on my tongue, and I palmed her little ass, hiking her body even closer to me.

Kissing my woman while still sitting on my bike, her body standing and pressed to mine, the feeling was one I would never tire of in a million years.

Eventually, she pulled away and ran a hand through her golden hair. "My goodness, that was so fun! I had no idea. The wind against your skin, the rumble of the engine, the road passing by... It was..." She smiled so big I could see the perfect row of her white teeth. "It was awesome!" she finished as though all the air had fled her lungs at the same time.

I grinned, pressed her back a couple feet, and got off the bike. I put my arm around her shoulders and kissed her temple, making sure to rub my nose along her velvet soft cheek.

"Bella, you kiss me like that every time we ride, and you'll never ride in my truck."

She blushed and looked down at the gravel. I stopped and put my hands on both of her hips. She scrunched up her nose and lifted her elegant face. I ran my hands through the hair at her temples and bunched it up at her nape and held her in place.

I got close to her face, and a panicked expression fluttered across her gaze. "Don't look down and away when you're with me. And don't be scared. I'd never hurt you. With me, you can be who you are in all things. You don't have to hide. You don't have to worry. You get to be nothing but free. Live in the moment. Be in the moment with me."

She licked her lips and bit down on the bottom one. "A lot of things about you scare me, Shane. You're very aggressive..."

"Only when it comes to something I want. That being you. Yeah, I'm going to make it well known I'm all in, babe. All fuckin' in."

Her fingers dug into my cut at my back. "But what if you find out I'm not what you think I am?"

"You mean you're not a beautiful woman who treats my daughter like a queen? A woman who takes her time teaching hordes of kids the art of dance and making 'em look like professionals out there. Getting them a stage to use to show off to their parents?"

"Well, yes, I did do that."

"The kind of woman who goes to a biker bar because her friend wants to let lose, sees her friend is tying one on and sips a warm beer all night, then steals her car keys and hires an Uber to pick you both up so you're both safe?"

"How did you know that?"

I smirked. "I have my ways. Look, I know we're just start-ing out, but you can't deny that, since the moment we laid eyes on one another, it was going to be you and me."

She sighed. "Shane, I'm not…" She shook her head, and I loosened my grip on her hair. "I don't know how to be what you need."

I got closer, pressing my forehead to hers. "You already are what I need. Does me being a single dad turn you off?"

"Goodness, no. Shayna is a dream."

I ran my nose alongside of hers. "Then how's about we just figure this out one day at a time, yeah?"

"One day at a time?" There was hope laced with a little bit of fear in her tone.

"Yeah, one day at a time. Can you do that for me, Bella?"

"Why do you call me Bella?"

"Because you're the most beautiful thing I've ever seen in my life next to the day I met my daughter."

She closed her eyes and wrapped her hands around my waist, bringing her body flat against mine. "I'll take it one day at a time."

"That's all I ask." I kissed her softly, sealing the deal.

When she was thoroughly kissed and weak at the knees, I reluctantly pulled away. "Come on, babe. Time to meet my family."

She nodded. "Okay, Shane."

"You know you can call me Whip?"

Anya shook her head and gifted me a sweet smile. "I like your name. And besides, everyone else calls you Whip. Everyone else calls me Anya. You don't. Now we both have something special."

I curled my hand around her hip and led her toward the

restaurant. "Everything about you is special, and I'm going to be the man to make sure you see it."

"Then I wish you luck, Shane."

"Don't need luck, babe, not when I've got facts on my side." I lifted up my hand and showed her one finger.

"Beautiful."

I lifted another finger. "Talented."

Another. "Great with children."

She beamed, and I lifted a fourth finger. "A great fucking kisser."

Those cheeks pinked up so pretty I wanted to press my lips to them to see if they felt hot to the touch.

"And the last one?" She bit down on her bottom lip, kind of getting into my game.

I swung her into my arms and caged her up against the wall like I'd done in the theatre. I palmed her ass and ground my stiffening cock against her. She mewled and wrapped her arms around me.

"Pretty sure my woman is going to be phenomenal in bed!" I thrust against her body. "Looks like I'm going to need to find me a sitter so I can take my woman out good and proper, take her home, and show her exactly how special we can be together.

"Shane…" Her voice shook.

I kissed her neck, then her lips, and the tip of her nose.

"Daddy! What are you doing kissing Misses M? Is she your old lady now?"

I grinned while Anya's entire face went white as a ghost.

"Yeah, baby, Misses M is Daddy's old lady now."

Anya frowned. "What's an old lady? I'm only twenty-three. Hardly considered old by anyone's standards."

I chuckled, pulled her to my side, and met up with my girl.

Her little face was beaming with joy. "This is so great! We

can have tea pawties and pway dwessup together." She jumped up and down. "Ohhh and maybe you can be my mommy!"

Anya slapped her hand to her chest and leaned her body heavily against mine. "Oh my…"

"Can it, Sunflower. Don't scare off Daddy's old lady just yet." I cupped her cheek.

"Okay, but I can still have ice cream, right?"

"Of course, baby. Go on and eat your pizza first."

She put her hands in the air and squealed. "Woohoo!" before scampering away.

"You okay?" I chuckled.

"That was a lot to take in."

I put my hand to the back of her neck underneath her hair and gave it a comforting squeeze. "You'll get used to it."

She inhaled fully and let it out slowly as we approached the room. Just as we stepped inside, she lifted her head and said, "You didn't tell me what being your old lady meant."

The entire room of brothers went dead silent.

Chapter 5

Anya

"HOLY SHIT, THE BIKER AND THE BALLERINA! LITTLE brother, you are too damn much! Come here, bro!" The beautiful brunette I met at the bar a few nights ago practically tackle hugged Shane. He dropped my shoulder and caught her up in a big hug. He lifted her off her feet, arching his back for a moment before setting her back down. I backed farther away and rubbed my hands over my crossed arms.

"I knew it when I laid eyes on you that night there was something special about you." Her grin was huge. She grabbed her brother's face and kissed his cheek. "Rock on! I love this."

"You remember my wild sister, Shay?" Shane rubbed his hand over the top of her beautiful mane of dark hair. I briefly wondered what it would be like to be a bombshell, every man's walking fantasy woman.

"I do. It's nice to see you again."

"Oh, it's *so* nice to see you. Seems like we'll be seeing a lot of one another now!" She moved out of her brother's arms and grabbed my elbow, tugging me toward a table to the side of the large party room. Her giant husband, Rex, sat in one of the chairs and nodded his head when I sat next to her. He held the most precious dark-haired little girl who was sucking on a pair of dog tags hanging around his neck.

"She's teething something awful," he said and kissed the top of her pretty head. Across from her, a little boy, quite a bit larger in size, was using a breadstick as a drumstick on the table, batting away.

"These are my twins. Swayze who's always with her daddy. Good luck getting any action. The only woman that seems to get any of her attention is my mother, but that's because she's Mags, who would get the Pope's attention during a midnight mass on Christmas Eve in St. Peter's Square."

I laughed and ran my hand down the arm of the little boy who stopped drumming and looked at me with the most gorgeous icy blue gaze. Then, surprisingly, he stretched his arms out toward me.

"May I?"

Shay nodded. "Of course. That's Trace, but we all call him Hustler."

I picked up the child that seemed around a year old if not a little more.

"Why Hustler?"

Shay grinned. "Because he tends to gets whatever he wants whenever he wants it. It's his superpower."

After she spoke, the boy shockingly placed his hands on my cheeks looked me in the face and gave me a sloppy open-mouthed kiss.

Most of the room roared with laughter. Me, I just stood there holding a baby that was trying to suck on my face, not exactly sure what to do or how to relieve myself of my predicament.

"Hold up, Hustler! She's my woman!" Shane chuckled and whipped the baby out of my arms and onto his hip with the confidence of a man that had done so rather regularly. He ruffled the boy's hair and kissed his forehead. "One day, bud, you'll get your own woman. Until then, don't be mackin' on my old lady," he mock chastised.

Rex answered in a deep rumbling tone, which seemed to vibrate through my chest. "He can't help it. He's a Crawford. When he sees a beautiful woman, he loses his mind," Rex said through a hearty chuckle. His daughter ignored the shenanigans and snuggled against his chest, pressing her head into his neck and closing her eyes.

"Babe, she's really tired. We can go if you want," Shay offered.

He shook his head. "Nah, she's cool sleeping on me."

Shay rolled her eyes. "Of course, she is. At least he has a rule that the babies are to sleep the night in their own room, or I'd never get any action. Swayze is a Rex hog!"

The big fella caressed his daughter's back, and her little mouth opened, letting the tags fall out and down her father's chest. "I'm okay with that. I get my little girl and my boy by day and their hot mama at night. Full fuckin' life. Best a man can hope for." Rex gave a sexy smirk to his wife. My cheeks heated at their overt display of sexual desire for one another.

When Shay leaned her entire body over the table to smack a kiss on her husband's lips, Shane looped his arms around me from behind. "The guy speaks the truth. You, me, my daughter, basically all I'd ever need in life."

I swallowed heavily, my body going tight. He pressed his lips to my ear. "Don't worry, we'll get you there, Bella. One step at a time," he finished while kissing my neck, which had the effect of sending a river of excitement rushing through my veins.

"Let's get some food in you."

"Where's Shayna?" I asked, not having seen the girl since we first arrived.

He chuckled. "If she's around the club, she's never with me. It's her time to entertain the brothers, but usually, she's with her Papa." Shane pointed across the room where there was a *Pac-Man* game machine. Riot steadied the little girl on her knees on a chair in front of the machine. She was still wearing her tutu, and tucked next the jeans-and-leather-vest-wearing man, she looked perfectly in her element.

"It's amazing, this family you've built." I scanned the warm room in awe. They all seemed to genuinely want to spend time together and enjoyed each other.

He nodded. "Definitely. Will feel like your family too. Real soon," he promised.

I hummed noncommittally. Shane grabbed my hand and led me to a table that already had a steaming hot half pepperoni and half cheese pizza. I looked at the pizza and frowned.

We sat side by side, and he gathered a couple plates, setting them in front of us. "Do you like pizza?" I bit down on my lip and shrugged. He nudged me with a smile on his face. "What's that supposed to mean?"

"Well, I wouldn't know. I've never had it."

"Say what?" He stopped with a slice of pizza from the steaming pie dangling in the air.

"I said, I wouldn't know; I've never tried it."

"No, I heard you. I just don't believe it." He shook his head.

"It's true."

He put a slice of cheese pizza in front of me. "How can that be? Every American from California to New York has had pizza."

I shook my head. "Maybe that answers it. I was raised in Alaska, and my parents are both Russian."

"Still, how can you be in your twenties and not have had pizza? It seems like a crime against humanity."

That had me laughing while he poured both of us a glass of beer from a pitcher sitting next to the pizza.

"I've been training my whole life. There are a lot of foods that were not allowed in my home. Pizza being one of them. My mother even packed my lunch during school. Then, when I was in the American Ballet Theatre, they provided our meals from a prescribed list of foods geared toward maintaining a specific weight, muscle tone, et cetera."

"That's crazy." He took a huge bite, almost eating half the slice in one go.

"That's sacrifice. In order to live your dreams, you must be willing to sacrifice. Fatty foods, things laden with sugar have never been part of my diet. I've never had a cupcake either."

His eyes got as round as the large pie in front of us. He dropped his slice to the paper plate with disgust. "That's fuckin' nuts. We're solving that shit!"

"You're sweet." I stood up, leaving the untouched slice on the table in front of me. I didn't have it in me to just throw away twenty years of training, and I wasn't altogether sure my body wouldn't revolt against the influx of fat and carbs.

He clasped my wrist. "Where you going?"

"To check the menu and see if there is a salad bar or pre-packaged vegetarian or vegan option."

His entire face screwed up into a mask of distaste. "You are fuckin' not." He tugged my arm until I sat back down. "Babe, try the fuckin' pizza. If you don't like it, we'll get you something else." He shook his head. "A salad. Vegan what?" he mumbled under his breath, his tone emphasizing his disbelief.

I stared at the pizza, and my entire body started to tremble. I sat up straight and lifted the gooey slice, attempting to find the courage to just take a bite. It was a simple task, but it felt like I was breaking the law. One I'd abided by for the last twenty years.

Tentatively, I leaned forward and sniffed it. It smelled delicious, but a lot of things that were bad for you smelled and tasted amazing. If I ate the slice, I'd have to find a way to get rid of those calories.

"What are you thinking about right now?" he whispered, and I set the slice back down and wiped my fingers on a nearby napkin. I put my hands in my lap while I curled in on myself protectively.

"How many calories are likely in that slice. How I'm going to have to work them off or be a half pound possibly even a pound over, due to just the amount of sodium, which will also have the added undesired effect of tacking on an abhorrent amount of water weight to my system...and how..." My breath caught in my throat. "And how I'm going to hate myself when I step on the scale tomorrow morning like I do every morning."

"Jesus Christ!" he swore and turned sideways on the bench seat to face me. He put his hands on my thighs. "If you don't want to eat the slice, you don't have to. Fuck, baby, I don't like any of what you're saying. Not because it might be true, but because it's fucked up. You should be able to eat something that tastes good and is loaded with fat because you like it. You're living."

"But that's not how it is for a prima ballerina."

"What happened to you?" he growled.

"How do you mean?"

"Why aren't you with the ballet company you mentioned?"

"I got hurt." The words were matter of fact, the best way

I knew how to explain what happened without breaking down and sobbing.

"Lots of athletes get hurt and jump right back on the horse. Why not you?"

I looked down at his hands on my thighs. "My injury was severe. I was hurt in a way that it is too dangerous for me to dance regularly in that capacity ever again. My body cannot handle it. Which puts me and any company I could work for at serious risk."

"So, you opened up a dance studio," he added, keeping me on track.

"It was always my plan after I'd lived my dream for a decade or so."

"Which means you're no longer living the same life or routines. You have a new life now. New opportunities. New things to try." He smiled softly and lifted his chin toward the untouched slice of pizza. "New things to taste. A new life to live."

And he was right.

Nothing that had come before was the same now. Everything was different. Just sitting here in a room filled with bikers, who were eating, drinking, laughing, and spending quality time together, was a new experience. Nothing like the hard and fast, stringent schedule I had to keep every day. I didn't have to go home right away, take a hot bath, and take care of my tortured feet and body in a way that would have me prepared to do it all over again the next day.

I realized then that I liked this portion of the change in my life. Loved seeing Shayna in her tutu, dancing from one big brawny biker to the next, offering them a private show of her ability to plié and pirouette until they clapped and congratulated her repeatedly.

I liked having a pair of hazel eyes running over my form as

if I were the prettiest woman in the room. Not because I was the best dancer or could stand *en pointe* the longest. Because of me. My company.

It took effort, but I inhaled fully, lifted the slice of pizza up in the air, grinned at Shane, and took a bite. The flavors exploded in my mouth. Sauce dripped down the side of my lip, and Shane thumbed the mess and stuck his thumb into his own mouth.

Wow.

That was hot. My temperature heated as I stole glances at Shane while he watched me eat my first bite of one of the most forbidden foods on my mother's exorbitantly long list.

I chewed slowly, allowing my very first taste of cheese pizza to settle into my memory bank. The cheese was salty and sumptuous. The sauce tangy and acidic. The bread chewy with just the right amount of texture.

"Well?" He tipped his head to the side.

I licked my lips, my mouth watering for another bite. "Amazing. I like pizza." I smiled.

He grinned and chuckled before leaning forward and kissing me thoroughly in front of the entire room. I didn't care. He tasted of the same pizza and a hint of beer, alongside a heady dose of Shane. A tasty combination.

When he pulled away, I hummed with my eyes closed. "I like pizza kisses too," I whispered.

He squeezed my thigh with one of his big hands. "Stick with me, babe, and I'll lay the world at your feet."

"Shane," I whispered. My heart clogged with emotion I wasn't able to understand because I'd never in my life had a person want to give something just to *me*. It was always what I represented to them or did for them. My father's perfect student. My mother's last chance at her DNA being the best ballerina in the world. A choreographer's muse. A director's prize performer.

I didn't know how to respond. It was all so much. I wanted to grab for what he was offering with everything I had, but I was afraid of the repercussions.

What if I gave everything and ended up losing him too?

What if I wasn't enough?

What if I didn't truly deserve what he was offering?

What if I failed…again?

He must have seen the darkness slide over my expression because he grabbed my hand and interlaced my fingers. "Eat your food. I wanna hear more about you. Then I have to get my woman and my daughter home."

"Where we going, Bella?" Shane asked me later when I was suited up with a helmet and my arms around his waist on the back of his bike.

"Peach Brook Commons," I answered.

"No shit?" He turned to the side so I could just barely catch his beautiful grin.

I nodded. "Yep."

He chuckled as he started the bike, but I had no idea why. The engine rumbled under my bum, and I squeezed my thighs against his.

"Fuck, I love having my woman wrapped around me on my bike. Now I know what it's all about."

"How do you mean?"

"You like being plastered to me, the engine roaring through your body while holding on to your man."

My body felt so much hotter, and I squeezed him tighter.

"Yeah, my woman likes it. Fuck me, I'm living a dream I never want to wake up from."

I rested my chin on his shoulder, and he slowly backed out of his position and jetted off into the night. It took no time at all to get to my apartment complex.

When we entered, I pointed to the left, and he ignored me and went to the right. I tried to get his attention, but he raised up his hand in a stop motion because there was no way I was going to be able to hear his words over his bike. Then he randomly pulled up next to a truck I recognized from the restaurant. I think it was Rex's truck. The same one he'd loaded Shayna and the twins into after dinner.

Shane stopped the bike, and I pulled off my helmet.

"Shane, honey, I don't live back here…" I started to say as I whipped my leg off the bike and stood on seriously shaky legs.

"No, but I do. This is my parking spot."

I frowned and crinkled my nose. "How can that be?"

He tipped his head back so I could see his long beautiful throat as he laughed. "Babe, I live in these apartments too. So do Shay, Rex, and the twins."

"You're kidding?" I said, deadpan.

He got off the bike and grabbed me by the hips until I gripped his leather vest, then he kissed me. When he was done making me swoon with lust, he allowed his cheek to graze mine as he pressed his lips to my ear. "You live alone?"

I shook my head as the small hairs on the back of my neck stood at attention while gooseflesh appeared on my skin. "No, with my best friend, Holly Hatfield. Your family calls her Holly Berry for some reason."

He looped an arm around my shoulders and started walking forward.

"What number is your place?"

"Twenty-four."

We walked through a breezeway of apartments. He looked up and lifted his chin. "My sister is 45, and I'm 44."

"You live next door to your sister?"

He inhaled deeply and then rubbed at the scruff on his chin. "Yeah, Shay and I don't do well living far apart from one another. When I was in the Army it was hell on wheels to be away from her. We like to be close. It's why neither of us has left the apartments. We're both in the market for houses, but we want to be close to one another. Same street at least. Rex thinks we're crazy but it's just the way with Shay and me. I think it's a twin thing. She's my best friend in the whole world."

"You were in the Army?"

"Yeah. Was gonna make a career of it but had to come back home after my first four-year tour."

"Why?"

"Because some club bitch I fucked while on leave got knocked up. Dropped the baby at my parents' clubhouse when she was born. She didn't even have a name. I ended up missing the first two months of Shayna's life before I could come home, but my parents, my sister, and the club stepped up. Took care of her until I could make it back."

I stopped at my door, completely in shock. Turning toward him, I grabbed his hands. "I can't imagine what it must have been like for you."

"Not gonna lie and say it was a walk in the park. I'd just started my life, was twenty-one years old, and found out I was a dad."

"What happened to her...um...her mother? I mean, not that it's any of my business." I looked away and frowned, chastising myself internally for the lack of filter. He likely didn't want to talk about the uncomfortable situation, especially with someone he barely knew.

Shane tunneled his fingers into the back of my hair and cupped my nape. "There is nothing about me you can't know. Unless it involves private club business, I'm happy to tell you anything and everything there is to know, and I expect the same from you."

I nodded, not sure how to respond.

"Jess was a pretty woman I slept with a few times. She was a club girl."

"Not sure I understand what that means. Like a book club but for motorcycles?"

Shane pressed me up against the door and nuzzled his nose with my own. "Damn, you're the cutest thing I've ever seen. But no, babe. Club girls are what you would call party girls. Some of them are straitlaced in the sense they have jobs and just love to fuck and party with bikers. Others are hoping to become claimed by one of the brothers. You see, when a biker claims a woman as his old lady, there is nothing he won't do for her and, by extension, her loved ones. The entire club takes on that woman as part of their family."

"And this Jess wanted to be your old lady?"

He shook his head. "Nah, she just liked fucking bikers and snorting shit up her nose. The drug bit we don't go for. We allow weed and booze, but those are legal in Oregon. We don't do illegal shit. Jess liked to party, drink, and fuck. One night, I did that with her. It ended up with her getting knocked up with Shayna."

My mind swirled with the ramifications of what these club girls were and how they had serviced the man I was quickly becoming very attached to. "Do you...um...still get with...um... the club girls."

"Fuck no! I'm no saint, and I never claimed to be. I like to get me some. I'm a man. I have a dick; I like using it. The women I've been with since Jess have no complaints and no strings."

"And what about me?"

"Just consider me your personal fucking puppet. I'm all strung up on you." He kissed me hard and fast.

"And Jess?"

"Apparently stopped doing drugs long enough to have Shayna then started right back up. Dropped my daughter in the arms of my parents on New Year's Day. My baby was born on Christmas Eve. In those few days she didn't even give her own daughter a name. We had to go through hell proving she was mine, which my sister did on my behalf since I was in Afghanistan. Then Jess bailed. Poof. Just gone. I came home and have been picking up the pieces ever since."

I struggled to speak. "But Shayna is your world. I can see it in every ounce of your being."

He cupped my cheeks. "Yeah, I have a thing for beautiful, blonde, and blue eyed." He smiled and kissed me softly. I wrapped my arms around him and tentatively deepened the kiss. He allowed me to lead this time, sliding my tongue along the seam of his lips. Him opening to me. I licked inside, tasting the man I was so quickly falling for second by second.

Shane's cupped my ass, and I smiled into the kiss. He liked one of his hands on my ass. Seemed to give him more leverage, but he didn't take over. For the first time, Shane was content to let me kiss him, and I did, with everything I had in me.

With every swipe of my tongue, I showed him how grateful I was to be there with him.

With every nibble of his lips, I conveyed my unwavering desire.

With every sigh into his mouth, I made a promise.

I was in this. I was committing to whatever this was.

Me. Him. Shayna. His club. His family. I wanted it all.

He finally pulled away and pressed his forehead to mine. "Damn, babe, gotta get back to my kid. Shay is cool to watch her, but it's her first recital, and I want to show her how much it meant to me. Make her special breakfast in the morning. Tomorrow night, I work at the bar. Would you come down and sit with me?"

I smiled and nodded. "I'd love to."

He kissed me hard and fast, his hand groping my ass and grinding his very large erection against my belly. I didn't know what to think about that since I had only had one experience before, but it made my insides melt knowing he wanted me as badly as I wanted him.

"Get in the house. Lock up. Take an Uber tomorrow. I'll be bringing you back to my place. It's Friday, and Shayna usually spends the night with her Auntie Shay and Uncle Rex on Fridays so I can work. I don't pick her up because it's often two in the morning. Which means I'll have you alone and in my bed."

My eyes got wide, and my hands started to sweat.

He grinned. "I can see it makes you nervous, but don't worry, Bella. I'll get you past that in one single kiss. I promise."

Chapter 6

Whip

THE MOMENT ANYA ENTERED THE BAR, THE AIR IN THE ROOM changed. My nerve endings sizzled in recognition of her nearness. I couldn't help the small smile that slipped across my lips as I served the couple in front of me. I flicked my gaze up toward the door, and there she was.

A vision in white.

Like it was my fuckin' wedding day or some shit. She stood across the room in a simple, very feminine white lace dress that fell to her knees. It was sleeveless but she had a piece of fabric draped against her back and over her elbows. I scanned her long form and noted the demur neckline didn't even hint at her small breasts underneath. I liked that my woman covered her skin but was still the sexiest thing I'd ever seen. Her hair was up in a loose bun, tendrils gracing the sides of her cheeks delicately. Her feet were encased in a pair of pale pink wedge shaped sandals that reminded me of her ballet shoes.

Sex on stilts.

I grinned her way and watched in utter fascination as she held her small handbag in front of her body, straightened her spine, pressed her shoulders back, and walked confidently forward.

My heart pounded out a thunderous drumbeat while my hands fisted and released. I wanted to run my hands all over her softness. Like a pure white butterfly shimmering through the grass, she maneuvered through the crowd. Effortless.

"Bella," I whispered as she set her bag on the bar top and smiled.

"Hi, honey." Her sultry, timid tone went straight to my dick, making my jeans feel tight as fuck.

Honey.

She's all the honey I'd ever desire.

In a move driven by pure need, I stepped on a crate near my side of the bar and bent over the wooden surface, cupping her cheek and chin, leaning her toward my mouth.

She kissed me softly, almost tentatively, as though nervous about the public display of affection, but I didn't care. This was my stomping ground and soon to be hers. I wanted every bastard in here to know this willowy beautiful creature was all mine.

I sucked on her bottom lip and enjoyed the little mewl she gifted in response before pulling away.

"You look amazing. Like my own personal angel."

Her cheeks pinked prettily as she thanked me.

"What would you like to drink?"

"What would you suggest? I don't imbibe often."

I grinned. "Another one of those things on the restricted list."

She placed her head in her hand and leaned on the bar, her sky-blue gaze on mine. "Exactly."

"This list you speak of," I asked, while grabbing a bottle of Prosecco. My woman looked like a fairy tale princess, so I picked a drink I imagined would suit her best. "You mentioned it being your mother's?"

A frown flitted across her lips as I placed a champagne flute in front of her.

"Yes, mostly. And other things are just good common sense. Most athletes have to be specific about what they put into their bodies." I noted a hint of defensiveness in her statement.

"True. I know a guy at Champ's gym who only eats boiled chicken, fish, veggies, eggs, and protein powder. Nothing else. He's a fitness guru of some kind. Cool guy but we don't roll in the same circles aside from the gym."

I pushed the glass in front of her. "Try it."

She smiled, and I swear, it lit up the entire room. I watched her closely to gauge her interest in the sparkling wine drink.

She smacked her lips together and nodded. "I like it. Bubbly and fruity at the same time."

"Prosecco. Kind of a cross between a sweet wine and champagne."

I enjoyed watching her lips pucker to take another sip. Christ, I wanted to watch those lips wrap around another, more demanding part of my body right about then. Grinding my teeth, I breathed through the desire to take her in the back room and fuck her up against the supply room wall. Inhaling a few breaths, I reminded myself that we had time. The anticipation of tonight would make the end result all the sweeter.

While she sipped her drink, I served a few people down the bar. The waitress brought me her orders from her walkabout, and I got started on making them while chatting up my girl.

"Why does everyone call you Whip?" she asked.

I pointed a finger to my temple and prodded there. "Smart as a whip."

She grinned. "Really?"

I leaned over the bar, resting my elbows on the wooden surface and thumped against the counter with my fingers. "You don't believe me?"

A shocked expression flashed across her face. "Goodness, no! Of course I believe you. It's just I expected something involving maybe an actual whip, like you wielded one." Her entire face flushed a rosy color all the way down her neck.

Her response had me chuckling out loud. "Nah. Back in school, I was a straight-A student. Shay used to get so pissed that I'd hardly have to study and get all high scores. Since I was on the honor roll and graduated with the highest marks, the club came up with the road name Whip. They gave it to me right before I left for the Army. Something to look forward to when I got to come back on leave."

Anya pursed her lips and took a sip of her wine.

"Tell me about your parents." I asked, wanting to learn more about her.

Her jaw tightened, and she straightened her spine as though she needed to prepare to speak of them.

She took a deep breath and played with the lip of her glass, running one long elegant finger around and around the lip.

"My father died when I was fifteen. Had a heart attack at work and was gone before he hit the ground."

I put my hand over hers on top of the bar and squeezed it. "Babe, I'm sorry."

She smiled sadly. "Thank you, but it was quite a while ago. Though I miss him. He was very easy to please, and I'm an only child. He only cared about me getting good grades."

"Very easy to please. An odd way to reference your dad, Bella."

She shrugged. "He was a good man. Worked hard for his family. Made sure I had what I needed, especially as it pertained to dance. Even so, he worked so much he didn't often get to attend my performances. When I was a teen, I don't actually remember him making it to one."

I wiped the bar two spaces down from Anya where a couple had finished their drinks and left. "Sounds sad. I couldn't imagine how tough it must have been for him. I don't want to miss even one of my Sunflower's performances. I mean, I might not be able to take and pick her up from her dance classes, but I give her what she needs, wake her in the morning, make her breakfast, lunch, take her to school and walk her in, make her dinner every night. I'd quit a job before I missed something important to her."

"Which is wonderful, Shane, but my father did what he could to provide for his family." Her voice took on a frustrated layer. "He died doing it…"

I lifted my hands. "Babe, I'm in no way bad-mouthing your dad. I'm just pointing out that it had to be hard for him not to be able to be as involved as he may have liked."

She nodded curtly, which didn't sit well with me.

"And your mother?" I asked, trying to change the subject and get the heat off my ass for putting my foot in my mouth about her father.

"My mother is a difficult person. She expects a lot, and I've repeatedly let her down," she said while running her fingers along a cocktail napkin, straightening the edges and wrinkles.

"How so? You were a prima ballerina, and now you've opened your own successful studio doing what you love. It may not be you dancing on the stage for thousands of people across the world, but it's you enriching lives and teaching very impressionable minds the art of dance every day. That, in my opinion, is more powerful than being the star of someone else's production."

She frowned deeply, and her full lips went into a thoughtful pout. "I've never thought about it like that." She rested her chin in her hands, cupping her cheeks. "You do that a lot, Shane. Make me see things in a different way."

I chuckled. "No, Bella. I make you see things the way they *are,* not the twisted-up version you've somehow manufactured over time. Life is beautiful and messy. There is no right and wrong way to do something. You used to dance, and from what I've seen, were probably the best at it."

"I did very well in my company." She lifted her chin with what I gathered was pride.

"And now you do very well in your own company, which you run. You're a business owner, babe. One who works with children. A woman who teaches them that their dreams are possible because you lived it."

"But only for a brief moment..."

"A couple years is not brief. I was in the service for four years, and it was not nearly enough. I didn't get to climb the ranks, make my parents proud of what I achieved. Life changed. It got messy. Then my dreams changed. Now all I want is a good woman, my daughter to be happy, run this bar, and spend time with my family and brethren. Maybe have a few more kids."

Her eyes rounded to the size of the crystal tumblers we served the top shelf whisky in. "A few more?" She brought her hand up to her chest, which I could see was rising and falling rapidly.

I laughed and grabbed both of her hands. "Relax. We can have as many or as few as you want, Bella. Just as long as they have your beautiful face and talent, I'll be happy."

"Me!" she gasped. "You want to have children with me?" Her question was tinged with awe.

I leaned over the bar and put my face right in front of hers, so we were only an inch away.

"Bella, what is it you think we're doing here?"

She swallowed as I pressed a tendril away from her stunning face and behind her ear so I could stroke my thumb along one velvety cheek.

"I didn't…I never thought about children."

"But you're great with them."

Her mouth opened and closed, but instead of speaking, she just nodded.

I grinned and pressed the last inch forward to kiss her. "Mark my words, Anya. One day you will be wearin' my ring and havin' my babies," I whispered against her lips, then sealed it with another sweet kiss.

We held hands as I led her up the stairs to my apartment. Anya stayed at the bar until I could leave. Thankfully one of the prospects took over so I didn't have to close. He was eager to make an extra buck.

Anya was quiet on the ride back. I'd taken my truck so I could hold her hand all the way home. She seemed at peace in the truck and content in my presence most the evening. While I worked, we caught up on one another's upbringing. Shared embarrassing stories of our teen years. Hers involved dance and costume malfunctions, mine involved erections at inopportune times and pranking my sister whenever I could. She told me more about her mother and how strict she'd been. Not allowed to have many friends. Holly Hatfield, our town's librarian had been the one and only friend she'd kept through the years. Mostly because they met when Holly was in Alaska as a foreign exchange student. Then they did all their correspondence via email and phone calls.

I felt sad for the childhood she'd had. Though she had nothing but good things to say about her father, her mother was another story all together. Sounded to me like her mother was a controlling bitch who was living her own life vicariously through her daughter. Putting unreasonable and oftentimes impossible goals to achieve on Anya's slight shoulders. And if she achieved the results, she'd gain a scrap of affection from the woman who bore her. I'd have to have a talk with Shay and Mags. My sister and my mother would wrap my woman in their biker babe arms and show her so much love she wouldn't even know what hit her.

I swore on everything I had in me I would not mess this up with Anya. I knew in my heart of hearts she was the woman meant for me. My soul sighed in her presence. Every inch of me wanted to touch every inch of her the second we were near. It was as if my body called to hers—and the damn call was loud, positively blaring. Hell, she even looked like she could be my daughter's mother, and one day soon, I hoped she would be.

Once I opened the door, I flicked on the light. She entered and stopped at the center of my small living room with her arms crossed, hands at her biceps rubbing them up and down in a self-soothing gesture.

"Bella, turn around and look at me."

Her head dropped forward toward her chest, and she spun around slowly on those sexy-as-sin pink stilettos.

"Eyes, babe, I need your eyes."

She let her arms fall, and the fabric shawl she wore slipped to the ground. I leaned against the wall and gave her space. I wanted to know that she was ready for this without my hands and lips convincing her. I wanted to love her body, but I needed to love her mind in order to secure her heart.

"Tell me what's going on in that gorgeous head of yours."

The compliment made her smile, and my heart started to pound.

"I've only ever had sex once. It wasn't pleasant, and it was five years ago."

I had to steady my hand against the wall to keep from falling over. My mind and body quaked with the endless possibilities. This information also changed things. A lot. My dick swelled against the fly of my jeans in an almost painful need to take, fulfill, and repeat.

Except I couldn't move fast with her. Already I knew she was a bit skittish and nervous. I'd figured it was because she was sweet and shy, not because she was lacking experience.

Hell, Anya was the most unearthly sexy and enchanting woman I'd ever seen. How she could go the past five years without a trail of men chasing her? I didn't know. But fuck if it didn't suit me just fine that she was inexperienced.

"Okay," I croaked.

One of her eyebrows arched. "Okay? That's it?"

I grinned wickedly. Those possibilities had flashed through my mind a moment ago and were now on the spin cycle like the *Wheel of Fortune*. So many winning options.

"Babe, I'm not going to be sad that you've barely been touched. It means everything you and I do will be off the charts amazing and down right memorable." I flexed the hand not holding me up, wanting to go to her, to twist my fingers into her golden hair, tip her head back, and suck on her shimmery white skin.

Her head lifted, and she straightened, puffing up her chest a little. "You're not disappointed I'm inexperienced?"

I couldn't stay away any longer, but still, I held every primal instinct inside of me in check. For her, until she was more comfortable with me, I'd do go slow. Though it might kill me.

I moved closer to her, like a cat prowling toward its prey, no longer capable of keeping my distance. "Not even a little bit," I finally said through my teeth.

Her shoulders dropped as though in relief.

"Elated," I grated softly while teasing the lace trim of the bodice of her dress.

Her breath caught as I walked around to the back of the dress and untied the satin bow cinched at her waist.

"Delighted," I whispered in her ear and ran my finger up the center of her spine until it caught on the zipper.

She shivered.

"Excited." I tugged the zipper down all the way to the crack of her small ass, revealing perfectly unmarred skin.

I pressed a kiss to the back of her bared neck while pushing the edges of the dress out and to the side. As I expected, it fell to the floor in a whoosh of lacy fabric.

Anya was long, lean, and ripe for the taking. I put my hands on the swell of her hips, and she trembled in my hold. Oh so slowly, I dragged my hands over her tiny waist and up along each slight indent of her ribcage. When I got to the bottom of her simple white bra, I unhooked the clasp. With as much tenderness as I could muster in my sexually heightened state, I kissed along her swanlike neck while looping a finger into each strap and dragging it down her arms until it, too, fell to the floor.

Goosebumps appeared across her skin, and she leaned back against me. I trailed my fingertips down her arms to her hands. Lifting the right, I brought it to my lips and kissed the pad of each delicate finger. Once completed, I repeated the move with the other arm and hand.

Feather-light, I slid my hands around her, encompassing her body from behind. She sighed and leaned more heavily against me, standing in only her lacy white panties and her heels. I glanced over her shoulders and had to bite my tongue at the vision of her small breasts heaving up and down with her labored breaths, the peachy pink nipples erect and begging for my touch.

So as to not scare her, I slid my fingers along her belly and up to cup each breast. My entire hand engulfed each mound. She arched into my hold, and I smiled against her neck, sucking on her pulse point. I circled her small berry-sized nipples with my thumb and forefinger and petted them lightly.

"Oh…" She whispered and arched higher.

I pressed harder, elongating her little tips with tender plucks. Her hips started to rotate, and she lifted one elegant arm up and behind her, clasping the back of my neck while I played with her petite tits.

She was magnificent.

"You are so fucking gorgeous." I burrowed my nose against her flesh.

Anya hummed when I pressed my fingers together a bit harder against her luscious breasts.

"Do you like me plucking your pretty tits, Bella? Do you want me to put my mouth on them?" I licked up the length of her neck and then back down to the ball of her shoulder.

"Yes," she sigh-gasped, her ass rotating against my stiff cock like its own personal merry-go-round.

I spun her around, clamped my mouth over hers, and hiked her up by her perfect ass. Her long legs wrapped around me, and I carried her through my living room, down the small hall, and to my king-sized bed. Anticipating this very moment, I'd left the small lamp by my bed on. It gave off a warm glow, but allowed me to see all her beauty in the warm light.

Kissing her deeply, I settled a knee to the bed and laid her down on my comforter. I let her go and whipped my shirt over my head. Her eyes seemed to darken as she took in my naked torso. She licked her lips in a way that made my dick painfully hard against the fly of my jeans.

"I feel the exact same way looking at your chest, babe." I grinned and unbuttoned my pants, shoving them and my briefs to the ground as I toed off my boots and socks.

Her mouth opened in a wide "O" when the sight of my hard cock made its appearance before her.

With one hand, I encircled my length and stroked a few times. Her gaze was riveted to the view of me stroking myself for her pleasure and mine.

Regretfully, I let my cock go, grabbed one of her ankles, and lifted her leg. There was no resistance whatsoever. That's when it dawned on me she could lift her entire leg up in an air split. I filed that bit of information in the back of my mind for future reference. With only one go under her belt, I wanted to make tonight a night she'd never forget, which meant it had to be all about her. Later, we'd test her flexibility.

I kissed her ankle and removed her stiletto, dropping it to the floor. I repeated the same with her other ankle and shoe.

Running my hands up her long, muscular legs, I reached her panties. I curled my fingers into them and glanced at her face.

"May I?" My voice was a timbre so low I barely recognized the sex-roughened tone.

"Please," she responded, her voice small but filled with desire.

I tugged the panties down her legs as I leaned over the mattress and kissed her belly, encircling her naval with my tongue. She smelled of mint, mixed with lavender, and a hint of a feminine musk unique to her. My mouth watered at the knowledge that she was so aroused I could scent her so easily.

With quick hands, I pushed her knees apart, spreading her open to my view. She immediately attempted to close them when she realized where I was headed.

"Shane...um...Shane, I've um...never..." Her flustered words came and dropped off into a long moan as I ran the flat of my tongue up her center.

She tasted like honey. Like the nectar of the fucking gods. And all mine.

I pressed my hands to her thighs, holding them open and went to town on her cunt. She withered under my ministrations and arched up into my mouth when I plunged my tongue into her heat.

"Shane!" she cried out, humping my face wildly.

"Oh. My. God. Oh my God. Ohmygod..." she chanted over and over as I took her higher and higher.

I sucked on her feminine lips. Licking each one individually.

I swirled my tongue inside her depths.

I tickled all around her hot bundle of nerves with the tip of my tongue.

I pressed a hot, wet kiss to her pink pucker.

I tasted *everything*. And it was perfection.

Then, when she was pressing my face to her flesh and calling out my name in an endless circle of pleasure, I wrapped my lips around her throbbing clit and sucked...hard.

Anya screamed, holding my head down, her hips bucked up into the air and went still. I kept at her, turning one orgasm into two, then into three before she begged me to stop.

When she was boneless, her eyes open wide, her mouth gasping air, I opened the drawer on the bedside table and grabbed a foil packet. I sheathed my weeping cock, pressed the tip to her entrance and waited for the right moment.

My Anya looked at me with tears in her eyes, her beautiful face aglow as she smiled and said, "Be with me."

I needed no further instruction. "Always and forever, from here on out Anya, that's my promise to you," I swore, then slowly eased inside my new home.

Anya wrapped her arms and legs around me, taking me deeper than I'd ever felt. She became a part of me, my body, and my heart.

"Make love to me. Show me what making love means," she whispered, her warm breath against my ear.

"I'll show you, Bella. I'll show you every day for the rest of my life."

Chapter 7

Anya

I WOKE TO MY HANDS STRETCHED ABOVE MY HEAD, MY LEGS spread, and Shane's warm torso centered between them. His lips were rhythmically suckling at one of my breasts. I arched into the spiraling pleasure and sighed when he circled one erect tip with the heat of his tongue.

"Good morning, Bella," he rasped before lifting up, dragging his muscular torso along the achy space between my thighs and pressed his lips to mine.

His tongue tickled mine at first, then moved into long, drugging swipes I could barely keep up with. When he had his fill, he ran his lips down the side of my cheek, my neck, and down between my breasts.

He hummed. "I'm struggling, babe."

I inhaled a full breath and sighed dreamily. "With what?" I glanced down my body where he had shifted up a bit so he could stare at my small breasts and between my thighs at the same time.

"Not sure what I want. More of these perfect tits or to gorge on your cunt." He smacked his chops, let go of my hands, and ran them over my breasts, giving them a little jiggle. "Decisions, decisions."

I smiled huge, knowing, after last night, both of those things were incredible. My legs started to tremble as he got up on his knees and ran a thick thumb over my center as though he was petting me there.

"So pink. So pretty. Every inch of you is peachy pink and so god damned pretty. Sometimes your beauty hurts my eyes, babe."

Feeling bolder than I ever had in my life, I ran my own hands down over my breasts and squeezed them together. "You don't have to choose, you know." He grinned and licked his lips.

"How are you feeling today?" He cupped the sides of my hips and gripped the small bit of fleshiness I'd gathered since my injury a year ago. I'd put on a total of maybe three additional pounds since my accident, and I hated every one of those pounds. At that moment, with his eyes full of lust and glued to the possessive hold he had there, I thanked my body for the additional womanly curves.

I ran my hands down my form until I covered his hands with my own. "Better than I ever have in my entire life. I never had any idea sex could be this...this..."

"Amazing. Incredible. Hot." His eyes practically twinkled with happiness.

"Life-changing," I whispered.

His expression flashed with male pride as his torso lifted. "Too true."

I smiled and bit down on my bottom lip. "I want more," I said shyly, my entire face flushing with heat I could feel moving down my neck and over my chest.

He growl-hummed. "My woman wants to get herself some." His nostrils flared, and he wrapped a thick hand around his long erection. "The question is, after last night's sexcapades, what is it you got a taste for?"

My mind flashed to the many times he'd taken me last night. The first time being soft and slow. The second hard and fast. The third, wild and unhinged, when he had me from behind, my hands curled around the wooden headboard, both of us up on our knees as he plunged me into oblivion so many times, I lost the ability to hold myself up any longer.

"What do you want?" I ran my hands up his strong, muscular forearms.

His body practically vibrated with whatever he was thinking about.

"Tell me?" I widened my legs, letting him see every inch of me, opened and ready for whatever he had in mind.

"Anything I want?" He cocked an eyebrow, his sandy brown hair falling into his face in sex mussed layers I wanted to run my fingers through.

"If I have it to give, I'll give it you."

Shane shuffled back on the bed until he stood at the end. He grabbed my ankle and tugged me to the edge.

"Sit up. I want your mouth around my cock before I fuck you into tomorrow," he commanded, his tone filled to the brim with lust.

I'm certain my eyes widened, and my entire form quivered in fear. I'd not attempted this activity before and though Shane had introduced me to so many things in one single night, I was worried this one would make him unhappy. I frowned deeply as I sat up and put my hands together in front of me, twisting my fingers, trying to figure out how to proceed without losing the best thing that had ever happened to me after only one night together physically.

"Bella."

I pursed my lips and kept my head down.

"Anya, look at me."

I shook my head as tears pricked the back of my eyes. Confusion, sadness, and fear raced along my mind, making me feel less than.

He lifted my chin with a curled finger. His face was a mask of worry and concern. "Babe, with me, you don't ever have to do something you don't want to do. Fuck, I'm sorry. I didn't re- alize this might be something you didn't want to do..." Regret laced his words, and instantly, I felt worse.

"No, I...uh...want to try; it's just... I've never done it, and I want to be everything you need." My chin wobbled as appre- hension seeped into my chest.

Shane crouched down and cupped the back of my head, placing his face only a few inches from mine. His eyes were a blaze of bright green and swirling golden yellow as he spoke. "You are everything I need. Just you. As you are. And anything you've not done in the bedroom is just an opportunity for me I cherish. It's a gift, Anya. I get to be the one to share new things with you, and babe, there is nothing I want more than to share everything a couple can do...with you. Including sex. We are fire and light. Everything we did last night was the best I'd ever had. Every moment I experience with you is nothing but beauty."

I cupped both of his cheeks. "I'm falling in love with you, Shane." My voice shook, but I had to say it. Couldn't hold it back another moment. "I know it's too soon, and it's so new..."

He tunneled his fingers into my hair and held my head so I couldn't move. "Anya, I was gone for you the second you lit up at seeing my daughter. I knew I had to grab that light, make it mine and Shayna's forever. Now that I've had you...tasted your kiss, felt your legs, arms, and heart wrap around me...there is no going back. You are my old lady. You are my woman. You are mine."

I kissed him then. Letting go of all the fear, anxiety, insecurities, and everything in between. Shane would take care of me. Shane would make it all okay. I didn't have anything to be afraid of when I was with him. Right then, I decided I'd be free.

Free to be myself.

Free to kiss him when I wanted.

Free to hold him as I desired.

Free to love him in my way, and in turn...be free to love myself as he did.

Shane wrapped an arm around my waist and one under my bum and shifted me back up the bed. He rolled over to the stack of condoms he'd carelessly left on top of the nightstand after last night. Then he sat up, ripped the package open, sheathed his member, and licked his lips.

"I want to fuck you hard. I want to fuck you wild. I want to fuck you until you feel every inch of me so deeply embedded in your body and soul, you'll never want to be free of me."

My heart pounded a staccato beat against my chest as I lifted my knees up toward my chest and stretched my legs out into a wide legged split.

"Jesus, fuck!"

I grinned, running my hands from crease where my leg met my bum and up my thighs, the back of my knees where my scar was and up to hold onto my calves.

"Does it hurt?" His gaze ran all over my body like a caress.

I shook my head. "Not even a little bit."

His gaze flared with so much heat, I feared I'd get burned but knew it would be in the best possible way.

"How long can you hold that position?" His voice was the thunder before a storm.

"How long can you fuck me?" I cursed for the first time since we'd met. It felt tawdry and dirty, but I loved the way it affected my guy.

"Oh, Bella, you're gonna regret teasing the beast," he grumbled, dipped his head down quick as a snap, and ran his tongue straight up the center of my cleft, leaving a sucking kiss at the tiny bundle of nerves that drove me mad with need.

I cried out in pleasure and then smiled. "Honey, I seriously doubt that." I pointed my toes, ran my hands up to my ankles, and brought them together before my body, straight in front of my face.

He growled.

My man *growled* at the sight of my flexibility and lewd display of my talents.

Inside, the sheer feminine pride I possessed had me soaring the moment I felt his large wide tip pushing through the tight clamp of my vaginal muscles. He wedged inside, gripped my ankles, and separated my legs so he could see my face. His big body leaned forward, pressing his weight against the back of my thighs. There wasn't so much as a pinch in my thigh muscles but there was an intense pressure at the heart of me. His length pushed so deep I lost my ability to catch my breath.

That's when I knew teasing the beast inside the man I loved would be a common occurrence if this was the reaction.

His forehead pressed to mine as he eased in and out of my willing body in a slow, torturous rhythm. "You okay?"

I dropped my legs, resting the backs of my knees on his brawny shoulders, and used the position as leverage to lift my hips and slam against his lower body.

A startled, blissful expression covered his face in a blanket of pleasure. "Woman, your flexibility is going to be the death of me," he teased and sucked on my neck, sending shivers down my spine. I locked my arms around his slick, sinewy lower back and held on.

Ribbons of heat soared through my system as I got into the act of slamming my hips up as he thrust in and out. Together we literally rode one another, our pleasure building to incredible heights I never wanted to leave.

The slapping of flesh filled the room alongside male grunts and female moans. We made lusty music, using one another's bodies as instruments.

It was beautiful, raw, and sheer magic.

Shane maneuvered my legs, still spread for him, back to the mattress. He lifted his body up, yet we remained connected on the most primal level. One arm was centered by my shoulder, holding his body up and bowed over me, and one hand gripped my waist. He circled his hips, screwing his length inside of me, crushing my clit with each perfect rotation. His gaze was plastered between us, watching his wet length plummet inside fully and retract to the flared tip. He watched with rapt attention as my feminine lips stretched to accommodate his thick shaft in what seemed like endless earth-shattering thrusts.

I started to pant. There was a heat building so hot between my thighs that every ounce of my being was focused on it. It was a ball of ecstasy ready to explode from where he was connected to me.

"I love fucking you, Anya. Love seeing my cock go in and out of your beautiful body. Love your pearly white skin turning pink where I touch, kiss, and bite. Love every damn thing about you, woman. My old lady. The perfect woman for me."

The ball of ecstasy between us flared double its size as I attempted to breathe between brutal thrusts of his intense length pounding relentlessly inside my over sensitized depths. I locked my inner muscles around his member, and his body bowed up like a growling lion. His hands moved to my hips, and he lifted himself up to his knees, tipped his head back, and roared while he manually used my body to jerk his cock.

I wrapped my legs around his waist, planted my hands flat on the bed, and let the ball inside of me explode, sending lightning blasts of sizzling euphoria out every nerve ending. This orgasm battled each one I'd had last night and topped them when he pressed his thumb to the throbbing knot above where he was taking me and spun a tight circle.

A soundless scream left me as the second orgasm blasted through me in a perpetually never-ending stream of sexual rapture. I couldn't move, just stared and watched as the chaos of pleasure overtook him.

Shane's entire body went rigid, his muscles straining, the veins in his forearms and biceps bulging with the effort to hold my body up as he held his pulsating length inside and let go. His teeth were bared in a snarl, eyes closed tight, sweat misting his gorgeous body in a glowing sheen. I wanted to slide my tongue across and memorize his taste for eternity.

Eventually it passed. His grip lessened, and his softening length slipped from me as he lowered my hips back down to the mattress. There, he plowed to one hip, circled his arms around me, and rested his head on my chest. His lips were pressed near the flesh of my breast, and every couple seconds, he'd kiss what he could reach there, his hot breath tingling across the still erect tips, leaving them feeling hot and prickly. I leaned my head forward and kissed his forehead then ran my fingers through his sweaty hair, dragging my nails along his scalp until he purred his enjoyment.

"Is sex always like this?" I asked, staring at the ceiling.

"No," was his one-word reply.

"I was hoping for a little more of a response."

"That's all I've got."

"No. You mean all the times you've had sex before, you can't compare to the handful we've had?"

"No. I can't. Because you obliterated all sexual experiences that didn't include you from my mind." He lifted his hand up and cupped it around my small breast.

He nuzzled my other one and kissed me right on the nipple saying, "Mine," under his breath before resting his head back again like a content cat.

"Shane, I'm being serious. I want to know."

He sighed heavily. "Babe, sex with someone who doesn't mean something to you is just a physical release. It's fun at the time, but ultimately, all you're focused on is the moment when you get off. With you, it's not like that. So no, sex is not like what we have. Not by a long shot."

I smiled and hooked a leg over his and turned to the side so he'd have to look at me. "What you're saying is that because you love me, it's different? Better perhaps?"

He smiled lazily. "You fishing for a compliment, Bella?"

Shock slithered through my mind as ire fed into my blood. "Absolutely not!" I fired back and pouted at my sudden frustration.

He chuckled and cupped the ball of my shoulder, sweeping his thumb across the bare flesh. "What I meant to say is that sex is just sex. It's fun. It can be really good sex if the person you're doing it with knows how to please you."

I frowned because I was still learning how to best please him. I hadn't even used my mouth on him yet for fear that I'd do it wrong.

He lifted my chin with his thumb and forefinger. "Sex with someone you love, someone who holds your heart in the palm of their hand, is when sex becomes a memorable experience.

I can honestly say sex has never been like it is with you, babe, because I've never been in love with the woman I was with. Sex with you, it's everything. It's sex for fun. It's making love. It's beautiful raw and wild fucking, made all the better because I want nothing more than to be doing all of it with you. My old lady. The woman I love. Does that make sense?"

I leaned forward and kissed him softly. "Thank you. It makes perfect sense. And I love everything about sex with you too. You make me feel things I didn't even know were possible."

"Come here, babe." He tugged me until I was leaning against his side, my arm over his chest, my chin setting against his pec. I snuggled in and was about to ask him more information about this old lady business when his body got tight, and he held me close.

Then the sound of pounding feet echoed off the hallway and a very feminine cry of, "Shayna, no baby!" before the bedroom door flew open and slammed against the opposite side.

Shayna's eyes were a brilliant bright blue with the navy dress and rainbow-colored leggings she wore underneath. Her hair was in a ponytail on the top of her head with a matching rainbow bow. If I wasn't naked and half on top of her father, in his bed, I would have told her how cute she looked. As it was, my insides were melting, and my mind was mush on how to best deal with this situation.

Then, of course, it got worse when she jumped up on the bed and rested on her knees right next to us. I grabbed the comforter and held it tight against my bare chest.

"Hi, Daddy! Hi, Misses M! I had the bestest time at Auntie Shay's. Wook!" she lifted up her hands in front of her face, frowned, and then turned them around. "Auntie painted my nails pink! So pwetty!"

"Shit, Shane, I'm sorry," Shay said from the doorway, half

out of breath as if she'd run through the house to catch the little sprite currently bouncing happily on the bed in front of two people who were clearly still naked.

"Jesus!" She covered her eyes and turned around. "It's three o'clock, bro, and I gotta get to the shop. Rex already has a handful with the twins, or I would have kept her home."

"Very pretty, Sunflower," he rumbled to his daughter.

She nodded. "Uh huh, and guess what I decided I want for my birfday?" She wiggled excitedly.

"Shayna, your birthday isn't for another few weeks."

"Mmmhmm."

"So sorry, Shane," Shay added miserably.

"It's okay, sis. If you could just get her settled with a show before you leave?" he said clearly with absolutely no hint of concern when my entire body was aflame with mortification.

She pounded on her dad's bare chest. "Daddy, I want to tell you what I want so you can give it to me!" she demanded.

He petted her cheek. "What do you want, baby?"

She looked at me and then looked back at her dad. "I want Misses M to be my mommy for my birfday! Then we can dance all the time and play dress up, and Barbies, and paint nails and..." Her eyes got huge. "We can do everything together! Like Auntie Shay with Grandma! Can I have that? Can I? Can I, Daddy?"

Dead.

Basically, I was pretty sure this was the moment when people die after they've done something horrible, and God wants to get back at them before he sends them to hell.

Yep. Purgatory. That's what this was. Only a living one.

"Christ!" Shane sat up. "Sunflower, we need to discuss this another time. Right now, I need you to go watch a show, and let Daddy and Anya get up."

Shayna lifted her hands in the air. "Woohoo! I wanna watch *Mickey Mouse Clubhouse!*" She got up and ran into the other room, leaving the door open.

Shay sucked in a sharp hissing breath. "Sorry," she said while closing the door.

I let my entire body fall to the bed and covered my eyes with my hands. "Kill me now."

Shane, on the other hand, laughed, kissed my shoulder, and then got out of bed and went into the bathroom, presumably to get rid of the condom he still wore. When he emerged, he was wearing a pair of plaid pajama pants. He threw a pair to me along with a t-shirt.

"Babe, I just got you. There's no way you're dying on me now. Get up. I'll make you some pancakes."

"Restricted list," I said flatly with zero humor. I wanted to curl up into a ball and disappear. How was I supposed to deal with this? His sister and his daughter caught me in bed with their brother/father, and I was naked. Naked! And Shayna thinks she wants me as her mommy.

"We're living for the moment, Bella. No more restricted list."

I flung off the blanket, grabbed the t-shirt, and threw it over my head. It fell to mid-thigh. "I'm going home so you can talk to your daughter about what she just saw...and said!" I shoved my leg through one pant leg and then the next. When I pulled them up and let them go, they immediately fell to the ground in a puddle at my feet.

Shane put his fist to his mouth and held back his laughter, but just barely.

"Not funny." I bent down and pulled them back up and then rolled them until they stayed up.

"So funny!" he countered and pulled a t-shirt over his head.

I crossed my arms over myself and bit down on my lip.

He came over and wrapped his big arms around me. Instantly, I felt safe and loved, the exact opposite of what I felt most days. "It's gonna be okay, babe. Promise. It's not gonna be an issue."

"Shayna just saw us in bed together. That is a huge issue!" I whisper yelled and poked his chest.

"Why?"

"Because you can't just bring a woman home and let her see them sleeping with her dad. It's inappropriate and confusing."

"Hold up. I've never brought a woman to my home before you. I've never introduced a woman to my daughter as the woman in my life and definitely not as my old lady. You are not just any woman, Anya. You are *my* woman. You are in my life for the long haul. It's time Shayna got used to that."

"Are you gonna be my Mommy now?" Came a little voice from the doorway. In our hushed argument we didn't realize Shayna had opened the door and was listening.

"Sweetheart, your father and I are in a relationship with one another that is just starting out..." I tried.

"Mmmhmm. Yep. You are my daddy's old lady. Like Grandma is to Papa and Auntie Shay is to Uncle Rex." Her little eyes widened, and the biggest smile I'd ever seen crossed her sweet face. "Oooh, that means maybe I can have a baby too! I want a baby. Can you give me one and be my mommy?"

The request slammed into my chest, and I took a step back and fell to a seated position on the rumpled bed, my hand to my chest as though if I didn't put it there my heart might pound its way right out.

Shane scooped up his daughter and spoke directly to her. "Daddy is in love with Anya, Baby, but in order for her to be your mommy, we have to get married. And we can't have babies until we're married. Make sense?"

She nodded. "So you can get marry-ed."

"Down the road, Baby. For now, how's about your dad makes his best girls some chocolate chip pancakes!"

"Woohoo!"

"I'll give you some time," he said to me with a smile.

"I may need eternity," I hissed, freaked out beyond reason.

"As long as we're together, you've got it."

I shook my head and waited until they moved out of the room and down the hall, Shayna happily chatting away.

What have I gotten myself into?

Chapter 8

Whip

THE PHONE RANG IN MY BACK POCKET AS I POURED A PITCHER of beer for the group of guys watching the game. It was two weeks after Anya and I had gotten physical. Two weeks since I'd told her I loved her. Two weeks since I'd made her my old lady. The best two weeks of my fuckin' life. Hands down.

I grabbed the phone and saw "Old Lady" on the screen.

"Woman, you trying to make me go hard?" I said smoothly into the phone.

"Honey…wait, huh? What?" She was breathless and sounded as though she was walking.

"Babe, any time your name flashes across my screen, I think of you. Tonight, all I can think about is the thing you did with your mouth last night and when the hell I was going to get that bit of Heaven again."

"My goodness, Shane…" Her tone was packed full of shock and awe. "You can't talk like that, especially now."

"Bella, I'll talk to my old lady any way I want, especially if she's the most beautiful woman I've ever seen, great in the sack, and damn good with her mouth. Which you are. You're an important role model to my daughter, and you're damn near perfect. Hence the reason I see your name and my dick goes hard. Now, what are you going to do about it?" I growled, heading toward the supply room. I had a hankering to wrap my hand around my dick to my woman's voice.

"Shane, speaking of your little girl, she's right here with me."

"What? Why?" I rubbed at my forehead, my dick softening at the mention of my girl.

"Honey, it's Thursday remember? Dance class on Tuesday and Thursdays. Tuesday evening, we met Holly at the library, and today, I promised a girl date. She had a lovely bowl of spaghetti to my salad, and we just picked up ice cream. Now we're walking home so I can get her bathed and in bed."

Damn. When I mentioned it been heaven the past two weeks, a lot had changed to help make it that way. One thing in particular is how much Anya liked being with Shayna. Right after Shayna and I'd had our talk about her keeping the mommy business to herself for a while as to not scare off Daddy's old lady, she'd been a perfect princess. I told her Daddy and Anya loved one another and loved her, and the rest would come with time. She seemed okay with it, but she started clinging to Anya in a way I was thrilled with. More so was how Anya reacted to the change of having an almost five-year-old want to be with her all the time in spades.

The two of them had become close, and more times than not, I heard the murmurings of how much they looked alike. Every time Shayna heard it, she beamed with pride. I know it's been hard on her not having a mom and looking different than the women in her immediate family. With Anya, my girl looked similar. Blonde hair, blue yes, peachy soft skin. Together they were two peas in a pod. Two beautiful flowers that seemed to glow everywhere they went.

"Aw, I'll bet my girls had a great time together."

"We did! But I'm calling because we have something to celebrate this weekend!" Her voice rose with her exuberance.

"Celebrate? Her birthday's not until next month, babe." I reminded.

She groaned in my ear. "Daddies can be so annoying," she said into the phone, but I know it was directed at my daughter.

"Totally! Hi, Daddy!" Shayna hollered, and I chuckled.

"Let me speak to my baby." I looked down the line of the bar and noticed Lacey, one of the club girls and also tonight's waitress, tapping her hand on the bar as though she was bored to tears. Her Pride t-shirt was cut at the neck and arms making it sleeveless and showing a reckless amount of her plastic tits. The shirt was tied in a knot at her back, showing off her tramp stamp of a motorcycle with flames coming out the back. The tat was sweet. Ink, a brother from the club, did the work, and his artistic ability was off the charts. Reminded me that my girl didn't have a speck of ink on her. Something I wondered if she'd change when I got her name branded next week at the club pre-Christmas Hog roast Mags put on for the club. Now that we had more members with kids and old ladies, Mags started talking about setting down some traditions. I was all for it as long as my kid and my woman participated.

Ever since I got with Anya, I'd been bailing on the club parties. Not because I would feel tempted to partake of any of the available pussy, but because I'd rather spend my free time with her and my kid.

When Lacey saw me staring her way, she leaned her tits to the bar so I could get a better view and waved.

Fuckin' hell. The woman would not let up.

Shayna got on the phone. "Daddy, you never beweave what I did tonight!!" My daughter screeched in my ear. I lifted a finger to Lacey in a wait-a-minute gesture. The little bitch rolled her eyes in defiance.

"What, sweetheart?"

"I learnded a big jetty in class tonight!"

"A big jetty? Sunflower, Daddy doesn't know what that is." I laughed and headed over to bitchface Lacey. Man, I wished I hadn't fucked her those few times. Every time I saw her here or at the club, I was reminded that I'd stuck my dick in that, and it gave me the creeps. She'd turned into such a bitch, and now that she'd seen Anya at her regular seat, spending time with me at the bar when Shay or my parents had Shayna, she'd been especially hard to deal with.

I heard Anya's melodic voice in the background, and it immediately calmed the irritation of having to see Lacey. "My darling, it's a *grand jeté*. It's French."

"It's a French jetty!" my daughter screamed into the phone, her voice rippling with excitement. "I did a French jetty, Daddy!"

I chuckled and grabbed the list of drinks Lacey had on her tray and moved the phone away from my mouth. "Go get other orders. I'll have this filled when you come back."

Lacey leaned even farther over the bar, smashing her tits on the wood as if she was serving them up on a platter for my taking. "Wouldn't it be more fun if I stood here just like this, and looked at your fine ass while you made those drinks? Huh, Whip? Or we could just sneak to the back room..."

I ground my teeth and tried to breathe through the rage settling over me. Lacey knew I'd claimed Anya. Knew I was making it official by getting her brand at the party next week. She was pulling this shit just to be a bitch.

"Who is that woman?" Anya's tone was direct and lacking the easy happiness it once held.

"No one, babe." I looked right into Lacey's scowling face. "Just a club girl crossing a line she shouldn't be, knowing I'm claimed by *my old lady.*" I said those last words loud enough to make Lacey cringe and back away.

"I'll just go get more drink orders," she sneered.

"You do that while I think about not canning your ass!" I grated through my teeth as I sucked in a fire hot breath.

"We'll discuss this later. I'm sorry to bother you at work..." Anya's voice sounded rattled, and I hated that I couldn't be right there to make her feel better.

"Bella, you are never a bother. I want you calling me as much as you want to hear my voice because I love hearing yours. And I love that you took our girl out and had a good time. Makes me happy, Anya. Everything you do makes me happy."

"I love you, Shane," she whispered softly into my ear. "You always say the perfect things."

"My job, one I happen to like a fuckuva lot. And you're going to have to explain this big jetty thing, because I don't know what the fuck my daughter was talking about."

Anya laughed, and it drowned out all the sound in the bar and filled me up with goodness and light. Just what I need after dealing with Lacey.

"It's called a *grand jeté.* And it's where a ballerina jumps from one foot in the air, spreading her legs out and landing on the opposite leg."

"Fuckin' hell, that sounds tough. My baby did that?"

"Yes, well, she did a very small jump, which, for her age, was a very big deal. So, my call was to tell you we need to celebrate."

"Woohoo!" I heard in the background.

I chuckled. "Sounds good to me. My girl does big things, we need to reward them."

"My thoughts exactly. All right, honey, we're almost home. I'll see you soon."

"Yeah, babe, soon is never close enough."

"Wake me when you get home," she whispered, her tone sultry and telling in the way it dipped to a lower timbre.

"With my mouth or my cock, baby?" I hummed in enjoyment as the vision of waking her with my mouth between her pretty thighs danced across my mind.

"Surprise me," she taunted.

"Don't wear any panties," I grumbled into the phone, my words demanding and filled with desire.

She gasped, and it took a moment before she spoke, dropping the gauntlet with seven words that seared right into my brain.

"I don't plan to be wearing anything."

Later that evening, my mother and father entered the bar. His arm was around her shoulders as always. He kissed her temple and whispered something in her ear that made her laugh out loud. After they made their way over to the end of the bar, my father pulled out Mags' chair, and she sat in it. He reached into her wild mane of hair and tugged her mouth to his in a searing kiss that lasted a full minute. Patrons be damned.

It had always been like that between my parents. Nothing but love, sass, hilarious bickering, and happiness. Anyone who viewed the two could easily see they were soul mates. I wanted that kind of happiness for myself, and with Anya, I finally felt like I'd found it.

"What can I get for you two love birds?" I set two coasters on the bar in front of them.

"Usual," my father said, and I went over and grabbed him a cold beer, popping the cap and tossing it in the trash bin.

"I'm shooting tequila tonight, son! Hit me with some Patron!" Mags waggled her eyebrows playfully.

My father shook his head with a shit-eating grin plastered across his face. "Fuck me! It's going to be a wild night."

Mags slapped the bar top. "Damn straight. You better drink up because I'm planning a good, long, *ride* tonight!"

I chuckled and got my mother the bottle of Patron and set the entire thing in front of my father who promptly poured his woman a drink. If he was around, he poured her beverages. He also ordered for her. It was old-fashioned, but I think my mother got off on him remembering what she liked best everywhere they went. It proved he paid attention, and paying attention to a woman's likes and dislikes went a long way. Happy wife, happy life, from what I understood. My mother was living proof.

"I'm going limes tonight, son!" she called out, and I grabbed a lime, cut it into slices and put half on a plate in front of her. Then I grabbed the bar nuts and put a fresh bowl in front of my father.

"So, son, how goes it with your old lady? Everything still up for you getting your brand on Saturday?"

I grinned and leaned into the bar. "Fuck yeah. I can't wait to get my woman's name on my body."

Mags laughed. "And did you tell Anya what was coming?"

"Yeah, sure. Told her we were going to her first club hog roast as a pre-holiday celebration."

Riot let out a long whistle. "Son, you are asking for trouble."

"You didn't tell her that, when a Pride member claims an old lady, they officially brand their chests with the name?" Mags blinked and tilted her head.

I shook my head. "I left out that detail. Figured it would be easier to ask for forgiveness than permission."

"Sheeeeee-it." Riot sucked back a long swallow of his beer.

"Dumb. Dumb as a box of rocks my kid is." Mags sighed.

"How you figure?" I smiled, knowing she was teasing me, and crossed my arms on the bar in front of them.

"Shot," she stated flatly, and my father promptly poured her another shot.

She tipped it back, taking the entire thing in one go, let it sit in her mouth a moment, then swallowed, following it up with a bite of the lime. My mouth watered at the thought of biting into a lime myself.

"Remember how Shay freaked out about Rex? And she'd seen her father's brand her entire life. You prepared to deal with your woman when she's gonzo?"

I smirked. "Gonzo? Who are you, and what did you do with my mother? I see the property vest, the biker tank, the tight jeans, and kick ass boots, but what I don't see is Mags."

She ruffled and fluffed her crazy waves of hair, reminding me of my sister. The women in my family were too damned beautiful for their own good. It had always been a challenge, especially as a teenager. All my friends either wanted in my sister's pants or were MILFing out on my mother. It was hell on wheels. I had beat up too many fuckers to count for inappropriate talk about my mom and sister. Now that I had the golden beauties in my life along with their dark beauty, I was doubly screwed.

"Mark my words: She's gonna freak."

I shrugged. "Then I'll deal with it when the time comes. All that matters is that Shayna doesn't see, so you need to settle up one of the club girls to play with her in her room when it goes down."

"Not a problem."

My phone in my pocket rang again, and I frowned as I pulled it out and saw it was Rex.

"Brother," I started to greet him with a joke about my sister letting him up for air when his bark of words cut me short.

"Get. Home. *Now!* Your sister's beating the ass of some blonde skank who accosted Anya and Shayna. Anya's with the twins and Shayna now, but she's a mess, man."

"Fuck!" I cut the phone off. There was only one blonde skank I could imagine would know where to look for me that Shay would lose her mind over. "Dad, you need to man the bar. I think Jess just showed up at my apartment. Got to get to Anya and Shayna. Rex says Shay's beating the shit out of her!"

"Dammit all to hell," Riot cursed.

"Serves the bitch right! Get her Shay-la-la!" Mags lifted her hands into the air in a cheer.

Dad followed me out to the parking lot, phone to his ear. "Jay's on his way to cover the bar. When he gets here, I'll head to your place."

I nodded, revved my engine, and set off toward my apartment, hoping like hell my sister didn't kill Jess. I wanted that honor myself.

Chapter 9

Anya

Thirty minutes earlier...

"A
FTER YOU BATHE, MY DARLING, I'LL READ YOU WHATEVER
book you want."

"Two books." She held up two, sticky, choco-
late coated fingers and smiled. A sloppy chocolate "o" circled
her mouth.

I beamed at the beautiful child I was coming to love like my
very own. The bond Shayna and I had built over dance, all things
girlie, and the great love we both had for Shane had sealed her
into my heart. I wanted to be this little girl's mother one day,
and if you asked Shane, it was a foregone conclusion.

We'd been taking things as slow as I could manage, but
Shane liked to do things at the speed of light. He was already
talking about moving me into his apartment with him and
Shayna. I firmly declined the invitation as I felt it was too soon.
Still, every night he talked me into staying in his home and in
his bed.

Shayna seemed no worse for the invasion of me in their

little duo, which made him feel vindicated in his decision to move me in as soon as possible. At the very least, I promised him when they moved into their own house, I'd consider it... down the road.

"All right, my darling, two it is. But after the bath, Ms. Sticky Fingers." I lifted her hand and playfully kissed at her fingers, the scent of chocolate invading my nose.

She giggled with the free spirit her father had raised her to have. Unlike me at five. My mother had me going from kindergarten to several hours of ballet, homework, very little dinner only from her prescribed list of appropriate foods, most lacking taste, and off to bed. No bedtime stories. No lullabies. Having spent the past two weeks enshrouded in Shane and Shayna's world, including seeing Shay and Rex with their twins Swayze and Trace, it made me see how completely joyless my upbringing had been.

I longed for the ability to cuddle in my mother's arms and have her tell me how much she loved me the way Shay did every time she was around her twins or her niece. Love and pride were the prevailing emotions around any member of the Hero's Pride club. They were a family, and they showed it by being there for one another and caring deeply about everything in their lives.

Shayna swung my arm as she held my hand and skip-walked through the breezeway of my apartment and off toward hers.

When we got closer, I could see a woman with ratty, stringy, dirty-blonde hair sitting on the steps we would have to use. Her face was nothing but sunken in cheeks and bone, bluish lips, and heavy circles under her dark blue eyes. She stood up when we were about fifty feet away. There was very little to her, and that's coming from someone who had been underweight her entire life.

The jeans she wore hung off her hips as though they could fall at any minute. The bones of her ribs were stark protrusions along her bare midriff, the crop top just barely resting under her small sunken in chest.

"My baby girl! I'd know my baby girl anywhere!" she cried out, and Shayna grabbed my legs and hid behind me.

"Who's dat, Anya?"

I shook my head. "I don't know, my darling, but I will find out."

"Why are you hiding?" the woman screeched. "I'm your mommy! Didn't Whip show you pictures of me? I'm your mommy. Come here, baby! Come to Mommy!"

"I scawed, Anya. I don't like her." Shayna's eyes filled with tears and fell down her cheeks. I leaned over and picked her up, holding her against my chest. Her little body was trembling in fear. A rage so hot flushed my entire system as I held my girl close.

"Get away from us," I seethed. "I don't know you. My child doesn't know you, and you're scaring her!"

"Your child!" Her face turned bright red and tinged with ugly as she gripped her stringy hair and tugged on a wail. *"Your child!* She's MY baby! I gave birth to her. I'm her mommy! Where is Whip? WHIP!" she screamed at the top of her lungs. "WHIP! Get your ass out here! WHIIIIP!"

Shayna balled against my neck as I held on tight and started to back away from the screaming lunatic. I looked all around for a place to run but was saved by a giant when Rex exited his apartment wearing nothing but cargo pants, a tight black tank, bare feet, and a massive scowl. His multicolored brown and gold hair was in waves around his face, falling to his shoulders as he stormed down the stairs.

"Bitch, shut the fuck up! You've woken my twins!" he barked at the crazy woman.

She pointed at me where I stood stock-still, cradling Shayna at my chest. "She's got my child! That's my daughter!"

Shayna howled and gripped me so tight around my neck I was sure I'd have marks from her nails, but I didn't care. I'd kick and fight and scream until this woman left my child alone.

"Rex, this woman is upsetting Shayna. She's shaking and crying."

He pounded over on bare feet and put his hand to her back. "Hey, pumpkin, it's okay. Uncle Rex is here. I got you." His voice soothed her enough for her to lift her tear soaked face out of my neck, but she didn't reach for him.

"Bad lady is scawy. She says she my mommy, but Anya is my mommy. Don't let her take me!" New tears ran down her face as a deafening pounding sound came out of nowhere. It felt like the Earth was shifting under my feet.

I looked over Rex's shoulder at the commotion, just in time to see Shay jump from the last four steps in a leaping dive toward the woman. The two of them hurled to the ground and rolled until Shay got on top of the skinny lunatic.

Then, she bellowed in her face. "How fucking dare you come back here after leaving my niece five years ago! Fuck you." She punched the startled woman in the face. Blood poured from the woman's nose, and she wailed in pain. "You left my niece without a *name* in my parents' arms while my brother was serving our country." She shook the woman who was barely putting up a weak fight, batting at Shay's more targeted strikes.

"I could kill you for what you did to him, you stupid bitch!" She grabbed the woman by the hair and tugged so hard a large chunk came free. It was so long and bedraggled it hung down Shay's hands to her mid forearm.

The woman squealed and tried to protect herself.

"Shit! Get Shayna in my house and keep an eye on the twins. I'll take care of this mess!" Rex demanded, and with my precious package in my arms, I raced up the stairs and into Shay and Rex's home. Holding Shayna, I found the babies' room and looked in. They were both sitting in one crib together even though they had two. Shay must have placed them together to keep them happy while she lost her mind on the woman I assumed was Shane's ex and Shayna's biological mother.

I sat down in the rocking chair and petted Shayna's hair and cooed to her as she cried, me rocking her back and forth while I hummed the first song that came to mind. It was Tchaikovsky's *1812 Overture*, one of my favorites of all time. I'd danced a piece to it in the American Ballet Theatre before my injury.

As I hummed and soothed Shayna, the twins cuddled up next to one another, lying down forehead to forehead until their little eyes drooped and slipped closed.

After what felt like forever, but was probably thirty minutes to an hour, Shayna was asleep on my chest and the twins still out like lights. The door to the nursery opened, and there stood the only person in the entire world I wanted to see.

Shane.

My heart cracked in half at his stern and withdrawn expression. His hair was a mass of messy layers, which proved he'd probably run his fingers through it a hundred times over the last hour.

I watched as he entered quietly and kneeled before me. He put his hand on his daughter's back then pushed her hair away from her sleeping face to check her status.

"I'm sorry you had to deal with that." His tone was filled with sorrow and an intense sadness I wanted to kiss and hug away.

Instead, I stayed quiet, content in his presence, which made the world right again, and listened to the deep, soothing timbre of his voice.

"I'm sorry I wasn't here for either of you." He covered my hand with his own where I held his daughter.

I shook my head and reached out to cup his cheek. "We're fine. We're more fine now that you're here."

He nodded and dipped forward enough so he could kiss me sweetly.

"You and Shayna are *everything* to me." His voice broke on the word everything as though admitting the knowledge pierced his soul.

"I know."

"Don't let this fuck with your head. I couldn't live with that, Anya."

"Okay."

"Promise me we'll talk about it," he said brokenly.

"I promise," I said, but I was wrung dry. All I wanted was to take our girl, clean her up, get her to bed, and fall into my man's arms and sleep for a week.

"Let's go home."

"Yes, home." I nodded gratefully.

He lifted Shayna from my arms, and her breath stuttered, but she eased into his hold, perfectly content within her father's safety and love.

I walked by the twins and ran my hand along their perfect heads, placing a kiss to my lips and then to their foreheads. They didn't so much as stir.

We exited through the kitchen where Rex was cleaning the side of Shay's face. Along her cheek were four jagged bloody lines that appeared to be oozing blood quicker than Rex could blot away.

"My god, Shay!" I gasped, putting my hand over my mouth in complete horror.

She waved a hand my way nonchalantly. "Nothing to worry about. *Believe me.* You should see the other bitch." She grinned huge, then winced as her husband cleaned a particularly sore spot.

"Shouldn't be getting into brawls on front lawns with junkies, pussycat," he chastised.

"Strung out bitches shouldn't be sniffing around my brother and scaring his family," she retorted instantly.

Rex attempted and failed to hold back a smile. He shrugged. "Fuck. She's got me there. Besides, you were brilliant, baby."

"Of course, I was. Set her running away bleeding and crying like the hobag she is!"

I straightened to my full height even though I was dead tired. "She got away?"

Rex shook his head. "Club's gonna find her, Anya. Don't worry your pretty little head about it."

"She accosted me," I said in a defiant tone. "Screamed her head off and freaked out my daughter! She's a menace to society and a danger to anyone who comes in contact with her. Did you at least call the police?"

Shane hiked Shayna up higher on his chest and grabbed my arm. "Bella, let it go. The Pride has this. She's not gonna get far with a busted nose and a battered body. Let's get our girl to bed so I can get my big girl in my arms and to bed too."

I harrumphed and stomped my foot, not even realizing I was about to have a full-on temper tantrum. "I want that woman behind bars!" I demanded in a voice I'd never spoken in my life. It frightened even me.

Shane and Rex shared a smirk. "We'll work to make that happen."

"She's not allowed around my daughter ever again." I pointed to Rex and Shane and back again. "You two better make sure of it."

"Feral momma, it looks good on you, sis," Shay said with the biggest smile.

That's when I realized all I'd said. All night I'd been referring to Shayna as my daughter and reacting as though I'd already earned the title.

A deep wave of stress flooded my system. "I need a glass of wine, a hot shower, and sleep." And I needed to think about all that had taken place this evening. I frowned and crossed my arms over one another protectively, no longer sure how to act.

"Thanks for taking care of the twins," Shay said.

"Of course. They're family," I said before thinking about my choice of words.

Shay grinned wickedly. "Rock on."

"Looks like my Pussycat has a new best friend," Rex murmured.

"Damn straight!" Shay grinned.

I let out a heavy sigh. Shane led me out toward his apartment. "Come on, Bella. Let's get you home where I can look after you."

"I can look after myself!" I blurted, still feeling salty and emotional.

He chuckled softly. "Yeah, you can, but I want to take care of my woman who had a hard, fucking night protecting our girl and our niece and nephew from a succubus who has nothing but drama and garbage stink on her."

I followed Shane as he put Shayna to bed fully clothed. Still, I went to the bathroom and got a warm washcloth and used it to wash off her tear stained cheeks and chocolate mouth along with her sticky hands. She sighed and opened her eyes for a brief moment. Her face showing a smile of recognition as she snuggled her favorite stuffed animal.

"I love you, Mommy. Thank you for keeping me from the bad lady," she said and closed her eyes.

My throat went dry, and I inhaled sharply. Shane cleared his throat at the doorway. I leaned forward and kissed her forehead. "Sleep well, my darling girl. Sweet dreams."

As I passed by Shane, he interlaced our fingers and led me down the hall to our room. I meant his room. *His. Room.* I reiterated internally.

"You okay with that?"

"With what?" I said tiredly. He handed me a full glass of red wine.

"With her calling you Mommy. You acted like a full-on momma bear this evening, taking care of her and my sister's kids so they could deal with Jess. You got her away from a woman who was coked up to the gills and unpredictable. Who knows what she could have been up to if you weren't the one with Shayna tonight? Hell, Rex said you wouldn't even let her go when he approached."

"She was scared. I'll do anything in my power to prevent her from feeling fear in her life."

He smiled and nodded. "Yeah, just like a mother should."

I sighed, entering the bedroom. "Why was that woman here? Why now when Shayna is doing so well? When you and I have something real."

Shane pulled off his shirt and tossed it toward the closet. It fell at the entrance to the room, and I didn't care enough to pick it up and drop it in the hamper for him.

"Far as I can figure, she wants something. Now I just need to figure out what it is."

I ground my teeth and got up into the bed where I sat

cross-legged. I sipped the wine and watched as Shane tugged off his boots and socks and let his jeans fall to the floor. He pulled back the blanket and held is hand out for the wine. He took a long drink and handed it back to me.

"I need to know what this means for us, Shane."

He frowned deeply and tipped his head to the side. "What do you mean?"

"Us. You and me. If Shayna's mother is back in the picture, what does it mean?"

He huffed. "Nothin' much. She hasn't been around Shayna her entire life. After two years of her being gone, I got her parental rights taken away on the grounds of abandonment. She has no legal rights over Shayna."

"And you? What are you feeling knowing she's back in town?" I bit down on my bottom lip and held the glass with both hands.

"Anya, I love you. I'm in love with you. I never gave a shit for Jess. Less so when she dropped off the child we'd made when the baby was only days old on my parents' doorstep and left without so much as giving my daughter a name or a birth certificate. We had to go through hell to get her a legal birth certificate and social security number since the bitch had the baby out of a hospital. We're lucky she's alive at all and wasn't junked up on meth or coke or whatever the skank was doing at the time."

"You can't hate her that much. She's still the mother of your only child…"

"No. My child has had three mother figures in her life. Mags, Shay, and now you. Not Jess. Those are the only female role models in her life. I'm thankful as fuck they are good ones, who will teach her how to be a good, honest, kind woman. And as luck would have it, I get to keep the last one and make her mine, giving Shayna a mother who will be there for her entire life. Lead her down the right path as a woman should. A good woman. I want that for my baby. More than anything. Jess does not factor into the picture."

"And if she cleaned herself up?"

He shook his head. "I can't speak on hypotheticals, Bella. We just don't know what's up with her right now. Her showing up the way she did, acting like a loon, scaring my daughter doesn't speak highly of her mental status. My daughter is not going to be around someone who loses their shit like that. Shay excluded. She had five years of pent up anger to shell out." He smiled softly.

I chuckled. "Shay was quite the bad ass."

"Ooh, my woman said ass! Call the papers!"

I pushed at his chest lovingly, and he caught my hand, grabbed the glass of wine and set it on the nightstand. He encircled my waist and tugged me down to the bed until I was prone. Then he straddled my body with his own.

"My old lady took care of our girl today. Protected her from an evil bitch."

"I'd give my life for hers, Shane. I want the best for her in all things."

He smiled and dipped down to press his lips to mine. "I know. That's why you're going to make a great mother, a kick-ass wife, and the best old lady."

I sighed into his kiss, letting his tongue tease and heat me from limb to limb with each delicious swipe. He peeled off my sweater and found my full leotard underneath.

"Fuckin hell, woman!" He grumbled at the bodysuit while I laughed heartily.

The leotard was no match for him. When he'd taken off my jeans, he simply sheathed his length with a condom, spread my legs under him, curled his fingers in the gusset of my leotard, pushed it to the side, and slid home.

I arched into the sweet invasion of his first thrust. Instantly everything in the world righted itself once again. As Shane made slow love to me, his mouth connected to mine, we held hands and whispered promises.

The promise to handle things together.

The promise to never let anything become between us.

The promise to do everything to make our family safe and whole.

The promise to love one another through it all.

And as I cried out in a slow, throbbing orgasm, he followed me over the edge, proving that we'd survive anything big or small. Any challenge. Any individual threatening our happiness. Anything life had to throw our way.

As long as we were together.

Chapter 10

OREGON

Whip

ALMOST A WEEK HAD GONE BY SINCE WE'D SEEN HIDE OR HAIR of Jess. Either she'd cut and run for the hills after the beating my sister gave her, or she was lying low. My gut said the latter was in play.

I served a happy couple then poured a few drinks and made sure everyone down the length of the bar was set. It was early. Just after dinnertime. Wednesday nights tended to be when my mother and father had one on one time with their grandkids. They took Shayna, Swayze, and Trace all together and either made dinner or took them out. Gave me and my sister some free time with our mates, which I was looking forward to. I'd only had Sunday with my girls; the rest of the week I worked. Anya and I were due for some alone time.

Speaking of my angel...

The door to O'Donnell's opened, and my old lady strutted in. My jaw dropped open, and I leaned against the bar. My dick paid close attention to every inch of her as she maneuvered through the patrons, nodding at some of my brothers and their current flings. Her entire body was encased in a sweater dress much like the first one I'd seen her in. This one, however, was candy apple red. Her lips were painted to match, and her golden blonde hair was pulled back on one side with a barrette or clip or some shit. Her eyes had a slim line of black kohl that went out to a point, making the blue pop. The dress hugged her curves all the way to her knees. The black suede "fuck me" boots were the perfect finishing touch.

My mouth watered at the desire I saw not only in her eyes but also in her body language. My beautiful woman wanted to fuck.

She swayed her small hips from side to side with each step, every man in the place watching her come to me. When she got to the bar, I lifted the side, grabbed her hand, and dragged her to the back.

"I'm on break!" I barked to the prospect who had come in tonight to help out. I'd already planned to leave early, take my girl to a private candle lit dinner, which I imagined was why she was so dressed up.

"Honey…where are we going?" Anya laughed as I pulled her down the hallway and to the back office. Once I got her inside, I closed and locked the door.

She was standing, facing the room. "Kind of a dark and dank room. It could use some paint and sprucing up…"

Her words fell off when I spun her around, tunneled my hands into her gorgeous locks, and crushed her body and mouth to mine.

She gasped, which was all it took for me to sink my tongue in for a long, deep, drink of her. Anya's arms came around me, and she lifted onto her toes. That's my girl.

I kissed her with every wanton need splintering through my system. My cock was rock hard and throbbing to the beat of my heart. I slid my hands down her sides and hiked up her dress to her waist.

"Oh, my goodness, what are you doing?" She tried to distract me, but I was a man on a mission. There was absolutely no stopping this train.

"Need to fuck you. Right here. Right now."

"Shane…" she mewled as I tongued her neck and drove my hands into her panties and squeezed her bare ass.

I pushed at her panties until they fell to the ankle of her boots, then I pressed her back until she hit my desk. I lifted her up and put her bare ass on the desk before I reached down and unhooked her panties, placing them in my front pocket, I grabbed for my wallet and pulled out one of the condoms I kept there.

"This is crazy," she panted, her lips on my neck, teeth grazing, fingers unbuttoning my shirt. Once she got it open, her warm hands slid all over the planes of my chest. She left my shirt and club vest on.

"I'm crazy in love with my woman," I growled, spread her pretty thighs, centered at her wet slit, palmed her ass, and thrust inside. Her entire body arched back, and she groaned.

"Lean back, baby, I've got you." I urged her to rest her body against the desk, her legs up and out wide. I used her hips to drag her on and off my cock. My gaze zeroed on the glistening pink flesh. I wanted a taste of that honey so bad, I pulled out, dipped my head, and covered her cunt with my mouth.

"Shane!" she cried out then covered her mouth with her forearm, biting right over the sweater to muffle her cries.

I sucked and licked all around the heart of her, paying special attention the hard, little pearl that made her buck against my face. I flicked at her clit a few times then flattened my tongue and rubbed it roughly. Her hips bucked against my face, and she held onto my hair while I feasted. Christ, she tasted like the finest desert and smelled like utter heaven. I wanted to be everywhere at once. Tasting her cunt and fucking her mouth at the same time.

I made a mental note to introduce sixty-nine to her repertoire in the near future. Just the thought made me bite down on her hard little knot until she screamed around her arm and held me down against her flesh while her orgasm tore through her.

When she stopped keening, I sank my tongue as far into her as I could, wanting to sear her essence in my mouth and memory until I could get her home and spend hours fucking her to exhaustion.

After I had my fill, I lifted back up, pressed my aching cock back inside and rode her hard. So hard, I leaned over her body and hooked my fingers around the other side of the desk for more leverage. She was right there with me as I drilled into her willing, hot center until her body started to shake.

"Honey, again, oh my god!" Her nails dug into the muscles at my back as she wrapped her long legs around my body. "So good, please, more..."

I grinned and sucked at the skin of her neck before moving my lips to hers. She kissed me, not caring that I still had her taste on my tongue. She sucked, nibbled, and ate at my mouth while I plunged inside, crushing her clit with every thrust. Her body strained, her muscles gripping tight all around me. From chest to back to cock, I was surrounded by her, claimed, loved.

I went over the edge on a hoarse cry into her mouth as she moaned through her second release.

After several minutes of kissing and simply breathing, I finally pushed off her, grabbed her hand, and lifted her up. I took off the condom, wrapped it in a tissue from the box that hadn't fallen off the desk, and tossed it in the trash. I went over to the supply closet and grabbed a clean bar towel to wipe between her thighs. She let me tend to her, as she attempted to fix her sex mussed hair and wipe at her lipstick that had, surprisingly, stayed well in place.

Once she was cleaned, she stood up and pushed her dress back down, hiding every one of her attributes behind the sweater material. Her nipples were still hard and looked impossibly sexy pressed against her bra and the fabric of her dress. I liked knowing I had made those little berries hard as stone even though I hadn't even touched them. I would...later tonight.

I buttoned up my pants, tucked in my shirt, and ran a hand through my hair. "You ready?"

"My panties?" She held out her hand.

I grinned wickedly and shook my head. "I like knowing you're bare under there so that, when we leave here and have dinner, you'll be sitting there with no undies, getting wetter by the minute, waiting for the moment I take you home and fuck you stupid."

"You're seriously not going to give me my underwear?" Her eyebrows arched up in question.

"No, Bella, I'm not. Now, come on. I have another hour before we leave Jay in charge of things so we can have our dinner.

When we entered the bar, there was one person sitting at the end of the counter with a hoodie up and her face down. I could only see the profile, but I'd know her anywhere.

White-hot anger skated down my spine and swirled in my gut. I ground my teeth and led Anya to the other side, walked her around, and sat her away from the bitch.

I crowded Anya at her barstool and forced her to look at me by cupping her cheek. "Jess is at the other end of the bar. I want you to stay here where Jay can tend to you for any reason."

Her pretty blue eyes looked startled and concerned. "What are you going to do?" She gripped both of my biceps.

"Gonna find out why the fuck she's back and what she wants."

"You don't think she wants Shayna, do you?" Fear coated her tone, and wetness shimmered in her eyes.

I shook my head. "Only one way to find out."

She pushed me back a little and stood up. "I'm coming with you."

"Fuck no!" I grated through clenched teeth and got close to her. "Can't risk anything happening to you. Who knows if she has a weapon or is going to pull some shit? Want you far away in the event she does."

Anya stood up taller and lifted her chin defiantly. Hell, my woman was about to throw down. I was equal parts proud and pissed off at her.

"You're not going alone. If I'm your old lady, which you claim is the highest honor, I have every right to address your ex."

I grimaced. "She's not my ex."

Anya crossed her arms over her beautiful body. "Don't care. I'm going to bear witness to whatever she has to say."

We had a stare-off for a full minute before I scowled, grabbed her hand, and held her a step behind me as we approached Jess.

Her once nice blue eyes were clouded and dark, the pupils bigger than they should be.

"Why are you here?" I grumbled low and direct.

Jess looked from left to right and then scratched at her arms. Her eyes were black and blue. There was a cut running down the side of her face, and her nose was twice the size. She'd been pretty once. Full of life and laughter. That woman no longer existed. In her place was an empty shell of what used to be a woman I would have called a friend.

"Need your help, Whip. Bad. Real bad." Her gaze kept flitting around the room as if she was worried someone was going to find her.

"Where the hell have you been?" I asked. Anya thankfully stayed a foot behind me and leaned against the bar, listening but not participating.

"Doesn't matter where I've been, man. Only matters where I'm going, and it's going to be six feet under if you don't help me out."

"What kind of help do you need? Rehab?"

Her entire face scrunched up into one of horror. "NO!" she said overly loud. A few of my club brothers looked our way. Tank and Champ being two of them. Anya waved, and they smiled back at her, either not aware of the shit going down between me and Jess or waiting to see if I needed backup.

Tank rose from his chair, crossed his arms over his chest, and glared at Jess.

Fuck.

"Then what do you want?"

Her hands shook as she rubbed at her eyes, wincing at the same time. "Money, I gotta get outta here. Far, far, away, man. You need to help me!"

I jerked my head back. "I haven't seen your ass for over five years, and you come back, scare my old lady and my daughter, and expect me to fund your get-out-of-town plan? Are you insane? Or have the drugs eaten away every moral cell in that small brain of yours?"

Jess sat up and reached out and grabbed my hand. "You have to help me or they're going to kill me!" Her nails dug into my arm.

"Let. Him. Go. Now." A scathing female voice laced with acid and hard as nails broke into our conversation. Anya had placed her small hand around Jess's wrist and was squeezing the life out of her. "Don't make me ask again."

Jess let me go instantly. "Who is this? Your newest club girl?" Her dull eyes ran up and down Anya's form. "We could be sisters," she scoffed.

Anya flicked her hair over her shoulder and glared. "Hardly."

I grabbed Anya just as Tank walked up behind us. He hooked an arm around Anya's shoulder and kissed her temple. "Hey, Twinkle Toes, you making new friends?"

Anya pursed her lips. "Define friends."

I waved at the two of them in annoyance. "Jess, you have a lot of balls to coming here after five years, having left your daughter with the club. Don't you even care about Shayna?"

"Shayna? That's her name?" Her tone expressed the briefest flash of interest, but then it disappeared along with her humanity.

An animalistic growl came up my throat and had me clenching my fists. I'd never hit a woman, but this woman tried my resolve with every word she spoke.

"Yeah, that's her name. After me and my twin…"

"You've always been pussy whipped by the women in your family. Oh, Shay and Mags could do no wrong, but you'd fuck all of us with not a care in the world." She looked around the bar again. "Are you going to help me or not? I need five thousand—ten would be better—to get myself far away from the Devil's Riders."

"Fuck me running," Tank spat. "You've been with the top outlaw one percenters around? Are you insane?"

"She left a stunning little girl at the doorstep of a motorcycle club. Of course she's got a screw loose," Anya added unhelpfully, though her sass was a serious turn-on. Something I looked forward to exploring another time.

Jess glared and scratched at her arms. "You don't know me. You don't know anything about me. I could come in here and take Shayna away. She is my daughter. Is that what you want? Huh, Shane?"

And I lost it. I grabbed the back of her hoodie along with her hair and forced her head back as I got right in her face, so close I could smell the stink of her rotten breath. "Don't. Fuck. With. Me. Or. My. Kid. I will destroy you."

She narrowed her gaze. "Then give me what I need, and you'll never see me again."

"You leave right fucking now or I call up the president of the Devil's Riders myself and tell them you're here."

She cried out and ripped at my arm to let her go. "No, no, no! You can't. They'll kill me."

I held her fast. "What did you do?"

"Nothing! Let me go!" she roared, fear controlling her reactions.

"I'll ask you one more time: What did you do?"

She shrugged and attempted to fix her messed up hoodie. "I took a pound or five of their coke. Sold it, smoked it, had a little party. No biggie, but they don't see it that way."

"You stole half a million dollars' worth of pure cocaine from the Devil's Riders?" Tank snarled in disgust and shock.

My heart sunk. Jess was in deep. Far too deep for the Pride to get her out, no matter what we tried to do.

"We can't get you out of a bind like that," I warned.

"I'm not asking you to pay my debts, I'm asking you to help get me out of town. They know I was here before I rolled with them. They'll be coming this way soon. I figure I'll get on a bus headed out East. Set up roots somewhere new. Lay low."

"And your drug use?" I grated.

"What's it to you? I took care of your daughter. Didn't do drugs when I carried her. You should be happy. You fuckin' owe me!" She grabbed for my vest, her hands shaking as she pleaded in a voice so delirious, I had no idea who the hell she was anymore or how I'd even gone to bed with her in the first place. "You owe me for Shayna!"

I inhaled full and deep and made a decision right there. No matter what, I couldn't let my daughter's biological mother get taken out by the Devil's Riders. Not without trying to do something to help. My conscience wouldn't allow it.

"Wait here." I spat. I hated what I was about to do.

I caught gazes with Tank. "You've got Anya."

He nodded curtly and stood in front of her.

"I'm right here; I can take care of myself..." she harrumphed, and it almost made me smile. Almost.

I gave her a quick, hard kiss on the mouth. "Stay with Tank and don't engage," I warned.

She smiled coolly. "I don't engage with wild animals."

Again, it took everything I had not to laugh, but this situation was like crawling bugs all over my skin. I wanted free of this woman and the shit storm she'd brought with her. Immediately.

I walked to the back room, opened the safe and pulled out twenty-five hundred dollars. It would come out of my cut from the club, but either way, I'd have to tell the guys I took it and what I did with it. Knowing my father and my brothers, they'd understand even if they hated it for me.

I put the cash in an envelope and folded the lip and hustled back out. By the time I got back, Shay and Rex were standing off against Jess who was behind Tank and cowering against the corner of the bar.

"Fucking hell, did you have to come tonight?" My shoulders sank as I made my way to the standoff.

"Champ called. Everyone's here 'cept your folks." Rex lifted his chin, and I scanned the bar.

It was wall-to-wall leather vests. Fucking shit fuck.

I lifted my hand in the air. "I've got this. Stand down."

The brothers did not sit. If anything, they became more imposing. I made my way over to Jess, grabbed her wrist, and she flinched when I slapped the envelope in her hand.

"Twenty-five hundred is all you're gonna get. I hope to fuck you don't snort it up your nose, but I don't care as long as you get far away from Grants Pass, out of fuckin' Oregon, hell away from the West Coast. Just go away. And you better not have told the Devil's Riders about Shayna. If they come for my daughter, a hellfire so hot will rain down on you so hard you'll feel it straight down to your soul."

She shook her head and pocketed the cash. "They don't know. I was between places when I left the Pride and found out I was pregnant. Stayed with a cousin who was heavy into church, made sure I took care of myself for the baby."

I inhaled a quick breath of relief. "Get the fuck out of here, Jess. And don't ever come back."

She nodded, and her dark, dead eyes lifted. For a brief moment, the woman I remember flashed to the surface. "I did love her, you know. I just knew I could never give her a good life. I didn't want to even taint her with a name I'd chosen. I wanted her to have her entire world created and gifted by you and the Pride. It was the only thing I had to give."

Anya's fingers interlaced with mine as the warmth of her body resting against my back, centered and calmed me to my core.

"Goodbye, Whip. Thank you."

I nodded, and the men in vests parted as Jess cowered through them to the door. She walked out, and I knew we'd never see her again. Whether she made it to the East Coast or got caught by the Devil's Riders, she was no longer my problem or Shayna's.

We had Anya now. I looped my arm around my woman and pressed her head to my chest where I could feel her from tits to toes.

My sister put her hand on my shoulder and then rubbed her hand down my back. "You okay, brother?"

I held my woman close and kissed the top of her head, the mint and lavender scent permeating my being as I kept her close. "I am now."

Anya's arms tightened around me, but she didn't move her body, content to let me hold her for as long as I needed.

Shay lifted the bar door and got behind the counter. "Who's ready for some shots? We're celebrating, people!"

The Pride cheered as Shay started laying out shot glasses by the dozens.

"What you did was honorable, Shane," Anya lifted her chin and gazed up at me. Her face was stunning. High cheekbones, almond shaped, clear blue eyes, rosy cheeks against pearly white skin, and her mouth with the red stain was beyond succulent. She was my living dream woman.

"If the situation were reversed, I'd like to think she'd help me. I had to give her a chance to get out. Every person deserves a second chance at a beautiful life, don't you think?"

She lifted up on her toes and pressed her mouth to mine. We kissed until we lost our breath, foreheads resting against one another's.

"You're my second chance." She beamed and ran her fingers through my hair.

"And you're mine, babe." I cupped her pretty cheek, letting my thumb trace her kiss swollen bottom lip.

"So yes, I believe everyone deserves second chances." She smiled. "And shots. I want to be wild and have shots and then have my man take me home and make crazy love to me!" My girl was feeling brazen, and I loved it. Having her here to take away the heavy of what just happened proved how much my life had changed for the better.

"Shay-la-la, get me and my woman a couple shots! We're celebrating!"

"Righteous!" She poured us both a double of Jameson's.

We clinked our glassed. "To second chances," I said.

"To second chances."

Chapter 11

Anya

"**I**F ANYONE SHOULD BE NERVOUS, LOVE, IT'S ME, AND I'M chuffed to bits to be attending my first biker soiree," my best friend Holly stated as we walked up the steps to the wooden lodge type building that housed the Hero's Pride.

Holly's British English word choices and accent had always been an endearing quality, matched with her superior intelligence and petite buxom curves, which made her an exceptional catch. Though she'd spent the better part of the last few years playing the field instead of finding *the one*. I never pushed, but now that I had Shane and Shayna and was planning to move in with them, sooner rather than later if Shane had his say, I wanted my friend to find her special someone too.

"It's not that I'm nervous, well, okay, maybe it is. This is a big deal. This is my first full party with Shane's club where everyone meets me as his *old lady*. I want to make Shane proud."

"Old lady," she tsked. "That colloquialism is a bit dodgy, is it not?"

I rolled my eyes and sighed. "Let it go, grammarian. Leave

the librarian at home for the night. Besides, it's the highest form of flattery in the biker world. I tried to make him call me 'young lady' instead, and he responded with one word: Babe. As though that answered all."

She fluffed her wavy fiery red-brown hair that reminded me of Julia Roberts in *Pretty Woman* and flashed me a sunny smile.

A blonde I recognized and loathed came to the door, her fake smile on display. She wore a micro mini denim skirt and a tube top, which left nothing to the imagination. The blonde would be pretty if she didn't try so hard to flaunt her assets.

Lacey let out a groan and held the door open. "Party's out back. Through the living room, down the hallway, and to the kitchen where you'll see the patio doors," she said with boredom coating her tone.

"Are your legs broken, mate? Can't spare a second to show us the way?" Holly griped, and I bumped her side with my elbow.

"Bugger all!" She rubbed at the now sore spot on her ribs.

Lacey huffed and looked up at the ceiling. "I'm not allowed to be seen right now. Girlfriends and old ladies only. I'm just here to open the door and do drink and food runs and be ready for any of the bikers if they get a hankering for a roll in the hay in their private room."

Holly's blue eyes widened to the size of teacup saucers. "Well, don't let us get in the way of your schedule." We locked elbows as Lacey shut the door and pranced up the stairs on hooker heels so high I silently hoped she'd tumble down the stairs, maybe conk some sense into her brain.

"Bikers have whores to shag at the ready? This party became bloody brilliant, and I just arrived. I can't wait to learn more," Holly teased with absolute glee and a hop to her step.

I shook my head. "Why do I feel like I'm going to regret bringing you?"

"Bollocks! I'm the best mate you've ever had. And I won't let you get rat-arsed and vomit on your hair. That pretty much makes me your angel."

"Right. Which is the reason I keep you around." I sighed as we made our way through the huge building to the back where we could hear music playing.

As we exited the kitchen door, Mags approached with two empty pitchers of beer. "Coming through, ladies!"

Holly held the door open for her. "Do you need any help?"

Mags stopped where she stood. "Holly Berry, how's all the words doin' for ya?"

"Right as rain. How's the biker babe business treating you?" she countered.

"Can't complain," Mags said right as Riot came up behind her, grabbed her around the waist, and kissed her neck.

Holly's eyes lit up at the sight. "Brilliant! I'll take one of these and get a drink for myself while I'm at it." Holly grabbed one of the pitchers from Mags.

"Hey, Twinkle Toes, how goes it?" Riot asked.

Holly followed Mags as Riot embraced me in a big hug. It felt almost as nice as the bear hugs Shane gave me but not quite. More fatherly. A pang of sadness squeezed my heart as I wished my dad could meet the man I'd chosen and his brethren. I think he'd like the family I'd entered into.

"I'm good. Thanks, Riot."

He let me go and lifted his chin across the yard. "Your man is waiting, practically drooling at the sight of ya," he teased on a chuckle.

I turned around, and there he was. Wearing a pair of tight-fitting jeans, a white t-shirt that stretched across his muscular chest, and his club vest. His sandy brown hair was a tussled mess of layers that I wanted to run my fingers through. Instead of running to him the way my heart desired, I calmly walked down the steps of the porch, through the grass to where he was standing with Tank and Shay.

Shayna raced past me, chasing a big brother named Champ.

"Hi, Mommy. Bye, Mommy," she said as she ran after her target.

She'd been calling me Mommy daily now. Every time she did, my heart sighed in relief, even though I believed it was far too soon for such an honor. We'd only been together the better part of a month. Hardly enough time for such accolades, but according to biker lore, a month was an eternity to officially claim your Old Lady and initiate her into the club family. I didn't agree, but I was so swept away in Shane's world that I couldn't put up much of a fight.

"Damn, you're a lucky son of a bitch." Tank shook his head.

Shane's smile and gaze burned as I made my way into his arms. Instantly, he wrapped an arm around my waist and hauled me against his chest, dipped his head, and kissed me soundly on the mouth. I accepted his kiss with a flourish, heat skating down every one of my nerve endings until he removed his mouth but kept his face only a few inches from mine.

"Hi, Bella." He grinned.

I smiled so wide my cheeks hurt. "Hi," I said huskily.

"You ready for the ceremony?" he asked nonchalantly.

"Ceremony? What's this? I thought you just introduced me to everyone as your old lady and that was it."

He inhaled and rubbed his forehead against mine. "Yes, that is what I'll do. However, it's a little different for the club members when they claim their woman."

"How so?" I cocked my head to the side and ran my hands down his chest, straightening his t-shirt and vest.

"Well, you see…" His tone was gruff, and he let me go to rub a hand over the back of his neck. "It's tradition…"

Warning signals started to blare in my mind at his unwillingness to explain this 'ceremony' to me.

"Fuckin' hell, man, just spit it out, Whip. You're freakin' her out!" Tank groused.

"I'm trying. If you'd shut up." He glared at his friend.

Tank put an arm around my shoulders and pressed me to his side. "What Whip is trying to say is when a brother claims an old lady officially to the club, he burns for her."

"Burns?"

A sadistic smile slipped across his full lips. His dark brown eyes sizzled with excitement. "Burns. As in he gets her name branded on his chest right where his heart is." He lifted his chin toward an area off to the side where I could see Riot and a couple of the prospects setting a fire in the fire pit. Riot held a long metal rod of some sort.

All sound disappeared as I put two and two together, and it equaled my man getting branded with my name on his body.

"Bloody hell! You're going to get branded like cattle with my best mate's name?" Holly blurted. She held two beers, one in each hand.

Tank let me go, and Shane scooped me into his arms and against his chest. I didn't speak. I didn't think. I didn't anything. I just listened to his heartbeat while the rest of what he was planning to do sank in. He was going to brand himself to me for the rest of his natural life.

It was unbelievable.

It was beautiful.

It was poetry and music.

It was true love.

Biker style.

The length to which he was going to prove his love to me was beyond any measure I could ever fathom. My eyes watered, and I my breath caught as I whispered, "My God, Shane, how can I ever, ever give you such a gift in return?" I gripped him around the ribs as I kissed his t-shirt over his heart.

He weaved his fingers through the sides of my hair and lifted my chin with both his thumbs.

Tears swelled and a couple spilled over.

He gasped. "You understand. Fuck me, you get it."

I nodded. It was the ultimate sacrifice. Shane "Whip" O'Donnell would burn for me. Scar his skin for life. Cement his commitment to me forever through the ultimate sacrifice.

"You're not doing it alone," I expressed evenly.

"Anya, I have to do it alone," he murmured and kissed my forehead.

I shook my head. "No. I'll be right there for it all."

He got so close his nose almost touched mine. "You're mine until the end of time. Say you're mine."

I swallowed the ball of cotton down my suddenly dry throat. "I'm yours and you're mine, until the end of time."

He grinned right as Riot called out above the crowd. "Fire's lit, gather round, Pride!" His voice was a booming echo through the crowd.

"This is utterly barbaric. I cannot wait." Holly's blue eyes were filled with excitement as mine must have shown devastation.

My man would burn for me. Literally. I understood it in a twisted, primal, animalistic way, but it didn't mean I liked the idea of Shane hurting for me.

Tank slapped Shane on the back. "Proud of you, brother," he said in a gravelly timbre.

"Hey, Romeo, how's about you help me find a good position and make sure I don't faint." Holly licked her pink lips and put on what I called her "Sex Face", which was a combination of sexy and hot, and prim librarian. Even now with her black slacks, red peep toe pumps, and silk tank she looked like a million dollars. Her hair fell down around her shoulders to the middle of her back in wild waves, looking redder in the sun.

Tank smirked and rubbed his hands together before putting out his elbow. "Don't mind if I do, pretty lady."

"I'm Holly," she said in a tone laced with interest.

"I'm Tank, and I'll be your shoulder to lean that beautiful body against anytime."

She grinned and gripped his arm. "Play your cards right, and I'll hold it against other more enticing parts, love."

"Jesus," he grumbled but led her away.

She glanced at me over her shoulder and mouthed, "So hot!"

Shane interlaced our fingers and led me to where the brothers, old ladies, girlfriends, and friends of the club were gathered around.

The crowd parted as Shane and I walked into the center.

"On your knees, Whip," Riot called out from across the way as he held the long iron rod in the fire.

"Babe, you're gonna wanna stand to the side. Mom?" He gestured to Mags who came over and grabbed my arm.

I shook her off as though the touch cut my flesh into ribbons. "No! Let me go. I'm staying right here." I growled and tugged at Shane's hand until I was kneeling on the ground in my blue sundress next to where he did the same. The grass was cool against my bare knees.

"Gotta let my hand go so I can take off my shirt and vest," he smiled.

I inhaled and let him go, but I swear it hurt to lose that brief connection. I started to shake, but Shane looped my arms through his vest so that I was wearing his most prized possession aside from me and his daughter. "Keep this warm for me, yeah?"

I graced him with a small smile and tugged the soft leather around my body. His chest prickled with goosebumps as Riot walked over. I reached out and took his hand again.

"Bones, you at the ready?" Riot gestured to a man who was standing nearest Shane, holding what looked to be a medical bag. He already had a stethoscope around his neck.

"Club doctor, babe," Shane whispered, and I sighed in relief.

I knew this would be bad but having him close helped relieve a glimmer of the fear bursting through my body at what was about to happen.

"This is vicious and fascinating." I could hear Holly's intrigued words from somewhere to the left of us.

I drowned out all sound around me and held Shane's hand tightly. He didn't seem frightened at all. My heart was beating so loud I could feel it at the edge of every nerve ending.

"You don't have to do this," I said under my breath then looked up into his beautiful face and mesmerizing hazel eyes.

"I want this, your name on my chest for all to see."

His words pierced my chest, and my anxiety pounded mercilessly through me as Riot spoke.

"Today we celebrate our brother, Shane "Whip" O'Donnell claiming his old lady, Anya Markova. The club accepts her into our club, our hearts, and our family. We will protect her with our lives, today, tomorrow, and forevermore. Bring me the iron." Riot held out his hand, and one of the prospects who had taken up holding the rod in the flame walked over proudly.

Shane lifted his chest up as if he couldn't wait to be branded.

I held his hand and lifted my own chest in solidarity. I brought his hand to my lips and kissed the top. "I love you, Shane."

"Are you ready? Anything you want to say?" Riot asked as he held up the red-hot glowing branding iron, which spelled my name in a four sweeping curling letters, the A at the beginning and end matching perfectly.

"I will love and protect Anya until my dying day. For now, I will burn for her." He nodded as his Dad who got close, hovered the glowing iron right where his heart would be.

"So be it." He pressed the iron against Shane's flesh.

I squeezed his hand, or maybe it was him who squeezed mine so tight I thought it might break every one of my fingers. I didn't care and would have been okay with it as long as Shane was spared.

He wasn't.

The agonizing sound of his love was seared into my brain and his chest. He took it, eyes closed, teeth biting down on a leather belt I had no idea he'd been given.

The entire thing happened in only a couple seconds. Riot moved away, and the man they called Bones, the club doctor moved in to treat the wound. He poured something on the wound, and Shane hissed, but he didn't cry out.

I pet his hand over and over while he was tended to. Eventually, he was treated and was about to receive a bandage when Shane shook his head and growled out a pained "Not yet."

"Stand up, Anya," Shane asked.

Tears ran down my cheeks in rivulets I didn't even realize were falling. My dress was soaked with them as I saw my name burned into my man's beautiful chest.

Shane held my hand and readjusted his body so that he was resting on one knee. I tried to pull him up with me, but he shook his head and held out his hand to his sister who was also crying. She sniffed and dug into her pocket and handed him something small.

I watched as Shane lifted up a white gold and diamond ring.

"Anya Markova, today I proved my undying commitment to you. I burned for you. For us. For our future. Now I ask before my family, my brothers, everyone I hold dear, if you would gift me the honor of not only being my old lady but of being my wife." His voice shook with the emotion coating every word.

While I stood there in shock, the pain of what he'd just done, the gift he'd given me still racing through my system, I saw Mags push through the crowd, Shayna standing in front of her. Shayna walked over to her father, got down on both knees then realized her mistake and adjusted so she was on one knee just like her father and held up another sparkling ring. This one said "Mommy" in cursive script across the white gold band.

"This is for you from me. I pickeded it. Will you be my Mommy for real? For ever and ever?" She held the little ring up proudly just like her father held his.

"Good job, baby," he whispered to his girl, and she gave him a beaming smile.

Two of the most beautiful faces gazed up at me with such love and devotion my heart split in two, because each owned a half.

I fell to my knees, tears pouring down my cheeks and a sob bursting form my lips as I put my arms around both of them, being careful not to touch Shane's chest wound. My entire world was held in two beating hearts within my arms.

"Yes, yes, yes, a million yesses!" I cried out, and the entire crowd roared and cheered.

Shane kissed me hard and fast then nuzzled his daughter who was laughing and kissing my cheek over and over squealing "My mommy!" At the top of her lungs.

It was the best moment of my entire life.

Epilogue

Whip

Three months later…

THE WIND WHIPPED ANYA'S HAIR WILDLY AS SHE STOOD overlooking the ocean, standing on the lanai in nothing but an orange bikini and a vibrant swath of fabric around her slim hips. The sun shone down across her skin as she lifted her chin to the sky. My wife was tanned a beautiful buttered toast color after a week of being on our honeymoon. My parents, Shayna, Shay, Rex, the twins, her best friend Holly, my best man Tank had all descended on the island of Maui last week.

I asked my woman what type of wedding she wanted, hoping to spirit her away to Vegas like Rex did my sister, but she wanted a destination beach wedding. And what she wanted, she got—in all things.

The day after we landed, we met the minister on the beach. I wore a pair of black linen pants and a short sleeved crisp white button up. Anya walked alongside my daughter. They wore similar white lace sundresses. Her hair was in a loose bun and away from her beautiful face, reminding me what she looked like when I first fell in love with her. My daughter's hair was also in a bun along with a halo of flowers around her head, streaming ribbons flying in the breeze as they approached hand in hand. Both of them carried bouquets of sunflowers, the only color beside the golden spun silk of their hair, the pink of their cheeks and lips, and the blue of their eyes, which perfectly matched the sky. The ocean was our backdrop. My mother, sister, father, her best friend and mine stood in a small circle of love as we said our nuptials. Nothing more was needed.

It was the third best moment of my life. The first being when I met my daughter for the first time. The second when Anya agreed to be my wife and the ceremony where I burned for her. The third was her saying "I do" in front of our much smaller wedding party. We'd have a big shindig back at the club when we returned, but this event, these two weeks were just for us and our very immediate family.

The only downside had been her mother's refusal to attend. Apparently marrying a biker who owned a bar and was a single dad was beneath her plans for her daughter. Anya didn't so much as shed a tear. She wrote her off. Said if her mother wasn't going to support her choices in life, the man she chose, the little girl she wanted to raise, then she didn't need her.

So far she hadn't mentioned regretting that decision. I'd keep my eye on her and talk it through more when we returned, see if we could try again with her mother, maybe over the next holidays, but for now, I was content in making my old lady...*my wife*, happy.

Anya crossed her arms over herself and leaned forward, gifting me a nice view of her small ass and the snarling lion tattoo just above her right hip on her lower back. The top said the words "Property of" and under it my name. Only instead of my road name she put my first name, Shane. Directly under that was our daughter's name, Shayna. Good thing she left room because I planned on giving her a couple other names to add to those one day.

I stared at my wife's ass and brand in the form of the club tattoo every old lady got. Man, the things her ass could do in the bedroom and on the dance floor.

I'd made her do ballet for me in our honeymoon suite in one of her sexy nighties, sans the panties, and then made her do it all over again bare ass naked. When my woman stretched her leg up and over her head, I dropped to my knees and worshipped at the altar of her body and talent. She worshipped me right back.

Everything about Anya spoke to me, lived inside of me as a pounding rhythm that soothed and grounded me to her.

I ached to tell her the news I'd just received from our lawyer back home. I clenched and unclenched my hands as excitement poured through my limbs. When I reached her, the warm breeze eased along my skin, and I wrapped my arms around her waist. She covered my hands with hers, content to just let me hold her.

My lips were against her neck as I spoke close to her ear. "Got the call we've been waiting for." I grinned as her body went still in my arms, and gooseflesh appeared across her tanned skin.

"It's done?" she asked, a little hiccup in her response.

I kissed her neck for a long moment. "It's done."

"She's mine." Her voice shook and cracked, the emotion hiding just under the surface beginning to pour out.

"She's ours," I reminded her.

"Our daughter," Anya sighed, the sound more beautiful than I'd ever heard it.

"It's official. The papers filed through the court, stamped, and signed by the judge. No matter what happens to me, you are Shayna's mother not only in my eyes and hers, but in the eyes of the law and within the power of the legal system."

I felt her body lean heavily against me as tears ran down her cheeks. "I want to have another baby." Her words were sweet and filled with love and hope.

I chuckled against her neck. "Bella, I just told you: Shayna is your daughter in every way that counts, and you want to double your bounty?"

Anya spun around and looped her arms over my shoulders. "My daughter wants a sibling. I want to give it to her."

"Babe, you can't just give her everything she wants out of life; she'll be spoiled rotten," I warned.

She shrugged. "Don't care. I want the three of us to have something new and beautiful to look forward to. We are moving into our new home when we get back, three houses down from your sister. A big house with five bedrooms. I'm ready to take that leap. Are you?" Her gaze was filled with excitement and love.

"You know I could never deny you something you wanted."

Her corresponding grin was beautiful as she leaned back, reached behind and untied the strings at her back and then at her neck before she flung her bikini top into the room. Her succulent breasts bounced into place like beaming beacons of light I wanted to wrap my fingers and lips around.

"Let's start now," she teased, baring her beautiful body and taunting me with it.

I reached for her, removed the little fabric skirt thing she wore around her bikini bottoms, picked her up by the ass as she wrapped her mile-long legs around my waist, and carried her to our king bed.

When I laid her down, I cupped her cheek and stared lovingly into her eyes. "Anya O'Donnell, you will always be my beloved, my old lady, my wife, my whole world."

"And you will always be my biker, my man, my husband, my everything," she said before I sealed our love with a kiss.

Nine months later, Anya and I introduced our son, Andrei Riot O'Donnell to our five-year-old and the rest of our family. He was named after both Anya's father and my own.

Shayna looked at the baby, pursed her lips, scrunched up her nose, and said, "He's pretty cute, and I will love him a lot. But, you're gonna have to ask God to make your belly big again with a sister."

My Anya was dead set on giving her daughter what she most wanted in life. So we did.

Two years and nine months later, we welcomed Holly Ann O'Donnell to our family. Our seven-year-old daughter Shayna was thrilled. "Bruiser" as we called Andrei, our two-year-old, didn't care either way. He was too busy rough housing with his cousin Trace aka "Hustler" and making a mess of the hospital room.

Me and my biker beloved were firmly grounded in our second chance at a beautiful life. We swore to one another we wouldn't let a moment of it go to waste.

And we never did.

The End

Keep an eye out for other *Biker Beauties* novellas, *Biker Babe*, *Biker Beloved*, *Biker Brit*, and *Biker Boss*. I plan to write these as complete standalones that can be read in any order and released whenever my muse fancies an insta-love insta-lust fix.

Until next time…Live wild, ride free!

Excerpt from *Biker Brit* (Biker Beauties #3)

Holly

"**S**EXY AS SIN LIBRARIAN. FUCK ME RUNNING," TANK growled into my mouth before sucking my bottom lip between his with an audible plop. "Jesus, your body is insane." He ran his hands down my sides and cupped my bum, fingers squeezing delectably.

I sighed and wrapped my arms around his thick neck and lifted my leg up toward his hip. He was too bloody massive to get a good lock. "Bed," I mewled as he ran his tongue down my neck.

"Not done," he murmured against my heated skin. He nuzzled down between my breasts where the low scoop neck of my silk tank opened. His hands glided back up my sides to grip both of my breasts, lifting them so that the fleshy globes spilled out the top of my tank graphically. I moaned as his hot tongue skated across each breast. His fingers were not idle. He kneaded and pinched at the erect peaks hidden behind the lace of my bra and top.

"Please, bed." I tried to hike my leg up to secure a delicious bit of friction where I wanted him most. "You're too bloody tall for me," I clenched my jaw, dug my nails into the back of his shoulders through his shirt and huffed.

Tank chuckled, a deep rumbling sound that I felt all the way to my toes. I barely categorized the heat of the moment when his hands left my breasts and fumbled with the catch at my trousers until he scored what he wanted. The fabric slipped down my legs and pooled at my ankles. Before I could move, he curled his giant hands around each ass cheek and lifted straight up. My red peep-toe heels fell to the floor when I wrapped my legs around his trim waist. He didn't even stop sucking at the flesh of my breasts, reacting to my weight as though I was light as a feather.

I locked my legs and ground over his jean-clad erection, moaning with delight.

He pressed me harder against the door of the room he'd brought me to in the ski lodge-style clubhouse. The party was in full swing outside in the heart of the club and inside this room.

I ran my fingers through Tank's loose black layers at the crown of his head. The sides had been cropped close, very military, which pressed all my buttons. There wasn't much to hold on to, but I twisted my fingers in as best I could and arched my body for all I was worth against that steely erection.

"Are we going to shag against the door or you going to let me have my fun too, Romeo?" I finished off with a yelp when he'd bit down hard over my nipple through my blouse.

Without a word, he pulled me away from the door and had me on my back on the bed. He ripped his t-shirt over his head.

My eyes bugged out of my head. "Blooming hell, you're positively gilded. A damn brick wall," I lifted up on one elbow and ran my other hand down the planes of his obscenely well-defined chest. It was beyond the realm of reason. "You're a bloody work of art. I'm almost scared to touch you." I couldn't help the awe in my tone as I traced each chiseled abdominal muscle until I reached the fine dusting of hair that went down into a perfect line toward his cock.

Tank grinned and unbuttoned his pants. "Take your shirt off. I wanna see your tits bounce while I fuck you."

Without preamble, I sat up and ripped my silk tank over my head and tossed it to the floor, attempting to hurry so as to not disrupt my view of the Adonis disrobing at the side of the bed.

He kicked off his boots, toed off his socks and, with an arched brow, pushed his jeans down his tree-trunk sized muscular thighs.

"Unbelievable," I gasped, my hand going to my pounding chest as his body blistered my vision with nothing but male perfection.

His large member sprung to attention, which led me to believe he either pushed his underpants down along with the jeans, or he didn't wear them. I fanned my face and licked my lips at the sight of my current obsession. It was long, thick, and glistening at the tip. I wanted it in my mouth more than life sustaining air at that moment.

"You keep looking at me like that, pretty lady, and you're gonna get your mouth fucked before I ever get a taste of you."

I shook my head, leaned back, spread my legs, and crooked a finger. "Hop on, Romeo. I'll take an IOU to get a taste of you first."

He cursed and brought a knee to the bed, then straddled me, a leg on each side of my chest, and his beautiful length centered right at my face. I glanced up his gorgeous body and smirked. "One thing you need to learn about me, soldier, I always get what I want first." I winked and then swallowed him down as far as I could go. No teasing. No flicks of the tongue just straight up gold medal, mind blowing suction right off the top. I had him coming in mere minutes, swallowing down his heated essence and humping the air as I did.

His head lifted to the sky on a long, drawn out groan. His beautiful body trembled for a few moments and then went eerily still.

I let his length slip from between my lips and laid back… waiting. For a full sixty seconds he breathed and didn't so much as look at me.

Right before my eyes, and much to my astonishment, his length hardened again. It seemed even larger than the first go.

I gasped, and he finally set his dark blue gaze on me. "You're gonna pay for that."

I blinked and smiled coyly. "In Euros or US Dollars?"

"Oh, pretty lady, this is going to be a long night."

I stretched like a cat, my arms above my head, bringing my still covered breasts together while I lifted my pelvis, reminding him that he was still straddling my mostly naked form.

"Do your best, Romeo."

He leaned down, his hands resting beside my shoulders, bringing his face closer to mine as he centered his form directly over mine. "Be careful what you wish for, baby. You don't know who you're playing with." He lifted one of his hands and stroked down the center of my body, his large hand snaking under my knickers where he instantly inserted two thick fingers.

I arched, pressing my lower half up hard on his hand and crying out.

"Fuck me, I think I met my match in the bedroom," he growled, fingering me hard and fast.

"Oh Romeo, Romeo, promises promises," I teased before his full lips crashed down over mine in a fiery kiss.

His fingers moved, hooked deep, and his thumb centered on my hot button. I cried out into his mouth as a quick but intense orgasm blazed through my body.

He lifted up, ripped my thong off and undid the front hook on my bra until my breasts were free. He grabbed a foil packet from the nightstand and put it over his length. "Baby, I'm going to fuck you so hard you're no longer able to quote Shakespeare."

"To be…or not to.."

"Be fucked. That is the ultimate question," he roared before he spread my legs and thrust home.

From that moment on, I was no longer able to quote Shakespeare.

I was having the shag of my life.

Get your copy of Biker Brit now and continue Holly & Tank's story.

Purchase
AUDREY CARLAN'S
Other Books

BIKER BEAUTIES
Biker Babe
Biker Beloved
Biker Brit
Biker Boss

INTERNATIONAL GUY SERIES
Paris
New York
Copenhagen
Milan
San Francisco
Montreal
London
Berlin
Washington, D.C.
Madrid
Rio
Los Angeles

LOTUS HOUSE SERIES
Resisting Roots
Sacred Serenity
Divine Desire
Limitless Love
Silent Sins
Intimate Intuition
Enlightened End

TRINITY TRILOGY
Body
Mind
Soul
Life
Fate

CALENDAR GIRL
January
February
March
April
May
June
July
August
September
October
November
December

FALLING SERIES
Angel Falling
London Falling
Justice Falling

Acknowledgements

To my husband **Eric** for thinking it's cool that your wife is writing about fictional alpha men who fall in love instantly, that also happen to be bikers. I will forever love you more.

To the world's greatest PA, **Jeananna Goodall**, because you get me. Completely.

To **Amy Tannenbaum** for being an incredible agent. You listen, you advise, but you never steamroll. I adore you.

To **Ekatarina Sayanova** with Red Quill Editing, for always taking care of me and my book babies. You go above and beyond the call of duty every time. Thank you. Big thanks also go to **Rebecca Cartee** and **Tracy Damron-Roelle** for the additional line and proof edit. Team Red Quill definitely makes a sparkling final product.

To my alpha beta team **Tracey Wilson-Vuolo**, **Tammy Hamilton-Green, Gabby McEachern** I don't think you ladies could understand how much your feedback moves me. I love you.

To **Jena Brignola** your graphics for redoing this cover a bazillion times until I finally found my Anya. You are a true professional.

To the **Readers**, I couldn't do what I love or pay my bills if it weren't for all of you. Thank you for every review, kind word, like and shares of my work on social media and everything in between. You are what make it possible for me to live my dream.

About
AUDREY CARLAN

Audrey Carlan is a #1 *New York Times, USA Today,* and *Wall Street Journal* bestselling author. She writes wicked hot love stories that are designed to give the reader a romantic experience that's sexy, sweet, and so hot your ereader might melt. Some of her works include the worldwide phenomenon Calendar Girl Serial, Trinity Series and the International Guy Series. Her books have been translated into over 30 languages across the globe.

She lives in the California Valley where she enjoys her two children and the love of her life. When she's not writing, you can find her teaching yoga, sipping wine with her "soul sisters" or with her nose stuck in a wicked hot romance novel.

NEWSLETTER

For new release updates and giveaway news, sign up for
Audrey's newsletter: audreycarlan.com/sign-up

SOCIAL MEDIA

Audrey loves communicating with her readers. You can follow
or contact her on any of the following:

Website: www.audreycarlan.com

Email: audrey.carlanpa@gmail.com

Facebook: www.facebook.com/AudreyCarlan

Twitter: twitter.com/AudreyCarlan

Pinterest: www.pinterest.com/audreycarlan1

Instagram: www.instagram.com/audreycarlan

Readers Group: www.facebook.com/groups/
AudreyCarlanWickedHotReaders

BookBub: www.bookbub.com/authors/audrey-carlan

Goodreads: www.goodreads.com/author/show/7831156.
Audrey_Carlan

Amazon: www.amazon.com/Audrey-Carlan/e/B00JAVVG8U

Made in the USA
Coppell, TX
24 June 2024

33886045R00173